SINGING BIRD

Old secrets, new friendships, and a journey to the heart of Ireland...

Twenty-seven years since she adopted a baby girl in Ireland, Lena Molloy receives a call from the nun who set up the adoption. Sister Monica claims that she merely wants to tie up loose ends before she retires, but Lena is intrigued and worried by the call. With her best friend Alma, she travels to the west of Ireland on a secret mission to trace the birth parents of her daughter. At first the trail seems to have gone cold, but then a chance meeting sets Lena on a journey to an outcome she could not have foreseen in her wildest dreams.

SINGING BIRD

SINGING BIRD

by

Roisin McAuley

Magna Large Print Books
Long Preston, North Yorkshire,
BD23 4ND, England.

British Library Cataloguing in Publication Data.

McAuley, Roisin
    Singing bird.

A catalogue record of this book is
available from the British Library

ISBN   0-7505-2233-X

First published in Great Britain in 2004
by Headline Book Publishing

Copyright © 2004 Roisin McAuley

Cover illustration Figure © Corbis
Background © Getty Images by arrangement with
Headline Book Publishing Ltd.

The right of Roisin McAuley to be identified as the author of
this work has been asserted by her in accordance with the
Copyright, Designs and Patents Act, 1988

Published in Large Print 2004 by arrangement with
Headline Book Publishing Ltd.

Magna Large Print is an imprint of Library Magna Books Ltd.

Printed and bound in Great Britain by
T.J. (International) Ltd., Cornwall, PL28 8RW

To the memory of Tony McAuley

Acknowledgements

My heartfelt thanks are due to Pamela Watts, who taught me a great deal about the craft of writing, and to John Boundy who generously imparted his encyclopaedic knowledge of opera.

Copyright Information

Chapter 1

We were drinking champagne in the kitchen when the nun telephoned. I rerun the moment. What if I hadn't decided to have a party? What if we'd simply locked up and gone elsewhere for a drink? Or if the house move had been a week earlier? Would my life have continued in the safe, familiar pattern?

Maybe. But she was a determined woman. She would have tracked down the new address and telephone number. We were only moving to the other side of the Thames. We are in the telephone book.

Or she would have left a message. And I would have replied. Because my latent curiosity only wanted an excuse. I would have taken the same path into the past eventually. She is not to blame.

I go back in my mind to the day of the call. It was our second last day in the old house. I got up early and made a lamb casserole. At eight o'clock I brought Jack a cup of coffee and drew back the curtains in the bedroom.

'The wind blew the runner beans down. They look all ragged and forlorn.'

'Summer always ends with a storm,' he

said. 'We're halfway through September, Lena.'

He bent his blond head over the cup and inhaled, before drinking.

'You spoil me,' he said.

'I like spoiling you.'

'Do you mind me going away?'

A blackbird flew up from the wreckage of the beans and settled on the garden wall.

I turned and smiled at him. 'Everything's under control.'

I had plotted the move on a spreadsheet, and pinned it up in the hall. After Jack left for the office, Alma and two of my neighbours arrived to help me pack up. We moved methodically from room to room, sorting, packing, and tying colour-coded labels to furniture and boxes.

Just before five o'clock, I tied a pink label to a box of cookery books. I took a bottle of champagne from the fridge and called out, 'That's the last one. Time to celebrate!'

It was Alma's birthday. I had made her a cake. It sat on the breakfast bar dividing the living space from the kitchen. A Victoria sponge. Cream and home-made raspberry jam in the middle. Soft white icing on top. Pink miniature candles matched the labels dotted around the room.

'How about some music,' Alma said. 'Some opera? Our favourite singer, perhaps?'

18

Rosemary and Janet clapped. I bowed to acknowledge the tribute to my daughter as I slipped *Mary Molloy Sings Mozart and Rossini* into the CD player. It was her first recording, and is still my favourite.

Mary's voice filled the empty space and floated up to the attics.

'Tell me fair ladies, what ails my heart?
Yonder cupid, is this his dart?'

Her entire personality is contained in that sparkling combination of music and words. Delight and wonder, perfectly conveyed. We had rolled up the rugs, leaving parquet and bare boards. There was nothing to deaden the sound.

'Yonder Cupid, is this his dart?' Mary reprised.

'It's like being inside a giant speaker,' Alma said.

We sat at the long oak table drinking champagne, drunk on the music. The sky cleared. Sunshine splashed into the room. Mary began the Cavatina from *The Barber of Seville*. I bathed in the afterglow of a job well done.

'Una voce poco fa,
Qu'nel cor m'risuonò,'

I looked at the bright sky and thought of Mary on her way from Stuttgart to Heathrow. In the innocent minutes before the telephone rang, I sat in the September sunlight in a house I loved, listening to my

19

daughter singing, in the company of friends, utterly content.

'*Sono obbediente, dolce, amorosa*;'

Alma said, 'Is that the telephone?'

'*...mi fo guidar.*'

'Mary?' said Janet.

'She should be in the air by now. Unless her plane is late.'

Alma held open the glass door into the hall, waving me through with a flourish of her right hand. I waltzed past her, made a mock curtsy, and lifted the phone off the hook, still slightly unbalanced.

'Mrs Molloy? Mrs Lena Molloy?'

It wasn't Mary. I steadied myself against the banisters and signalled to Alma to turn down the music.

'Yes. This is Lena Molloy.'

'Sister Monica Devine speaking. Do you remember me? Saint Joseph's Home?'

I sank on to the staircase. My heart was thumping.

Sister Monica. The nun who gave me Mary.

Alma quietly closed the kitchen door. I mouthed amazement at her.

'Mrs Molloy? Are you still there?'

'Yes. You've just taken me by surprise, sister.' That was an understatement. Thoughts and memories chased each other round my brain. 'What can I do for you? Is there a problem?'

'No. No. Not at all. It's just…' she paused, 'well, I'll be retiring soon. I was reorganising my office, tidying a few loose ends, and I just thought it would be nice to catch up on all my babies.' Catch up? It was twenty-seven years since we'd last spoken.

'You're lucky you found me. We're moving house.'

'Well, now isn't that great. Tell me now…' the brogue accentuated by the telephone, 'what name did you give her?'

'Mary,' I said, glancing towards the kitchen. Janet was lighting the candles on the cake. 'I'm sorry, sister. I'm a bit busy just now. Can I call you back? I'm in the middle of getting things organised. But I could call you back.'

I tucked the telephone under my chin and reached for the message pad on the table. My hand shook as I wrote down the number. I fumbled at the handle of the kitchen door.

Alma said, 'What's wrong?'

'It's the nun who gave me Mary,' I said. 'Sister Monica. She ran the home where Mary was born.'

'Is everything all right?'

'She said there wasn't a problem. It was just a catch-up call. But I'm going to call her back.'

Janet topped up my glass and Rosemary handed it to me. Their eyes were like saucers.

21

'Blow them out before they go out on their own,' I said to Alma.

She drew up her shoulders, and with one gust of breath blew out all the candles. Rosemary, Janet and I raised our glasses and chorused, 'Happy birthday, Alma.'

'When were you last in Ireland, Lena?' said Alma. 'You haven't been for a while, have you?'

'Ireland?' said Janet.

'Was the nun ringing from Ireland?' said Rosemary.

They knew Mary was adopted. It wasn't something we talked about much. When Jack and I moved to Stratton Road, and Mary began playing with Janet's children and we got to know each other, I told Janet. As my circle widened and took in Janet's friends, they all came to know too. It was simply another fact that got passed around and absorbed by our small circle. Like Janet's mother being Canadian, Harry's ex-wife being an actress, and Rosemary's husband, Phil, dancing too close to his wife's friends at parties.

Alma, of course, had known about Mary from the beginning of our friendship. I had told her about meeting Jack, falling in love, getting married, and trying for a baby. Trying and failing. She'd heard all this a long time ago. She knew we'd adopted Mary in Ireland.

'We haven't been over for ages,' I said. 'Not since Mary was small. When we realised how musical she was, we started going to summer schools and festivals in the holidays.'

'You adopted Mary in Ireland?' said Rosemary.

'Yes,' I said. 'And it was all quite sudden and miraculous.'

Looking back, it still seemed like a miracle. Something meant. Jack's food-importing business was beginning to show a decent profit. For the first time since we'd got married we had plenty of money. Jack still spent weeks away from home looking for new suppliers, but he'd hired more staff. I didn't need to spend as much time in the office. It was the perfect time to have a baby. But it didn't happen. There was no hi-tech fertility treatment in those days. We tried not to think about it. It was just a shared sadness in our lives.

'Jack had a cousin who was getting married to a girl from County Offaly,' I told them. 'We flew over to Ireland for the wedding. But we went early and took a holiday at the same time. Our feet hardly touched the ground. We flew to Shannon and drove up the coast to County Mayo to stay with a cousin of Jack's father. Ned O'Connor. A charming man. He died about ten years ago. He was taller even than Jack.

He carried a hawthorn stick. He knew every bend in the road. We had a wonderful time. One day he drove us along a flat peninsula in Mayo. About as far west as you can go. We were right on the edge of the Atlantic. Next stop Newfoundland. There wasn't another car in sight. We took a side road and it ran out at the shoreline. There were the ruins of a church, and this shrine in a field. A faded plaster statue and a well with a hedge round it, on a bit of stony ground near the sea. There was grass everywhere else in the field, even inside the ruins, except for this stony bit. It wasn't a rock. Just dry ground and pebbles. Ned said, "Grass doesn't grow on the grave of a saint. It's an old saying."'

As I told the story, I recalled every detail of the scene. The irises lining the stream that ran down through small fields to the sea. The sunlight glittering on the water. The wind whipping my hair into my eyes. The ancient, faded sign – Saint Dervla's Bed. Jack and Ned walking down the field and clambering over the dry stone wall on to the rocky strand. Me whispering, 'Dear God and Saint Dervla give me a baby.'

'I asked the saint for a baby,' I said. Alma, the great rationalist, was smiling. She'd heard it all before. The others had settled into relaxed, listening mode.

'The next day we drove to the wedding. Maybe Ned said something to Sister

24

Monica. She was at the wedding. A relative of the bride's mother. A cousin, I think. She came over to me at the reception afterwards and said, "Mrs Molloy, I believe we can help each other." It turned out she was in charge of a home for unmarried mothers. Somewhere near Tullamore. There was this girl who'd just had a baby and she'd decided to give it up for adoption. It was a fine healthy baby. Did I want a baby?'

Rosemary gasped. Janet nearly shot out of her seat. I carried on with my story.

'Jack and I had talked about adoption. We'd even approached an agency in London. They told us there was a long waiting list. Years. And here was this nun saying, "Do you want a baby?" I was so stunned I didn't even ask if it was a boy or a girl.

'"I know you are good people",' she said. '"My cousin has known your husband's relatives all her life. You'll give this innocent child a good home."'

'I've never heard anything like it,' said Rosemary. 'What did you do?'

'Jack and I sat up half the night talking. What should we do? It really was the answer to a prayer. But we weren't prepared. Mentally or any other way. Jack was more reluctant than I was. He was worried about the legalities. We didn't know what the law was. I assumed it must be OK if the nun could make the offer. We decided if it was all right legally, we'd adopt the baby. The funny thing was, Jack didn't ask if it was a boy or a girl either. It was as though I was pregnant and we didn't know the sex.

As I recounted the story, I felt again the nervous exhilaration of that night. Jack pacing the hotel room, me sitting on the edge of the bed, gripping and regripping the blue candlewick bedspread.

'Next morning, Jack telephoned a cousin who was a solicitor in Dublin. He told us the law was perfectly straightforward. There was nothing to stop us adopting the baby if the mother had given consent. Then we told Sister Monica we wanted the baby. And then we asked if it was a boy or a girl. She said, "It's a girl."'

I paused, remembering my tears, Jack gripping my hand. Sister Monica producing a folded white handkerchief, big as a tablecloth, from a pocket in her black robe.

'Tears of happiness I hope,' she said.

'I don't know how we managed,' I continued. 'We rushed about buying baby clothes and a carrycot and nappies. A cousin of Ned's was a chemist and he gave us bottles, and tins of baby milk, and plastic pants, and baby cream. We had boxes full of stuff. And then we went to this solicitor's office in Tullamore.

'The solicitor gave me a chair to sit on. I heard a car pull up outside the office. I shut my eyes I was so nervous. When I opened them, there was a young nun standing in front of me, holding a tiny baby in a pink blanket. "Here she is, Mrs Molloy," she said.'

I have always thought of that day as Mary's birthday, although she was about two weeks old by then. I took her in my arms. She gave a little murmur. I said, 'Does she have a name? Has she been baptised?'

'Yes,' said the nun. 'She was baptised in the hospital. Her mother called her Frances Mary.' Her hand jumped to her mouth. 'I'm not supposed to tell you that.'

'You get an amended birth certificate,' the solicitor said, 'with the name you give her.'

'We'll call her Mary,' I said. 'Can we add Dervla too?'

'You can call her whatever you like,' the solicitor said. 'It's an entirely separate document, a copy of her entry in the Adopted Children's Register. It becomes her official birth certificate.'

I looked at Jack. 'Frances Mary Dervla Molloy sounds right to me.'

'Me too,' said Jack.

'Dervla,' said the nun. 'My name's Dervla.'

'I thought that was a good omen,' I said. 'In fact, you'll think I'm silly, but I thought it was a sign from the saint.'

'I don't think you're silly at all,' said Rosemary. 'That's an amazing tale.'

The sun had dropped. Our shadows angled sharply across the table, and stretched across the floor to the skirting boards.

'What do you think the nun wants?' said Janet.

'I've no idea,' I said.

'Maybe she's been asked to pass on a message. Maybe Mary's – maybe somebody's got in touch and wants to know about her.'

She was going to say 'real mother'.

'You mean Mary's birth mother might have contacted her?' I lightly emphasised the preferred term. 'That's possible.'

'Maybe she's an opera singer herself,' said Rosemary. 'All that talent must come from somewhere. Of course you and Jack encouraged her and made it all possible. But you know what I mean.'

'Isn't it nice you're going to be able to tell her that Mary's happy and successful,' said the ever-tactful Alma.

'Has she never telephoned before?' said Janet.

'Never.'

'Sometimes things happen in your life that make you want to revisit your past,' said Rosemary. 'When I turned fifty I got this great urge to contact all the girls I'd been at school with.'

'Maybe she's ill. Maybe she wants to find out about...' Janet rooted around again for the right word, 'about the baby she gave up. Before she ... before she...'

'Dies?' I said. 'That's an uncomfortable thought.'

There was a moment's silence. Then we heard a car door slam outside.

'That'll be Harry,' said Janet. 'Time to go home. Give me a ring if you need any more help. And let me know what happens.'

'Me too,' said Rosemary. 'I'd better get back as well.' I walked with them to the front door, reiterating my thanks, and waved them goodbye.

Chapter 2

When I went back into the kitchen, Alma handed me another glass of champagne.

'Drink up. It's a cure for everything.'

'They're sweet and we wouldn't have managed without them.'

'Feet don't enter a closed mouth,' said Alma. She scanned my face, concern in her dark grey eyes. 'Are you OK? Has the phone call upset you?'

'Not really,' I said. 'I'm just curious. Well, maybe a bit worried. I don't like to think it might be something to do with Mary's birth mother. Some illness. Maybe something that would affect Mary. Something hereditary we don't know about. I suppose I am a bit anxious.'

'Call now,' said Alma. 'I'll wait.'

'There's a second bottle in the fridge,' I said. 'As you say, it's a cure for everything.'

I switched on the light in the hall, read the number on the message pad, steadied my breathing, and dialled. Sister Monica answered almost immediately.

'Thank you for calling back, Mrs Molloy.'

'Did you have a particular reason for your call, sister? I wondered if you'd been asked to pass on a message.'

'Oh no,' she said. 'I just wanted the information for myself. I've placed a lot of babies in my time. I want to retire knowing I've done a good job. Signing off, you could say.'

The knot in my stomach loosened. I waved at Alma through the glass door and raised my thumb, more relaxed now.

'What would you like to know?'

'Whatever you'd like to tell me,' she replied, in a pleasant tone.

'She's an opera singer,' I began. 'A mezzo soprano.'

I heard a quick inhalation of breath.

'Marvellous.'

'She's based in Stuttgart. But she's coming home tonight. On her way to San Francisco. She's got a part in *Suor Angelica*.'

'Puccini,' said Sister Monica approvingly. 'A great favourite with my brother and me.'

'At San Francisco Opera.' Excitement pitched my voice higher. 'With Adela Contini!'

'That will get her noticed.' I could tell Sister Monica was impressed.

'She's noticed already. She has two CDs out, on the Adagio label. And she's sung for the Pope.'

'A great honour,' said Sister Monica. 'The Adagio label, you said?'

'Yes. *Mary Molloy sings Mozart and Rossini*, and *Arias from the Baroque Era*.'

'I'll look out for them,' said Sister Monica. 'Tell me, is she married?'

'Not yet. But she's a beautiful girl. A golden girl.'

'Some man doesn't know his luck yet,' she said. 'You must be proud of her.'

'Immensely proud. I bless the day we met you, sister. When do you actually stop work?'

'Not for another few months,' she said. 'But it takes a long time to tidy up.'

She took down my new address and telephone number, and rang off.

Alma jumped up from the table and gave me a hug.

'Is it all right?'

'Yes. Just a catch-up call. Before she retires.'

'I'll go home, then,' she said. 'I'm expecting a call from Gerry.' Her shoulders slumped. 'I've only seen him twice in the last three months,' she said. 'The department was reorganised. Then the eldest graduated. Then he was away with the family on holiday.'

Gerry had been a fixture in Alma's life for six years. They'd met at an Open University summer school. He was clever, charming and married with three children. In the beginning it was a heady affair of stolen meetings and illicit trips to London and Paris. Even Boston once, for a conference. In the last few years it had settled into a pale pretence of domesticity. Gerry usually spent Tuesday nights with Alma in a London hotel. Jack called him Mr Tuesday.

'He always goes away with them in the summer,' I said. 'Stay and eat with us.'

'No. You three should have a family dinner without me moping around.'

'Mary's agent will be here as well. Eddy. He's meeting her at Heathrow.'

'They'll want to discuss work.'

'They can do that in the car. Stay and have dinner.'

'No.'

'I'll run you home.'

'No. You've had at least two glasses of champagne. And you have to cook.' She tapped a number into her mobile.

'There's a casserole in the oven. I only have to heat it up and toss a salad.'

'Taxi to Hope House, Stratton Road. White gate posts.' She gave me a wan smile. 'Twenty-five minutes? OK.'

'Sit down and talk to me while you're waiting. I'll wrap this last piece of cake for you.'

'Things haven't been good all year,' she said. 'He promised to see in the Millennium with me. Then he said his wife had organised a party and he had to be there. Then he stopped calling me every day. I call him more than he calls me. He didn't telephone this morning.' Her eyes glistened with tears. 'My birthday. And he didn't call me.'

'Maybe he'll call tonight.'

'You think I'm a fool. You've never approved of Gerry.'

'I just think a man who can live a lie for six years isn't a good bet.'

'They've bought a house in France,' she said. 'He didn't even tell me. I heard it from a colleague. The fucking Lot-et-Garonne. Apparently it's *the* place to buy at the moment.'

Alma doesn't swear often. She doesn't cry often, either. I reached across the table and squeezed her hand.

'He doesn't deserve you.'

'I just want someone to come home to,' she said. 'To be domestic.'

33

She stood up and began to clear the table.

'The ironic thing is, the last time I saw him was a meeting about the syllabus and next year's reading list. Attitudes and Approaches to Marriage in the Nineteenth-Century Novel. It's going to be one of the modules. Did you know there isn't a single happy marriage in Jane Austen? Yet we all assume Elizabeth and Darcy will live happily ever after.'

She carried the plates and glasses to the dishwasher.

'What about the Gardiners in *Pride and Prejudice?* That's a happy marriage. And the admiral and his wife in *Persuasion?*'

'Exceptions prove the rule,' she said. 'Shall I put the CD away?'

'Please. In the box marked A to M.'

'I've set a new book about marriage as a corrective to all those romantic nineteenth-century novels. Bloody *Jane Eyre*. Do you know wives do all the work? If they bring home the bacon they have to cook it as well. Married men earn more, they're healthier and they live longer. Married women, on the other hand, are more depressed than single women.'

'I'm not depressed,' I said.

'You're another exception that proves the rule. You don't know how lucky you are.'

She flipped through the CDs and records in the box.

'I didn't know you liked country and western,' she said, pulling out a long-playing record. 'This might fit my mood. Can I put it on?'

She handed me the sleeve. Four men with sixties haircuts and a girl in a miniskirt sat on a stone wall. *The Melody Kings: Ireland's Premier Showband with Ireland's Queen of Song.*

'Probably Jack's,' I said. 'He never gets rid of records. He must have bought this ages ago. On one of his trips to Ireland. Put it on if you like.'

Alma placed the shiny vinyl disc on the turntable.

'Mary likes country and western,' I said. 'She says the plots are the same as opera. Love, betrayal, secrets, loss.'

The needle sank on to the grooves. A husky female voice sang,

'Sometimes it's hard to be a woman,
Giving all your love to just one man.
You'll have bad times,
And he'll have good times,
Doing things that you don't understand.'

'Nothing like a bit of homespun sentiment to cheer me up,' Alma said, drying her eyes, and beginning to laugh.

The doorbell rang. She downed her glass and took her jacket from the back of a chair.

'Thanks for the party and the cake,' she said. 'It was a really nice thing to do.'

'Thanks for helping.'

She gave me a hug. 'That's what friends are for.'

I met Alma when Mary was ten. I wanted to kick-start my brain and was curious about the Open University. Alma was working as a tutor counsellor while she studied for her Ph.D. I didn't enrol in the end. Jack wasn't keen.

'Knocking shop,' he said. 'I've heard about these residential study weeks. I don't want my wife running off with her tutor.'

'This tutor is a she,' I said. 'And I'd never have an affair. Even if she was a he.'

'I know,' he said. 'You are the most wonderful wife. I think you're perfect as you are.'

To tell the truth, I didn't mind Jack being possessive. He wasn't one of those men who watch their wives obsessively. He liked to see men flirt with me at parties. 'I'm going home with the most desirable woman in the room,' he'd say.

'I've got the vocabulary of a ten-year-old,' I told him. 'I'd just like to exercise my brain.'

'I need someone to write a brochure,' he said. 'Will you do that for me? You could come into the office when Mary's at school. Get more involved in the business. That'll exercise your brain.'

That's how I learned marketing. I'm quite good at it now.

When I told Alma I wasn't going to enrol in the Open University she said, 'Why don't you come to our women's group? We meet once a week.'

So I went along every Monday night, clutching a copy of that week's recommended reading. We read feminist theory and the poetry of Sylvia Plath and Emily Dickinson. We examined Shakespeare's attitude to women, and discussed Virginia Woolf's *A Room of One's Own*. We went in an excited group to hear Germaine Greer and Andrea Dworkin. We talked about Northern Ireland, the miners' strike and the women protesters at Greenham Common. I wasn't too hot on feminist theory, but I enjoyed the poetry. I kept a commonplace book and wrote down lines that particularly appealed to me. After each meeting, we'd go to the pub for a drink and general gossip. One summer evening there was a particularly gory chat about childbirth. We were sitting outside. Alma went inside to get more drinks. I got up to help her. Being small and faun-like, she finds it hard to get served in a crowded bar. Besides, I wanted to escape.

'I feel a bit left out,' I said, as I stood with my hand in the air, waiting to order. 'I'm not the real McCoy. Mary's adopted. I'm all right as long as we're talking about bottles and prams and toilet training. But I can't compete on stitches and sore nipples. I feel a bit of a fraud.'

'I don't have any children,' said Alma. Her tone was bright, but her dark grey eyes were sad. 'I'm not married. I don't even have a man in my life to complain about.'

Suddenly we were swapping life stories. We've been friends ever since. When Jack was away on trips, Alma kept me company and entertained me with stories from the dating jungle. I was easy to talk to and I kept her secrets, she said. I found her great fun. She brought a whiff of the world I left behind when I married Jack. A world of sharing make-up and confidences. A world of parties and blind dates. She was the little sister I never had.

On the surface we are different. She is bohemian, feminist, agnostic and analytical. I am domestic, careful, Catholic and instinctive. But deep down, I believe we share the same view of the world. We come at things from the same emotional angle.

Chapter 3

I listened to Alma's choice of record as I laid the table for dinner.

'I don't want your lonely mansion with a tear in every room,

*All I want's the love you've promised beneath
  the haloed moon.*
*But you think I should be happy with your
  money and your name,*
*And hide myself in sorrow while you play your
  cheatin' game.'*

This hadn't been a lonely mansion, I thought. Mary had filled it with laughter and happiness. I was about to choose something more cheerful, when the telephone rang. I went into the hall to answer it, closing the door against the downbeat song with the incongruously upbeat tune.

'Hello, Mum. How's the move going?'

'Darling, where are you?'

'At Heathrow. Waiting for my bags. Mum, I've got a friend with me. Can he stay? Is that all right? He's on his way to Chicago. We travelled from Stuttgart together.'

'Of course he can stay. He can help us celebrate our last evening in the old house. Maybe we'll see him in the new house as well.'

'Mum,' she said, on a rising note of warning, 'you're trying to marry me off again.'

'You haven't mentioned anyone for ages. What's his name?' I wondered if she was living with him in Stuttgart.

'Hugo. He's a percussionist. You'll like him. Whoops. There's one of my bags! We'll be with you soon. *Wiedersehen!*'

Jack walked through the front door as I

put the telephone down. I loved his daily homecoming, the fizz of excitement I felt when his broad, handsome face signalled his pleasure to be home.

'Who was that? Have I time to shower and change?'

He was backlit by the evening sun flooding through the twin glass panels in the door. I returned his imagined smile.

'Mary. She's at Heathrow. You've got about an hour and a half.' I opened the kitchen door. The plangent tones of Ireland's Queen of Song drifted into the hall.

Jack hesitated at the foot of the stairs. I realised he wasn't smiling. The corners of his mouth twitched. He bit his lip.

'What's the matter? What's wrong?'

'Nothing.'

'Come on, Jack. What's up?'

The music began to irritate me. I hurried into the kitchen and stopped the revolving turntable. The song died in mid-sentence. I looked over my shoulder at Jack, framed in the doorway, looking uncomfortable.

'Tell me what's wrong.'

'I'll be away a bit longer. I'm going to New Zealand as well as Australia.'

I lifted the record from the turntable, suppressing the urge to snap the disc in two.

'Why?'

'I talked to a rep at the Wine Trade Fair this morning. He has his eye on independent producers the supermarkets and Bibendum haven't signed up. He thinks I should go over myself. If they're as good as he says they are, and if I can sign an exclusive contract with them ... it's too good a chance to miss.'

I walked across the room to put the record in its box. Jack said, 'Come on, Lena. It's all part of the plan. The more business I tie down the more we'll have when I sell.'

'I suppose I can stay an extra week with Alma.'

'Ten days.'

'Go upstairs and change,' I said.

'I have to go to North and South Island. Ten days. In exchange for more money when we retire. Then I'll be home all the time.'

'I've sent out the invitations for the housewarming.'

'I'll be back by then.'

'Only just.'

'I'm sorry.'

'Go and change.' I said.

I laid an extra place for dinner. I washed another lettuce and dried each leaf carefully on a tea towel. I straightened the tablemats. Then I went upstairs. Jack had just stepped out of the shower and was towelling his hair.

'I hate you being away. The bed's too wide. I don't want to cook for one.'

He wrapped the towel around his waist and stepped up to me.

'Where's my homecoming kiss?'

41

I trailed my fingers across his damp chest. 'How come you have grey hairs on your chest but not on your head?'

'This is the last big trip. I promise.' He pulled me to him and locked me in his arms. 'I'll make it up to you. When we sell the business we'll travel the world together. Then I'll never be away from home.'

Half an hour later I said, 'Mary's bringing a friend to stay overnight. A percussionist. His name's Hugo.'

'Boyfriend?'

'I don't know,' I said. 'I rather hope so.'

'I've always thought Eddy had a soft spot for her,' Jack said.

'Eddy's got a posh girlfriend in PR. And Mary calls him steady Eddy,' I said.

'Steady can be exciting,' said Jack, 'when steady has long legs and golden hair.'

'Eddy has dark hair,' I said.

He laughed and hugged me tighter.

'Alma probably won't mind if I stay a bit longer,' I said. 'She might be glad of the company. Gerry's bought a house in France.'

'The writing on the wall,' Jack said. 'Big enough for even Alma to see. Mr Tuesday was never going to leave his wife. If he didn't leave in the first flush of the affair he never will. He'll end up with his wife. Men usually do.' He pulled his arm from under my shoulder and sat up.

42

'Are you talking from experience?' I was teasing. I never doubted him for a moment. 'Are you thinking about Phil? I thought he was all talk and no action?'

'Nobody you would recognise,' he said. 'But I know men as you know women. They can both be fools for love.'

'I'd like Alma to meet someone else,' I said.

'Why don't you take her to La Colline?'

We had bought a house in the south of France, near Antibes. Our plan was to retire in three years' time, when Jack was sixty. We would spend the winters there, our summers in England. We were already spending our holidays and free weekends in La Colline. I knew what buying a house in France implied for Alma's relationship with Gerry. And how she would feel about going to France.

With a sigh of regret, I dismissed our pink house with its blue shutters, the walled garden, the rooftops below it, descending like irregular steps into the valley, and the Mediterranean shimmering in the distance.

'I don't think France is the right place for Alma at the moment.'

'Go somewhere else. There's time.'

'That's what you think,' I said. 'I've got plenty to do.'

'Nothing that can't wait.'

'I'll think about it,' I said. 'Now. I've got to make up a bed for Mary's friend. They'll be here soon. Where will I put him? Do you think...?'

I had never faced the prospect of my daughter sleeping with a boyfriend under my roof and had counted myself lucky when friends had agonised about it.

'Put him in the spare room, Lena,' Jack said. 'He can pad along the corridor in the middle of the night if he wants to. You won't know a thing about it. And you won't be encouraging immorality.'

'I wish Mary would tell me more,' I said. 'I was looking forward to nice girly chats. I want to be her friend.'

'Mothers are mothers and friends are friends,' Jack said. 'Be glad you're a mother.'

'I am,' I said. 'I am.'

Chapter 4

Mary, Eddy and Hugo tumbled through the door in a commotion of chat and suitcases. They were almost identically dressed in blue jeans, T-shirts and black leather jackets. Mary had bundled her blonde hair into a knot on top of her head. Her dark eyes took in the rolled up rugs, the paintings stacked against the wall, the bare windows.

'I'm glad I'm here to say goodbye to the

house,' she said. 'I love my little flat in Stuttgart. But I still think of this as home.'

'Our new house will be home to you as well,' I said.

'I know, Mum. Home is where the heart is.' And she gave me a great big hug.

Jack emerged from the kitchen, filaments of creamy flowers trailing from his hands. The scent of honeysuckle tickled my nose, and filled my throat with sweetness. He tucked a curling tendril of green spears and yellow-tipped blossoms into Mary's hair.

'Flower power,' he said. 'For my golden girl.'

Mary laughed. Eddy and Hugo clapped. Jack pulled first Mary, then me, into his embrace before breaking free to shake hands with Eddy and Hugo.

Hugo was from San Sebastian. He had a big-boned face and crow-black hair that swept his collar. Over dinner, he regaled us with stories about temperamental conductors and drunken oboists. Eddy was his usual quiet self. He listened, occasionally brushing a brown wing of hair from his forehead, while Hugo flirted and flattered with compliments.

'Maria, I move in with you if you cook like your mama.'

Mary gave Hugo a dimpled smile. That's one question answered, I thought.

'Mary has beauty from her father and

brains from her mother,' said Hugo. 'Or maybe the other way. Yes. The other way. Beauty from her mother.'

I glanced at Mary. She hadn't told him she was adopted.

'Everybody says how alike we all are,' she said.

After dinner we took our drinks into the drawing room. Eddy said, 'Will you sing before I go, Mary? The Habanera from *Carmen*? Will you accompany her, Hugo?'

I retrieved candles from a box in the kitchen and put them in the candelabra on the mantelpiece. I dimmed the lights and lit the candles. Jack, Eddy and I took our places on the sofa, smiling in anticipation. Hugo sat down at the piano. Mary pulled the ribbon from her hair and shook it free. Honeysuckle flowers fluttered to the floor. She stood beside the piano and sang,

'Love at best is a bird in flight
That cares not what you do or say.
Call it back, and it's out of sight;
You point, it flies the other way.'

She was all fire and sparkle. She swayed to the tango rhythm of the Habanera as her voice rose with ease, and descended thrillingly to the dark, lower notes.

'When it's ready to leave the nest
Nor you nor I can make it stay.
That's love! That's love!'

Mary finished with a triumphant toss of her

head. She looked magnificent. Jack and I applauded. Eddy jumped up and hugged her. 'Knock 'em dead in San Francisco, Mary.'

As I saw him out, his broad face flushed and eager, he said, 'I wanted you to hear how her voice is developing. I'm sorry I have to go. I could listen to Mary singing all night.'

'Me too,' I said.

Eddy's departure broke up our little party.

'Do you mind I go to bed now?' Hugo said. 'I like to phone my partner. He is singing at the Met. He will be on stage in thirty minutes.'

I hope I concealed my surprise and disappointment.

'I told you he was just a friend,' Mary said, when Hugo left the room. 'Didn't you guess, Mum?'

'I had no idea,' I said. 'I thought maybe you and he... I couldn't tell.'

Jack said, 'Don't look at me, Lena. I can't tell, either.' He sat down at the piano. 'Will we have a swansong for the old house?' He began to play and sing, *'Bless this House O Lord we pray,*
Make it safe by night and day.
Bless these walls so firm and stout,
Keeping want and trouble out.'
Mary and I joined in.

I saw all three of us reflected in the wide bow window. The perfect picture of domestic harmony.

Chapter 5

In the middle of the night I woke up and realised I had forgotten to tell Jack and Mary about Sister Monica's call. Jack stirred beside me.

'You're very restless,' he said, sliding his arm under my shoulders. I nestled into the crook of his neck.

'Sister Monica telephoned.'

'Who?'

'The nun who gave us Mary.'

His grip tightened. 'Good God. What did she want? Is there a problem? Is that why you can't sleep?'

'I don't think there's a problem. I had a long chat with her. She just said she was retiring and wanted to catch up on all the babies she'd placed for adoption.'

His arm relaxed. 'I don't even remember what she looked like. They were all dressed like crows. They all looked the same to me. But I don't suppose she was more than forty, forty-five max. Do nuns retire?'

'They do if they've been working, I suppose. It's like any other job. I suppose she has the right to be curious. I'm just a bit worried.'

'I'm sure everything's all right,' Jack said. 'Wouldn't she have told you if there was anything to worry about? Have you told Mary?'

'Not yet. There wasn't time last night. I forgot all about it.'

'It might make her interested in finding out about her birth parents. Would you mind?'

'It wouldn't bother me. Would it bother you?'

'No.' He kissed my forehead and disengaged his arm.

'Sometimes I think I'm more interested than she is,' I said.

Jack went back to sleep, but curiosity about Mary's origins lurked like a salmon in the dark pool of my brain, and so I lay thinking how little we'd been told about the girl who had given Mary up for adoption. I say 'girl' because I had always pictured her as a young student, schoolgirl even. Frightened by the pregnancy. Unable to tell her parents. Anxious to return to her studies. Knowing in her heart she couldn't cope with a baby. Realising adoption was for the best.

I concentrated on retrieving my conversations with Sister Monica, projecting myself back into the cheerful crowd milling around the entrance to the hotel. Hearing again the oohs and aahs of admiration as the page boy and flower girls followed the bride

49

up the strip of red carpet on the wide stone steps. 'Always other people's children,' I said, my throat tightening. 'Never our own.'

Jack muttered, 'No need to tell the world our trouble. At least try to look as though you're enjoying yourself.'

Sister Monica was tall. I noticed her making her way towards me along the gauntlet of guests waving and throwing confetti as the bride and groom scampered, hand in hand, to their car. As the car pulled away, with old boots and saucepans bumping over the gravel and Just Married lipsticked on the back window, she said, 'Wasn't Noreen a lovely bride? She's got herself a fine fellow. A relative of yours, I believe?'

'He's my husband's cousin,' I said. 'Jack Molloy. I'm Lena Molloy.'

'I'm Sister Monica. A cousin of the bride's mother. I'm delighted to meet you, Lena. You've been heaven sent.'

I was intrigued. 'How so, sister?'

'I hope you don't mind, but I understand you are anxious to have a baby.'

I recoiled. 'I don't think that's anybody's business but my own.'

'Now, dear,' she said – she was just old enough to be able to say that to me. 'Don't be angry. Gossip can be bad. But sometimes it's well meant. I believe we can help each other.'

Guests were beginning to gather round the

piano in the lounge. She gestured towards a quiet corner, away from the music.

'I run a home for unmarried mothers,' she said. 'I find homes for their babies. Good Catholic homes.'

My heart beat faster as she continued.

'I have a baby at the moment. The mother is a talented girl. From decent people. The father is a very distinguished man.' She sighed. 'The poor infant needs a home right away. I know you'll give this innocent child a good home. My cousin has known your husband's relatives all her life. Would you think about it?'

She had astounded me.

'I'll have to talk to Jack,' I managed to say. 'And we're going back to England at the end of the week.'

'I know,' she said. 'And please God you'll be taking this little bundle with you. You're staying in the hotel, aren't you?' And she glided away. We never learned any more about Mary's birth parents.

In those early days, when Mary cried, or wouldn't take her bottle, I would whisper, 'What do I do now?' And close my eyes to conjure up the slight, hazy figure of a girl in a summer frock with the sun behind her, her features in shadow.

I couldn't look after her. Do what you think is best, she seemed to say. After a few weeks, I

51

grew more confident. The figure faded to a blur. But sometimes, when I lifted Mary out of her cot, I thought of a girl wrapping her baby in a pink blanket and handing her to a nun.

Why had Sister Monica telephoned after all these years? The more I thought about it, the less I believed it had been a simple matter of catching up. I considered Janet's suggestion that Mary's birth mother was terminally ill, and had contacted Sister Monica for news of the baby she'd given up for adoption. What if she had a hereditary disease? Something Mary needed to be told about. But Sister Monica would have said, wouldn't she? She would have said. If there were some condition Mary could inherit she would be bound to say something. Or could it be the father who had got in touch with Sister Monica? Maybe he was the one who was dying, and weighing his life in the balance. 'A very distinguished man.' Sister Monica's words floated to the surface of my mind. Her description made him sound older than Mary's natural mother. I tried to imagine him. But the shadowy figure of a girl in a summer frock was all that came to mind.

Chapter 6

After breakfast, I sat on Mary's bed as she reorganised her suitcases. I told her about Sister Monica's call.

'I hope you told her I was a great success,' Mary said.

'Of course. She was delighted. Maybe you'll go and see her some day,' I said.

Mary folded her pink blanket and put it in the bag she would carry on to the plane. I felt a tremor of jealousy. I thought of the teddy bear my mother knitted for me. I take it everywhere.

'You'll want to know some day,' I said. 'Don't you wonder where you got your voice? Your mother or your father, or both, must have been very musical. They gave you a great gift.'

'You're my mother. Dad's my father.'

'You know what I mean.'

'Look, Mum. You've given me all your time and attention. Who knows what would have happened in other circumstances? Maybe I'd be singing country and western, or karaoke in a bar. Or just singing in the bath.'

'Oh, I don't know.'

'I'm grateful, Mum. All that slogging round festivals. All those singing lessons.'

'As long as it was worth it.'

'Worth it? I studied with Vera Rózsa. I'm going to sing at San Francisco Opera.'

'Are you nervous?' I said.

'A bit. It's a small part, but a big stage. The thing is,' she said, 'my voice is getting bigger. I'm extending the range of my voice, my tessitura, all the time. My voice teacher thinks I could be a soprano.'

'Mary, that's wonderful.'

'I want to be a soprano,' she said.

I loved it when Mary confided her hopes in me. 'You could be the next Adela Contini,' I said, excitedly.

Mary flushed. She fingered the single strand of pearls round her throat.

'Mum,' she began.

Jack put his head round the door. 'Is this girls only, or can I join in?'

'Mary's going to be a soprano,' I said.

Jack took her hands and kissed her forehead. 'We're proud of you, Mary. You're going to shine in San Francisco.'

'Taxi's here!' Hugo called from downstairs. They were all three travelling to Heathrow together. Mary hugged me.

'I'm the happiest woman alive,' she said.

'Go ahead, I'll bring your case down,' Jack said.

He stroked my hair. 'I'll telephone. If you

54

go away, take your mobile. Didn't we have a lovely evening?'

'Yes,' I said. 'I'll miss this house.'

'Me too,' he said. 'But we'll be just as happy in the new one.'

At six o'clock, I waved goodbye to the cheery trio of removal men and went back inside. I stood for a while in the kitchen. The house was quiet. I opened the French windows and walked to the end of the garden. The brickwork glowed pink and gold in the evening sun. A frill of red leaves curled down the edge of the back wall. The scent of rosemary filled the air. I walked back up the path, wrapping my memories around me, like a cardigan.

When Jack and I stepped hand in hand over the threshold thirty years ago, I had my eyes scrunched tight because I wanted to share his surprise.

'Pleased? Like it?' I asked.

'It's fantastic!'

While I supervised the work on the house, Jack had been visiting fisheries and smoke-houses in the west of Ireland. He hated having builders and decorators around all the time. He had wanted to buy a modern house. But the agent had seen my eyes linger on the colour photograph of Hope House with the Virginia creeper glowing on the front and gable wall.

'Sounds like a home for fallen women,' said Jack.

'I like the name,' I said. 'It's a good name for a house.'

The agent smiled politely. 'It was named for the man who built it,' he said. 'Jeremiah Hope. He owned the brickworks that supplied the brick. It's a bit out of your range. But it is rather splendid. The owners want a quick sale and might accept less than the asking price. We've had a lot of interest. Plenty of room for a family,' he added.

And so we were persuaded to buy this large Victorian semi-detached house, in much need of modernisation. I remembered how Jack had kissed me in the hallway. 'You've done a wonderful job, Lena. We're going to be happy here,' he said.

We were still trying for a baby at the time. Trying. A strange and terrible phrase for an act of love. But it's what people said, smiling inquisitively, 'Are you trying for a baby?' I hated those words.

Jack wanted a family as much as I did. He was an only child, brought up by his widowed mother and grandfather. 'Let's have our children when we're young and able to enjoy them,' he said.

When we got married, we did nothing to prevent my getting pregnant. We just expected it to happen. Girlfriends who got married around the same time got pregnant. 'Honeymoon baby,' they would say, with rueful smiles. After two years, I began to worry. Dada recommended Mr Granger in Harley Street.

'You're a fit, healthy young woman,' Mr Granger said. 'A little on the thin side for your height. Everything all right in the...' he paused, 'love department?'

'Fine,' I said firmly.

I became an expert on fertility. Jack sighed, as the pile of books by the bed grew higher.

'I'm not a performing seal, Lena. I can't always do things to order. If it's going to happen it's going to happen. Try to be happy as you are.'

'It's my fault,' I said.

'Lena, let's have none of this your-fault-or-my-fault stuff. This is something we share. Relax,' Jack said. 'We have plenty of time.'

I grew desperate. He grew sad. The room I'd chosen as a nursery reproached me every time I climbed the stairs. 'A house is not a home,' I said to Jack.

We made an appointment with an adoption society and sat in a cramped, airless office near Westminster Cathedral while a social worker took our details. Photographs of beaming couples with babies hung on the wall behind her desk.

'How long might we have to wait?' I asked.

'There is a vetting procedure. If you are considered suitable, your names will go on the waiting list.'

'How long?' I said.

She put her pen down and looked at me and then at Jack, before addressing a midpoint between us.

'There are more couples wanting to adopt than there are babies for adoption. You should expect to wait about three years.'

I cried all the way back to Hope House.

A year later, Mary turned our house into a home. I carried her, still wrapped in the pink blanket, into the nursery at the top of the stairs. 'This is your room, Mary,' I whispered to her. 'I picked it for you, before you were born.'

Now, twenty-seven years later, I stood in the doorway of Mary's room. Even after she left home to go to the Royal College of Music and then the London Opera Centre, I kept it ready in case she telephoned and said, 'Mum, I can drive up tonight. There's a bit of a break in rehearsals.'

Here she had hung her signed photographs of Placido Domingo and Kiri Te Kanawa, her posters from music festivals, her diplomas and awards. I smiled at the bright patch of wall where the old German upright piano had stood. When we discovered Mary's prodigious talent for music, we bought a grand piano, and moved the upright piano to her bedroom.

'You can get rid of the furniture in my room,' she said, when I told her we had sold the house. 'But I'm taking my old upright. It's my good luck charm.'

I closed the door and went downstairs. I put a jar of my green tomato chutney on the breakfast bar in the kitchen. 'I hope you will be as happy in Hope House as we were,' I wrote on the card for the new owners. 'Best wishes from Jack and Lena Molloy.'

I stood for a moment in the dark hallway. Car headlights swept over the windows and disappeared into the night.

'Goodbye, house,' I said.

Chapter 7

Over the next few days, I fell into a gentle routine with Alma. I spent my mornings in the office and my afternoons shopping and comparing swatches of fabric for curtains in the new house. In the evening I cooked dinner.

On Wednesday afternoon, Mary telephoned from San Francisco.

'Change of plans, Mum,' she said. 'I've just spoken to Eddy. He's got me a concert tour with the Frankfurt Symphony Orchestra. American Century, all American composers. In Europe. Starting the week after next.'

'But you've only just got there.'

'It's Gershwin songs, Mum. Isn't that exciting?'

'I thought *Suor Angelica* was a big break,' I said.

'I was only one of the nuns. The Novice Mistress.'

'But you were singing with Adela Contini.'

'This is better. And I can show off my figure in a nice frock.'

She laughed. But I thought I caught an edge of anxiety.

'Can you opt out just like that?'

'Oh yes. My replacement is lined up. She's delighted.'

'Are you sure this is the right move for you?'

'It's an emergency. Dawn Upshaw has dropped out.'

Trust Mary to help someone out of a tight spot, I thought. 'And Eddy thinks it's a good move?'

'Yes, Mum.' She sounded more definite. 'All the European capitals. London on the fourteenth of October.'

'That's the housewarming,' I said, dismayed. 'I've sent out the invitations.'

'You could come to Dublin,' she said. 'The tour starts there on Monday week.'

And then I had my big idea.

I would go to Ireland and look for Mary's birth mother. Excitement surged through me. This would be my gift to Mary! A surprise. Absolute proof of my love. I half listened to her chatting about flights to Frankfurt and rehearsals and meeting the conductor. The idea thickened in my head. I saw myself meeting Sister Monica. Maybe even Mary's natural parents. No. That would be going too far. I would leave that to Mary. I would content myself with finding the names and addresses. I would put it all in a letter I would give to Mary when she admitted interest in her natural parents. I would give a copy to my solicitor. The letter would be there for Mary – even if she put off looking for them until I was dead. I was thrilled with myself.

'Mum?' Mary's voice brought me back to the present. 'Are you listening? You haven't said a word. Are you there?'

'Yes, darling,' I said. 'I was just thinking about flights to Ireland and hotels and hire cars. I might take a holiday at the same time.'

'Mum, you're coming! That's wonderful. You never take enough time for yourself.'

'Call me from Frankfurt,' I said. 'Lots of love.'

I was peeling potatoes when Alma got back from London.

'Just what I always wanted,' she said. 'A wife to come home to. What are we having this evening?'

'Tarragon chicken, green salad, new potatoes, raspberries and cream,' I said, with some pride. I am a good cook.

'Divorce Jack and marry me,' said Alma.

'Wine and glasses on the table. I'll join you as soon as I've put the potatoes on. I can't divorce. I'm a Catholic. How was your day?'

Alma flopped on to a chair and poured herself a glass of wine. She looked tired, unhappy, and almost as old as her years.

'I'm a feminist,' she said. 'I've got a good brain, a good job, great friends, freedom,' she said. 'Why isn't that enough?'

'How did you leave it with Gerry?' I said.

'I burst into tears at breakfast and ran out of the dining room. I feel such a fool. I'm forty-three, for God's sake. My life's a mess.'

I abandoned the potatoes, sat down opposite Alma and poured myself a generous slosh as well.

'Feelings don't stop at forty,' I said. 'Or fifty, or sixty. Feelings never stop. People in their eighties fall in love and get jealous and fight and cry. Your emotional life's a bit messy. The rest of your life is fine. You have a good job and a nice house. You're fit and healthy. You just need time to think. Take a holiday. When did you last take any leave?'

'I took a week in April when Gerry had

that conference in Geneva.'

'And nothing since. Right? You definitely need a holiday. And not with Gerry.'

'Some chance,' she said. 'And I'm fed up going away on my own. Bloody ramblers, the refuge of the single. Or health farms. The book in the dining room, the waiters feeling sorry for me, the dreaded single room supplement.'

'Come with me to Ireland,' I said.

'What?'

I told her about Mary's change of plan. 'I'm going to see her in Dublin on Monday week. I thought I'd take a holiday at the same time. Go early. Maybe stay in Dublin for a while. I haven't been to Ireland for ages. Oh, Alma, come with me. Please. It's better than sitting beside the bottle of gin that never rings.'

At least I'd raised a smile.

'I'll think about it,' she said. 'I'm going into the garden for a cigarette.'

'I thought you'd stopped.'

'I've stopped smoking in the house. And I've cut down to about two a day,' she said. 'Just now, I feel I need one.' She rummaged in her bag for a packet of cigarettes and a lighter, picked up her glass and went outside.

She'd clearly given my suggestion a lot of thought by the time we sat down to eat.

'When would we go?'

'This weekend?'

'Does the nun have anything to do with this sudden decision?' She looked me straight in the eye. She knows me well.

'Why shouldn't I go to Ireland and see Mary?'

'Lena,' said my best friend, 'you are the most organised person I have ever met. You know exactly what you're doing every day for months ahead. You never do things on impulse.'

'I did once,' I said, 'and never regretted it.'

She dismissed my daughter with a wave of her hand.

'You know what I mean. Generally speaking, you prefer things organised well in advance. I can see you flying over to Ireland for a couple of days to see Mary. But a holiday at the same time? Don't tell me you haven't three dozen things in your diary for the next two weeks.'

'Nothing I can't change,' I said.

'Are you thinking of going to see whatser-name, the nun?'

'Sister Monica. Yes,' I said. 'I'd like to find out more about Mary's birth parents.'

'Is that wise?'

'It's for her sake.'

'Look,' said Alma. 'I understand why you want to do this. Believe me, I do. But you can't be sure Mary wants to know.'

'I think she wants to know.'

'You think.' Alma pounced on the word. 'You don't know.'

We were both silent for a moment.

'What does Jack say?' said Alma.

'I haven't told him yet.'

'But you will?'

'Of course.' Alma knew I had no secrets from Jack.

'So. Will you come to Ireland with me?' I said.

She thought for a moment. Then she smiled.

'Why not? It'll do me good.' She raised her glass. 'Mud in his eye. Cheers!'

After dinner, I sat by Alma's computer as she booked flights and car hire and a hotel in Dublin.

'Just for the first night,' she said. 'Things shouldn't be too busy at this time of year. If we don't like it we can change. We don't have to decide about going anywhere else until we get there. I'll get a couple of guidebooks tomorrow.'

Alma doesn't like to tie herself down too much. I'm the opposite. But I felt released from self-imposed constraints. I was embarking on a great adventure, prepared for the unexpected.

'Fine,' I said.

Alma gave the mouse a final click. 'There. That's done. And stuff Gerry,' she said.

Chapter 8

'Mary's leaving San Francisco,' I told Jack when he telephoned the next day. When Jack and Mary were travelling, I was the conduit for family news. 'She's doing a European tour with the Frankfurt Symphony Orchestra instead. Starting with Dublin on Monday week. Gershwin songs.'

'I hope she's doing the right thing for her career,' he said. 'Singing with Adela Contini was a big deal.'

'Mary says this is bigger. We can't see her in London. It's the same date as the housewarming. But I could go to Dublin. I thought I might take a holiday at the same time. I've asked Alma to come too.'

'That's great, Lena. Do you both good. Ireland should be lovely at this time of year. When are you going? How long will you stay?'

'We're flying to Dublin tomorrow. Alma has to be back on Sunday week. I'm staying on for the concert. I thought I could go and see Sister Monica.'

'I don't think that's a good idea,' he said.

'Why not?'

'It's for Mary to decide when and what

she wants to know.'

'But supposing she leaves it too late?'

'Lena, you can't manage other people's lives. You want everything to be perfect for everybody and life is not like that. Life is messy. People make mistakes.'

'I know,' I said.

'No you don't. You think every problem has a solution. They don't. I'm sorry, my angel. I know why you want to do this. But I think you should leave it. Have you told Mary you're thinking of going to see Sister Monica?'

'No.'

'Why don't you ask her what she thinks? She might want to do it for herself.'

I knew Mary better than Jack did. She would always feign indifference about her natural parents. A knot of stubbornness formed in my mind.

'I'll talk to her in Dublin,' I said. 'If she rings you, don't say anything. I want to be able to sit down face to face and have a proper chat about it.'

'I won't say anything to Mary if you leave well enough alone.'

I reluctantly agreed.

On Thursday afternoon I sank into a sofa at the hairdressers, already relaxed and in holiday mode. I was looking forward to going away with Alma. We'd had a giggly girls' weekend in Paris, about ten years ago, and a couple of overnight trips to London for the theatre and an exhibition. We'd never taken a proper holiday together. I picked up a magazine from the coffee table and idly flicked through the pages. Lots of photographs, not much text.

'Kyle and Shiralee pledge their love in Las Vegas ceremony.' 'Wills and Harry favourites at Goodwood.' 'Adela Contini at the Villa Ermosa.'

I wondered if Mary had been a guest at the Villa Ermosa, and felt immediately connected to a more glamorous world. The double photo spread featured the diva perched on a Louis Quinze chair. Black eyes glittered from a giant white powder puff on her knee. Her husband leaned against a marble fireplace. A gilded mirror reflected formal gardens falling in terraces towards a lake. *'Adela Contini with Puccini, her beloved bichon frise, and actor husband, Ricardo Marsili, in their 17th-century villa on Lake Como.'*

'Alwyn's lady?' said a young Goth with spiky black hair, and a steel stud in her nose. 'I'll take you through.' I took the magazine with me.

'Amazing or what?' said Alwyn, looking over my shoulder as I scanned the text. *'...Puccini looked after in her absence by devoted ... laughingly admits to her fiery temper ... denies gossip ... stormy scenes.'*

'It's another world, isn't it?' He fluffed up my hair and examined the effect in the mirror. 'Happy with the colour? Same again? Has your daughter met her?'

'She was going to sing with her in San Francisco, but she's doing a concert tour instead. Gershwin.'

'Lovely,' said Alwyn. 'And a lot safer. Have you seen the story in today's paper?' He pulled the *Daily Express* from the magazine rack beside the mirror and handed it to me. It was folded to a half page of brief items from around the world. He tapped the sub heading: SPARKS FLY AT SAN FRANCISCO OPERA.

I devoured the text.

Staff at San Francisco Opera acted quickly to douse a fire which broke out during rehearsals for Suor Angelica. *The management declined to comment on rumours that hot-tempered diva, Adela Contini, deliberately set fire to the curtains during a dress rehearsal for Puccini's tearjerker about a woman forced to abandon her illegitimate child and join a convent.*

It is rumoured the diva was inflamed by reports that her husband, actor Ricardo Marsili, was having an affair. Backstage staff extinguished the fire within minutes. The diva and her husband have been unavailable for comment. The Management of San Francisco Opera also declined to comment. The opera, now dubbed the hottest show in town, is a sell-out.

Sell-out or not; I was glad Mary was no longer in *Suor Angelica*.

We left for Dublin the next morning.

'Fasten your seat belt,' said Alma. 'We're going to have a great holiday with lots of excitement. Let's order some champagne for a start.' She pressed the overhead buzzer to summon a stewardess.

I was feeling mellow as the plane began its descent over the Irish Sea. It was a clear, sunny afternoon. As we came in over Dublin Bay, I shut my eyes against the blue skies above, and seagulls circling below, and pictured the places I had visited with Jack just after we were married. The quiet roads winding down to rocky inlets. Bright boats rocking in small harbours. The blue smear of peat smoke against a pale grey sky. The pungent, oily tang of the salmon smoke-houses.

'You'll love the peace and quiet,' I told Alma.

'Not too peaceful, I hope,' said Alma. 'I need a bit of fun.'

'You'll have plenty of fun,' I said. 'But it's a nice peaceful kind of fun. Lazy afternoons in the pub, good conversation, that kind of thing. Stress-free driving. Fresh air.'

We drove into Dublin bumper-to-bumper on a six-lane motorway.

'Must be rush hour,' I said.

'Must be the shamrock-tinted spectacles,' said Alma. 'It's only three o'clock.'

An hour later we were still crawling along the quays on our way to the hotel, overlooking the river Liffey in the centre of the city.

'Parking is a bit of a problem,' conceded the brisk young woman who checked us in. 'We recommend the multi-storey round the corner.'

'Don't be going there late at night,' said the porter as he carried our bags to the room.

'Dublin's changed,' I said. 'There's a lot more traffic than when I was last here. And it's a lot noisier.'

'That's the roar of the Celtic tiger you're hearing,' he said. 'He's a bit mangy now. But he brought an awful lot of changes. You wouldn't know the place from ten years ago. If it's peace and quiet you're after,' he added, 'you'll need to go west.'

We set out to find a cosy pub and a glass of Guinness. I had in mind the sort of Irish pub I'd gone to with Jack in the early days of our courtship and marriage. A pub with opaque glass windows etched with the names of whiskey distillers, polished wooden counters, panelled snugs and ceilings stained brown by years of cigarette smoke. Pubs where men perched on stools, watching reverentially as the barman went through a ritual as familiar

71

as Mass. The pint glasses standing in a line waiting for their creamy collars. The soft murmur as a finished pint was placed in front of a customer.

It was Friday evening. The offices were emptying for the weekend and the narrow cobbled streets were lively and bustling. We wandered past brightly painted houses, loft developments, art galleries and craft workshops in search of an old-fashioned pub. The bars and cafés were temples of modernity. All chrome, pale wood and polished steel. Full of boisterous twenty-somethings roaring at each other.

'Is everyone in Ireland under thirty?' said Alma. 'All this gilded youth is depressing me.'

We emerged from the pattern of narrow streets on to a wide road leading to O'Connell Bridge. The traffic was slowing to a halt at traffic lights. I steered Alma across the road towards a pub sign in a laneway.

'We might find an older crowd in here,' I said, pushing open the door. The interior was a near match of the pub I'd carried in my head. There were more young women in sharp suits than old men in tweed caps. But a line of pint glasses stood on the counter waiting to be topped up. The sun through the stained glass window made purple and yellow diamond patterns on the brown walls. And the hum of conversation seemed to have a tune in it.

'This is more like it,' I said.

We squeezed into a corner and ordered two glasses of Guinness.

'I haven't been in a pub for ages,' said Alma. 'Gerry and I used to meet in pubs in the early days.'

Traffic noise intruded as a small band of drinkers pushed through the doors.

'Dublin sounds and smells like any British city with a brewery,' Alma went on. 'I want it to be foreign, to smell different.' Despite her bright pink windcheater, she looked strained, and disappointed.

'What we need is a pub like this with a nice view, no traffic and the smell of the sea,' I said. 'Shall we check out tomorrow and head west?'

Alma nodded. On such quick and simple decisions do the patterns of our lives turn.

Chapter 9

By ten o'clock the next morning we were on our way west out of Dublin. Alma hunted for the weather forecast in the *Irish Times* as I drove along the banks of the Royal Canal and crossed the Liffey on the motorway into County Kildare. There was a cap of cloud overhead, with a fringe of bright blue sky.

'"The day will start cloudy with sunny spells and scattered showers, clearing from the west. Maximum temperature fourteen to sixteen degrees Celsius." We're heading in the right direction,' Alma said. She tossed the paper into the back seat, took the map from the glove compartment and opened it on her knee. 'The route's pretty straight-forward. We should get to Athlone about lunchtime. And that's more than halfway to Galway.'

'I remember when Athlone was a station on the wireless,' I said. 'Before transistors and FM. Dada would tune the big wireless in the kitchen and I'd read all the names off the dial. Paris, Athlone, Hilversum...'

I had a sudden image of my 1950s childhood. Sun shining on the checked tablecloth below the broad sash window. My head not much higher than the sill. Rows of peas and beans in the vegetable garden at the back. The orchard beyond. Mama taking a roast chicken out of the oven. 'I'll just let it sit while I make the gravy.' Dada tuning the brown Bakelite wireless on the windowsill. 'I'll just get the weather forecast before we eat. We might take a run out in the Rover before teatime.' The familiar, safe rituals of a happy home.

'The traffic's not too bad,' said Alma, as the

motorway ended and we joined the two-lane main road. Cars swished past us, travelling back towards Dublin. Five minutes later we passed a sign saying Road Works Ahead: 2 miles, and found ourselves at the tail end of a long queue of cars. Ireland had not yet worked its magic and we fidgeted for fifteen minutes making almost no progress, as cars slowed up behind us.

'I think we can get out of this and take another route,' said Alma, scrutinising the map as we inched along. 'Take the next turn left. Here. We can take a minor road for a while and rejoin the main road after the road works.'

I flicked the indicator and turned left on to the side road.

'Great. At least we're moving now,' I said, steering the car around a series of potholes. No cars elected to follow our example, and I realised our move was probably not a wise one. But there wasn't much point in going back to rejoin the queue, there was no obvious place to turn, and it was pleasant to be away from the traffic.

The road surface improved slightly. Rampant hedgerows, speckled with scarlet berries and tinged with the brown of autumn, lined the road. Every half mile or so, a gap revealed a half-built bungalow in a field – always a dull grey square of breeze blocks on a hard standing of cement, the

75

wooden ribs of a roof that waited to be tiled, and a pile of bricks. I had never seen so much new building. A white van inched out of a gateway to a yellow brick bungalow. I stopped to let it out. A mob of dull grey dwarves in assorted sizes, miniature grey castles and grey Grecian statues crowded the front garden. A sign said Ornamental Concrete.

'The perfect example of an oxymoron,' said Alma. 'I was expecting thatched cottages, like the brochures,' she complained.

'You'll see them in the west,' I promised.

The hedgerows and bungalows vanished. Now ranch fencing ran along fields where glossy horses grazed. A cock pheasant scuttled across the road and disappeared behind a gatepost. A graceful Georgian house stood at the end of a driveway lined with copper-gold trees. Wood pigeons fluttered out of the trees as we drove past and a magpie glared at us from the five-barred gate.

'Hello, Mr Magpie,' Alma sang. 'How are Mrs Magpie and all the little magpies?'

'You should always greet a single magpie,' she said.

A cluster of magpies swooped and hopped through a field on our left. We began to count out loud: 'One for sorrow, two for joy, three for a girl, four for a boy, five for silver, six for gold, seven for a secret never

76

to be told.'

'Seven?' said Alma. 'I've hardly ever seen seven magpies in one go.'

'Me neither.'

I hesitated at an unsigned crossroads.

'Right should take us parallel to the main road,' I said.

'But it turns left again and ends in a forest park, according to the map,' said Alma. 'Try going straight over and take the next right.'

Fifteen minutes later, we were lost in a labyrinth of minor roads where the signposts pointed to places we couldn't find on the map.

'Just drive until we reach a main road,' said Alma. 'There's bound to be a signpost for a big town.'

The land was flat. The road was straight and fell away into ditches on either side. I realised we were driving across a peat bog. Caterpillar trucks crawled over the surface of the bog, harvesting turf. About a mile away, smoke rose from a peat-burning power station.

'I think I know where we are,' I said. 'I think we're quite near where the wedding was.'

'What wedding?'

'The wedding where I met the nun.'

As I spoke, we drove past a new housing development of neo-Georgian brick boxes, packed into rows set back from the road, and emerged onto a main road near a church, on the outskirts of a small town.

'I recognise that church,' I said, excited and surprised. 'This is definitely the town where the wedding was.'

It was bigger and busier than I remembered. But the shape was the same. The road widened in the centre of the town. Side streets ran at right angles from the rectangular market place.

'Do you still know people here?' said Alma. 'Do you want to stop?'

'We never really knew anyone here,' I said. 'This was the bride's home town. Jack was the groom's cousin. I don't even remember her name. The reception was in a hotel somewhere else.'

I drove on, through the market place, to where the road narrowed again and led out of town.

'I've found us on the map,' said Alma. 'If we turn left at the end of the town we'll come to a main crossroads in a few miles. There should be a signpost for Tullamore.'

I glanced at her. Her head was bent over the map. She clearly didn't remember Tullamore. I wondered if the solicitor's office was still there.

'Yes,' Alma decided. 'Head for Tullamore. Then we can choose which way to go. It's a nice day,' she said. 'The sun's out. It doesn't matter if we take a roundabout route.'

A canal shone like a silver ribbon on the flat brown surface of the bog. In the distance, the land rose gently towards a ridge of mountains. We drove through a couple of small villages. There was hardly any traffic. I began to relax. Alma was humming softly, eyes closed.

And then I saw the sign: Saint Joseph's. A blue metal finger pointed down a driveway lined with shrubbery. On an impulse, I turned into the drive. Gravel crunched under the car. Alma opened her eyes, saw the laurels and the rhododendrons and turned to me in amazement.

'Where are you going?'

'This is the home,' I said. 'This is Saint Joseph's. It must be the same place. Where Mary was born. Where Sister Monica is. This is meant to be. Why would we have ended up here otherwise?'

The driveway swept round a two-storey Georgian house, fronted by a wide lawn, and ended in a car park at the back where a single-storey modern annexe adjoined the older building. The car park was hard-surfaced. Beside it was a paved rose garden, with wooden garden benches. Beyond that I could see playing fields, a school playground, the irregular edges of a town and a half-built housing estate.

I imagined Mary's mother looking out of a second-storey window, seeing the car bearing her baby away, watching till it dwindled out of sight on the black road beyond the fields. I pulled up beside a sign: Saint Joseph's Residential Home for the Aged. Parking for Visitors.

Alma said, 'I'll wait in the car.'

I walked up a ramp to the entrance of the annexe. As the automatic glass doors slid open, the sound of a piano rippled out to meet me. The music was coming from upstairs. It was punctuated by the occasional clatter of saucepans and plates. Through an open door leading off the lobby I could see staff carrying trays of food from a serving hatch. Another half-open door said Staff.

I tapped lightly on the door and looked into a small office.

'Can I help you?' said a nun, turning round from a filing cabinet.

'Sister Monica?' I said.

'Have you an appointment?'

'No, sister,' I said. 'I was just passing and saw the sign.'

'She's playing the piano,' the nun said. 'She often plays for the residents during mealtimes. I'll ask if she can see you. Have a seat.'

I took one of a row of chairs opposite the open door to the dining room. A few grey heads were bobbing in time to the music. Most of the residents were women.

The music stopped with a bravura run of notes, a dramatic pause, and a chord. I looked up and saw the nun from the office beckoning to me from the top of the first flight of stairs. I made my way up to her and she led me past an open upright piano on the landing, and along a panelled, polished corridor.

'You've come at a good time,' she said. 'They're all in the dining room. The residents eat earlier than we do. They'll have tea at five o'clock. A lot of them like to go to bed early and watch television. There's TV in all the rooms.'

I hung back while she put her head round a door at the end of the corridor. She held the door open for me.

'In you go,' she said. 'Perhaps I'll see you on your tour.'

The nun who rose, straight-backed, from her desk to greet me was taller and bonier than I remembered. She wore a black pleated skirt, a grey blouse and a long, black, hand-knitted cardigan. A short black veil concealed most of her grey hair. She had a dry, firm handshake.

'Please sit down,' she said, gesturing to one of two armchairs beside a round glass coffee table at the window. 'Mrs...?' It was clear she didn't recognise me.

'Molloy,' I said.

She took the other chair and said in a

friendly way, 'You're enquiring about a parent?'

'About a child,' I said.

She looked puzzled. Then apologetic.

'I'm afraid we don't take any children. Only the disabled elderly.' The last word lightly emphasised.

'I'm Lena Molloy,' I said. 'You telephoned me last week. In England.'

For the first time in my life I understood what was meant by the word thunderstruck.

She stared at me for what seemed like minutes.

'Why have you come here?' she said. Her tone was decidedly cool.

My words came out in a rush. 'I'm here on holiday. I was passing. I just wanted to ask you... When you telephoned me, I thought... I was worried. Maybe there was some problem. Some illness.'

She looked rattled.

'Who mentioned illness?' she said.

'Nobody. I just wondered if that was why you rang me.'

She got up abruptly, walked over to her desk and, with her back to me, rifled through some papers.

'I thought perhaps the mother had been in touch,' I added. 'That there was maybe some hereditary condition Mary needed to know about.'

The cool tone returned. She was still bent

over her papers. 'No. I was, as I told you, reviewing my...' she paused and shuffled the papers into a neat pile, 'my work.' Another pause. 'I'm retiring at the end of next month.'

'I'm sure you achieved a great deal,' I said. 'I hope you enjoy your retirement. I'm glad I've caught you before you go. I want to trace Mary's natural mother. I'm hoping you can help me.'

She stiffened, swung round and looked at me in amazement.

'I'm afraid I cannot help you. Adoptions are confidential.'

'Surely you can tell me something?'

'The law is clear, Mrs Molloy. You accepted the terms of adoption at the time. You are wasting your time.'

She resumed her seat opposite me.

'Does your daughter know you are making this enquiry?' she asked.

I shook my head.

'And do you think she would approve?'

'I know she will want to know who her natural parents are,' I said.

'How do you know?' she said.

I took a deep breath. 'Because I'm adopted too,' I said. 'And not a day passes but I wonder who I really am. I didn't try to find my mother until it was too late. I don't want that to happen to Mary. I want to give her that knowledge. With my love.'

Sister Monica was not silenced for long.

'Knowledge can be a burden,' she said.

'It's a burden I would gladly carry,' I cried.

'You would carry?' she said sharply. 'Is this about you? What about your daughter? What about the mother who gave her to you? How do you know she wants someone to come knocking on her door?'

'I can't believe she wouldn't want to know what happened to her child.'

'She knew all those years ago she was giving her child a better chance in life. Didn't that child have a good upbringing with you? Isn't she a success?'

It was my turn to be silenced.

'Be grateful for what you have got,' said Sister Monica. She rose to indicate the meeting was at an end, and moved to open the door for me.

'Goodbye, Mrs Molloy,' she said. 'Enjoy the rest of your holiday.'

And I found myself, snubbed and silenced, on the other side of the closed door.

I was trembling as I made my way downstairs. By the time I reached the lobby, Sister Monica was playing the piano again. The tune was unmistakably 'Count Your Blessings'.

Chapter 10

Alma was leaning against the car, chatting to a young woman in a pale blue nurse's uniform. They were both smoking.

'This is Maureen,' said Alma. 'She likes the occasional cigarette too. This is my friend Lena.'

'Hello,' said the nurse. She gestured to the building. 'It's no smoking inside. The auld ones can smoke in a special lounge but the staff aren't allowed. Sister Monica would kill us.'

I tried to keep the anger and frustration out of my voice. 'What's she like to work for?' I said carefully.

'Her tongue could clip a hedge,' said Maureen. 'We're all terrified of her. The Health Board's terrified of her. They've been trying to get her to retire for ages.'

'She must be well over retirement age,' I said. 'What's retirement age for women here? Sixty-five?'

'Sixty,' said Maureen. 'And she's more than sixty-five. Or so I'm told. She's a law unto herself. Mind you,' she added, 'they say she's not well and she'll be going sooner rather than later.'

I digested this interesting snippet before asking, 'Were you here when this was a home for unmarried mothers?'

'Before my time,' said Maureen. 'It's been an old people's home as long as I remember.' She wasn't more than twenty-five.

There was a sudden burst of whooping and yelling as children poured into the school playground.

Maureen dropped her cigarette on the tarmac and stubbed it with the toe of her white trainers. 'One o'clock,' she said. 'I'd better be getting back.' She looked up at the sky. 'You have a nice afternoon for your journey.'

'How did you get on?' asked Alma, when Maureen was out of earshot.

'Blood from a stone,' I said bitterly. 'I felt like a ten-year-old being ticked off in class. She as good as told me it was none of my business.'

Alma put her arm round me and squeezed my shoulders.

'I'm sorry,' she said. 'I'm really sorry. Maybe I should have stopped you. I wasn't expecting you to do it. You acted on impulse. She wasn't expecting you either.'

'She told me I was being selfish.'

'People don't react well to being surprised. She didn't have her answers ready. You could try writing to her.'

'She was quick enough with her answers,'

86

I said. 'I don't think writing will get me much further. She was really cold and off-putting. Not all grace and charm like she was on the phone. I felt I was back at school. She made me feel small.' I mimicked the sarcastic tones of a nun I had particularly disliked. 'Helena Houghton, is this a new fashion? Holes in your cardigan as well as your stockings? What gives you the right to ask these questions, Mrs Molloy?'

'I don't know any nuns,' said Alma. 'It's an odd career she's had when you think about it,' she added. 'The first half looking after babies. The second half looking after old people. Nothing in between. No men. No romance.'

'It's her own choice,' I snapped.

'Come on. Get into the car,' said Alma. 'We're on holiday. It would be nice to get to the west before sunset. And I'm hungry.'

I drove to Tullamore in a silent rage. Alma talked out loud.

'We could visit the Cliffs of Moher. Or maybe take a boat to the Aran islands. As long as the sea's calm. I'm not too good in small boats. The guidebook says the sea stays warm through September. I'd love a swim. Oh look! A heron!' Eventually she gave up and lapsed into silence like me.

We lunched in a hotel off the main street. Alma spread the map over the table.

'We've come a bit further south than we

intended,' she said. 'We could cross the Shannon here,' stabbing the map, 'and take this road across the Burren to the coast. It's supposed to be beautiful. There are plenty of places to stay.'

'Fine,' I said. 'You choose somewhere.' I didn't care where we stayed. Or how we got there.

'OK. I'll pick a hotel and book us in. Will you at least choose something to eat?' she said, handing me the bar menu. 'Or do you want me to do that, as well?'

'I'm sorry, Alma,' I said. 'I'm furious with myself. I let her give me the bum's rush.' I made a show of studying the menu. 'I'll have the same as you,' I said. When the smoked salmon sandwich and a glass of stout arrived, I realised I was hungry.

'Tullamore is where we picked up Mary,' I said, as we made our way back to the car. 'I just want to see if the solicitor's office is still there. It's only round the corner.'

We walked to where I remembered the office had been.

'E. J. Murphy,' I said. 'E. J. Murphy and Son. Maybe the son is still in practice.'

But a sandwich bar had replaced E. J. Murphy.

I closed my eyes and pictured a crane, a pile of rubble and yards of hoarding plastered with posters.

'Are you all right?' Alma said. 'You look a

bit pale.'

'After Mama died,' I said, 'I went to Croydon to look for the home where I was born. It wasn't there any more. It was knocked down. You see what happens when you leave things too late,' I cried.

'There must have been records,' Alma said. 'Who ran the home?'

'Nuns,' I said. 'I don't even know where they went when they closed it.'

Alma drove the rest of the way, keeping up a commentary on the scenery, leaving me to my thoughts. I was only half conscious of the change from watery plains to forested hills, to open uplands criss-crossed by dry-stone walls and dotted with clumps of gorse. We stopped at the barred gate of a railway crossing and waited for the train to pass. As it rattled along I seemed to hear repeated in the rhythm of the wheels Sister Monica's verdict: 'Is this about you? Is this about you? Is this about you?'

The French have a word for the riposte that comes to mind too late. *L'esprit d'escalier* – staircase wit. I had been down the stairs and across the car park before even beginning to think of an answer to Sister Monica's accusation. I reran the mental videotape and rose to my own defence.

'You have no idea what it feels like not to know your origins. It has nothing to do with ingratitude, or selfishness. I loved Mama and Dada. I know they gave me a good life. I know my real mother acted for the best. This is about feeling complete. I know Mary loves me and loves her dad. But I also know one day she'll want to know about her birth mother. Unlike you, I know what it feels like to adopt and be adopted. And to bring up a child. So don't preach to me.' There. That was telling her. I felt better for thinking the words I'd failed to say. And with them came a determination to rout Sister Monica and erase the memory of her scorn.

'Hundreds of girls must have been in Saint Joseph's before it became an old people's home. There must be a way of contacting some of them,' I said out loud. The barrier rose.

Alma put the car into gear, released the handbrake and drove on.

'Internet,' she said. 'Try the Internet. I bet there's at least one site about adoptions.'

Chapter 11

The sun was low in the sky when we reached the edge of the Burren. A great, treeless plateau sloping westward to the sea. Terraced slabs of pale limestone shone pink and purple in the evening light. The road wound past dry stone walls squaring small fields speckled with boulders, and stone cottages capped with blue-black slate or yellow thatch.

'Thatched cottages, at last!' said Alma. This was more like the Ireland of the picture postcards.

We stopped the car and got out to look at the square, stone ruin of a four-storey tower house rising steeply beside the road. Seagulls circled slowly above the crenellations, crying faintly. Alma inhaled deeply through her nose and pronounced, 'Wet grass with a hint of thyme, damp wool and sheep shit, peat smoke, molasses, salt.' She blew air from her puffed cheeks, smiled in satisfaction and flicked through the guidebook.

'Lemaneagh Castle,' she read. 'It belonged to Maire Ni Mahon, Mary MacMahon, known as Red Mary. The Cromwellians killed her husband and brought his body home to her. I'll have no dead men in this house, said Red Mary, and shut the door on them. She married a Cromwellian trooper, and got to keep the castle and the land. According to legend, when the new husband annoyed her, she pushed him out of a window.'

Our eyes travelled up the stone façade to the four windows at the top.

'Gosh,' I said. 'I wonder what he did to annoy her?'

'I don't know,' said Alma. 'The book doesn't say. She was probably jealous. Maybe he was making eyes at her maid.'

'I can't imagine being jealous enough to push Jack out of a window,' I said.

'Oh, I can,' Alma said, her eyes still focused on the black, empty spaces of the mullioned windows. 'I had a boyfriend at university who took my flatmate to a rock festival. I was so angry I went round to his flat – it was on the third floor too – and I got all his favourite records and I was going to throw them out of the window when his friend stopped me. He said I'd regret it.'

'You didn't do it,' I said. 'And they were records, not an actual person.'

'They were mostly Bob Dylan and Van Morrison,' Alma said. 'I think that's what stopped me. Haven't you ever been jealous, Lena?'

'Not really,' I said. 'Jack never gave me

any cause.'

Alma clicked her fingers and began to sway and sing,

'She gives me love, love, love, love, crazy love,
She gives me love, love, love, love, crazy love.'

I joined in. We swayed and sang and smiled at the spectacle of ourselves. Two mature women, one tall, one small, both relatively trim, dancing in the road. We stopped when we became aware that a mobile phone was ringing.

'Mine's switched off,' I said.

Alma ran to the car, reached through the open window for her handbag and fumbled for her mobile. The conversation was short. She switched off the phone and tossed it into the back seat of the car.

'Gerry,' she said, answering my unspoken question in a flat voice. 'I was hoping he would call and now that he's called I realise I don't want to speak to him.'

I didn't say anything. I moved to the driver's side of the car.

Alma said, 'It's over, Lena. Really over. It's been over a long time. I was just afraid to let go.'

'Get in,' I said. 'My turn to drive.'

'I need some crazy love again,' she said.

'No you don't.' I was looking back at the brooding height of the castle. 'You need some steady love.'

Thirty minutes later we had our first sight of the sea. I parked in a lay-by on the crest of a hill and we got out to take our bearings. The sun was hidden behind the dark, low shapes of the Aran islands set like smooth stones in the steel-grey sea. A weather front had started rolling in from the Atlantic. Black clouds billowed towards the land. The smell of peat pricked my nose. I felt the first specks of rain on my cheeks and tasted salt in the wind.

'That's where we're going,' said Alma, pointing to a ribbon of lights on the coast below us. 'The hotel is down there some-where. We'll be there in time for dinner.'

It was raining hard when we pulled up on the gravel sweep outside the detached Victorian house on a low hill about a mile from the sea. The black edge of the coast was just visible in the distance. Two carriage lamps illuminated green Celtic lettering on a cream board above the porch. Double glass doors opened on to a vestibule with a second, glass-panelled door beyond. Through the side window of the car I saw the luminous outline of a lamp on the reception desk and the splayed shadows cast by a vase of roses on the wall behind.

'Here we are,' said Alma. 'Happy holidays.' The headlights picked out a stone cupid supporting a birdbath, and the edge of a lawn that sloped into the darkness. I turned off the engine. The roar of a river in full spate joined the drumming of the rain. Droplets of rain clung to the windscreen. We left our suitcases in the car and sprinted for the shelter of the Atlantic House Hotel.

There was no one at the desk. The lobby smelled of peat and roses. Alma pressed a bell that said Service and a man's voice from down the hallway called out, 'I'm in the bar.'

We followed the signs to a narrow bar with a fireplace, old leather armchairs, small round tables and a few stools. A turf fire smouldered in the grate, and the rain rattling on the window added to the impression of cosiness. A dapper, elderly man was polishing glasses behind the bar.

'Terrible evening,' he said. 'Are you the two ladies who phoned earlier about a room? My wife will be back in a while to look after you.'

We advanced into the bar and made for a table by the fire.

'Will we be able to have dinner?' said Alma.

'She'll sort you out,' he said. 'I'll bring your things in.'

'You'll be well sorted if Eileen's cooking for you,' said a voice behind us.

'You're back, Donal,' said the man behind the bar. 'Did your friends get away all right?'

'Oh, fine, Michael. The plane was on time.'

I looked round and saw a tall, slightly

balding, lanky man divesting himself of a raincoat. He put the wet coat over a stool and proffered his hand.

'Donal Sweeney,' he said. 'Eileen's a great cook. I come here every year and she just gets better and better. Isn't that right, Michael?' he said.

'Alma Copeland,' said Alma, shaking Donal's hand and raising her other hand in salutation to Michael.

'Lena Molloy,' I said, doing the same. 'Are you staying here too, Mr Sweeney?'

'Donal please. I've been here all week. My friends have gone back, but I'm staying on for a bit.'

There followed that particularly Irish style of conversation in which the participants explore all the possible ways they could be related through blood, friendship or mere acquaintance. We established where friends of Donal had settled in England; Alma remembered a long-lost school friend who had married a doctor from County Cork; and I was beginning to explain my dearth of relations when a small cyclone of energy breezed into the bar.

'Right,' she said. 'Dinner. I have two fine trout, the last of the season. And I have three guests tonight. That means one of you will be disappointed. But only if you call a ten-ounce sirloin steak from the finest grass-fed beef cattle west of the Shannon a disappointment. I'm Eileen Collins,' she added. 'You must be Mrs Molloy and Mrs Copeland.' She paused to draw breath.

'Ms,' said Alma.

'I hope you enjoy your stay. Now. Ladies first. Trout or steak?'

'Call me Lena,' I said.

'Alma,' said Alma.

'Trout,' we said simultaneously.

'Steak for you, Donal. Medium rare?' said Eileen.

He inclined his close-cropped grey head towards her in assent.

'Broccoli, plain boiled potatoes and runner beans,' she said. 'Michael will sign you in.' She vanished down the corridor. The words 'soup', 'dinner' and 'twenty minutes' drifted back towards us.

'Enough talk for two sets of teeth,' Donal whispered. 'But a great cook.'

We three were the only guests that first night in Atlantic House. It seemed churlish not to invite Donal to eat with us. In any case, when Eileen collected us from the bar and led us into the dining room, we saw she had foreseen our invitation and laid a table for three.

'There's two groups arriving tomorrow,' she said. 'A group of walkers from the North, and a group of women going to Lisdoonvarna for the matchmaking. I doubt you'll see much of them. They'll be driving

97

back late and getting up late. I'll leave you the wine list.'

'Matchmaking?' I said, when we sat down.

'Oh, just a bit of codology,' said Donal. 'The matchmaking festival over in Lisdoonvarna. Drinking and dancing and singing. The whole of September. It's based on tradition. Farmers used to come here to the spa to look for brides when the harvest was over. But those days are long gone. It's been revived for the tourists rather than the farmers. Are either of you ladies interested in netting a bachelor farmer?'

'I think my husband might object,' I said.

'Alma?' His eyes checked her left hand for a ring.

'I've gone off men,' she said.

'If I were Sherlock Holmes I might deduce a recent unhappy experience.'

Alma flushed.

'If you were Sherlock Holmes you'd be dead,' she snapped.

'If looks could kill I'd be dead,' said Donal. 'My late wife used to say I'd a talent for putting my foot in it.'

It was Alma's turn to look discomfited.

'I'm sorry,' she began.

'She's been dead five years,' he said. 'A car crash. She was on her way home from baby-sitting our first grandchild. She skidded on black ice and the car hit a bridge. They told me she died instantly.'

He raised his hand to forestall our halting condolences. 'We had twenty-five good years together and three fine boys. She lived to see them all go to university, and the eldest one married with a child. Sure it's not a bad way to go,' he said. 'Now, will you let me get the wine?' he added, opening the wine list. 'Michael keeps a small but decent cellar. White with your trout?'

'What about you?' I said. 'Is white OK for you?'

'Tell you what,' he said. 'I'll get a bottle of white and a bottle of red. We can all start on the white. I'll have red with my steak and you can have the rest of the white with the trout and we can all finish the red with the cheese.'

That was the beginning of a memorable evening. We moved to the bar after dinner and sat round the fire. Alma softened and lost the edge I'd heard in her voice since she'd decided to ditch Gerry. The memory of Sister Monica's sarcasm faded from my mind. Donal charmed us with jokes and stories and information about the area. He lived in County Kildare and worked as a solicitor in Dublin, but his parents had been from the west of Ireland. He had spent his childhood holidays not far from where we were. We swapped the simple details of our lives. Alma's job, my decision to come to Ireland to see Mary in Dublin.

'Mary Molloy?' said Donal. 'Of course I've heard of her. *Mary Molloy sings Mozart and Rossini.* I have the CD. So she's replacing Dawn Upshaw? I have a ticket for that concert. And you're her mother? That's fantastic.' I warmed to him even more.

'Does she get that awesome talent from you?' he said.

'No,' I said. 'I love music. But I'm not a singer. Mary is my adopted daughter.'

I turned away from his steady gaze and looked into the fire. The last sods of turf flared briefly red before collapsing into grey ash. I said, as casually as I could, 'Do you know much about adoption law in Ireland, Donal?'

'A bit,' he said. 'I get the odd client who wants to trace the details of an adoption.'

I took a deep breath. 'I adopted Mary in Ireland twenty-seven years ago. I want to help her trace her natural parents. As a gift to her. My gift to her,' I said quickly. 'And before you ask if I'm sure she really wants to know, I am sure. I know. She's just like me. Because I was adopted too. I never got to find out about my parents because I left it too late and I don't want that to happen to Mary.' It was all out in a rush. My impulsive visit to Sister Monica. The hurtful brush-off.

Donal was silent for a moment. Alma lit a cigarette.

'I'm sorry you had such a bad experience,' he said. 'The religious orders here feel under attack. The papers are full of stories about child abuse, and cover-ups in institutions and schools. All from thirty or forty years ago. The mother and baby homes, run by nuns like your woman, around the same time, are getting a lot of stick as well. They're accused of cruelty, and putting pressure on girls to give up their babies for adoption and so on. They're all on the defensive. And you caught her on the hop.'

'What does the law say?' said Alma. 'Has Mary the right to know who her birth parents are?'

'It's not straightforward,' said Donal. 'Look, I'd prefer to go over it with you when I'm more clear-headed.' He hesitated a moment. 'What are you two planning to do tomorrow?'

'Alma thinks there'll be websites about adoption,' I said, glancing at her.

'There might be an Internet café in the town,' she said.

'I thought I could go there after Mass,' I said.

'We were planning to walk in after breakfast,' Alma said.

'Oh,' he said. He sounded disappointed.

'I'd really like you to explain the law,' I said. 'If you have the time. I'd be really grateful. But I don't want to spoil your holiday with my obsession.'

'I have my own obsession,' Donal said. 'Golf. I took it up after Kathleen died, and now I'm addicted. I'm playing at eight thirty in the morning, but I'll be off the course before half past twelve.' He cleared his throat. 'I could take you to a good seafood pub just up the coast, if you like? We could have lunch there. And I'll tell you what I know. Though it's not much, I warn you.'

Alma and I looked at each other, smiled and nodded. Donal looked pleased. 'One o'clock, here, in the bar?'

And so we agreed to rendezvous at Atlantic House the next day.

Chapter 12

'He's a nice man,' I said to Alma, as we were getting ready for bed. 'I'm sorry I put a damper on the evening with my questions. Don't you think he's nice?'

'Lena,' she warned. 'Don't be getting ideas. I'm not interested. No bat squeaks.'

Bat squeak was Alma's term for instant attraction. Soon after we'd met, I had told her about my first meeting with Jack. Six of us squeezed into Daphne Dawson's Mini. Jack's eyes boring into the back of my neck.

My skin tingling. Procul Harum playing 'A Whiter Shade of Pale'. Jack standing beside me at the bar.

'What would you like to drink?'

'Pimm's, please.'

'I'm with someone.'

'Oh.' Not knowing what to say. My heart leaping with recognition. Writing in my diary when I got home. *Tonight I fell in love with Jack Molloy.*

I remember saying to Alma, '*I knew he would ask me to dance, and I would say yes, and he'd ask to see me again. I felt confident and powerful, and all of a tremble at the same time.*'

'A bat squeak,' said Alma.

'What?'

'You heard a bat squeak. It's from *Brideshead Revisited*. Evelyn Waugh. When Charles meets Julia for the first time. *In the air was the thin high bat squeak of desire.* It's a great phrase,' she said.

And so it passed into the shorthand of our friendship. 'Any bat squeaks?' I'd ask when Alma told me about a party, or a new male acquaintance. Months later, I read *Brideshead Revisited* and saw that Waugh had written *the thin bat squeak of sexuality*. But I preferred to think of the high bat squeak of desire. It conjured up a meeting of minds and souls, making instant attraction more romantic and mysterious than mere animal instinct.

'Don't you find Donal attractive at all?' I asked.

'Not my type.'

'But you don't mind his company?' I persisted. 'I think he quite likes ours. He must be lonely now his friends have gone back.'

'I've spent plenty of holidays on my own,' said Alma. 'I know all about it. I don't mind if he wants to join us.' She yawned. 'Kindness is in our power. Fondness is not. As Dr Johnson said.'

'Well, I think he's nice,' I said.

'Only because his wife's dead and he's available.'

'Don't be so cynical,' I cried. 'What's wrong with wanting you to meet someone who's free to marry you? Somebody nice. Somebody you deserve. Somebody who deserves you, more to the point.'

'I'd like me to meet someone too,' Alma said. 'But right now I'm off men. I'd take up golf if it weren't for the ghastly clothes they wear.' She clicked off the bedside light, and turned over to go to sleep. 'Will you switch off the main light?' she said. 'Goodnight, Lena. Sweet dreams.'

'You too.'

I moved to the door and switched off the overhead light in the room before feeling my way to the tall sash window. I pulled back the edge of the long curtain and looked out.

The rain had stopped. The sky was clearing. A few thin clouds scudded across the face of the moon. Orion's belt was diamond-clear. I could see foam on the fast-flowing river through gaps in the willows that lined its bank beyond the sloping lawn. I pressed my forehead against the window frame and angled my head to glimpse the distant shimmer and curl of the sea. Despite the whiskey and the wine, I felt restless, not ready for sleep. I opened the curtain to let the moonlight fall across my bed and lay listening to the rush of the river to the sea.

I wondered if Mary was looking at the same night sky in Frankfurt.

'She's just like me,' I had said to Donal. Even when I went a shade lighter to disguise my grey hairs, people still said, 'I can see she's your daughter.' I thought about how, when she was little, Mary would follow me round the house, copying everything I did. She had a habit of tapping her cheek when she was thinking deeply, just like Jack. I reminded myself that I knew her better than anyone else in the whole world. I was sure a fierce curiosity burned beneath her apparent indifference to her origins. For hadn't I been like that? Hadn't I been equally careful not to disrupt our happy family by asking awkward questions?

When Mama looked up from her embroidery one evening and said, 'Do you ever wonder about your real parents?' and I said, 'No. I don't think about them at all,' I was lying. I was twenty-three years old. Mama was ill. I had guessed how bad it was before she told me. She was about to begin the wearying cycle of radiotherapy, sickness, chemotherapy. I was determined to show that she, and she alone, occupied my waking thoughts.

Dreams were a different matter. I sometimes dreamed of walking by myself along the avenue towards the convent school. Above me, the soft blue sky was studded with faceless statues of the Virgin Mary holding the infant Jesus. In my dream, I craned my neck backwards to study each statue, looking for a feature that would render one of the figures different from the others. But they were always all the same. The same white veil, the same head inclined towards the same plump, larger-than-life-size baby cradled, asleep, in the left arm of the hooded Madonna. So I didn't believe Mary when she said, 'I don't think about it, Mum.' I knew better.

When Mary was old enough to have a conversation, Jack and I decided to tell her she was adopted. We sat her down between us and told her how we had met Sister Monica at the wedding. How Sister Monica had told us about a special baby. How we felt God had chosen us to be the parents of

106

this special baby. She listened to us, eyes shining like plums. She tapped her cheek. She said, 'Where is this special baby now?' We didn't know whether to laugh or cry.

Mary knew I was adopted too. I told her when she was about fifteen and beginning to show a serious interest in boys. Time for a talk, I thought. Time to lay down some guidelines and elaborate on the bare facts of life I had imparted much earlier.

'Oh, Mum,' she said, when I began rather hesitantly, 'we've had all that in class. Boys' hormones and girls' hormones. Girls have to be in control and all that.'

I was relieved. The nuns had given no practical guidance when I was at school. My generation was given a booklet called *The Devil at Dances*. The cover showed a handsome man in white tie and tails twirling a laughing girl in a ball gown round a dance floor. The man had one black patent leather shoe, and one cloven hoof. Alma said you could construct an entire thesis on it. There were warnings about impurity, and occasions of sin, but no indication of how to be impure, or what to do should an occasion of sin arise.

'Nuns are clued up these days,' Mary told me. 'They know all about the sexual revolution.'

'That's good,' I said, because I'd hate her to get pregnant. It had happened to her birth mother, and to my birth mother, I said.

'So you're adopted too?' she said.

'Yes. And I'm sure my birth mother loved me and wanted the best for me. Just like your birth mother. They made a great sacrifice. But they knew we would have a better life in a family with two loving parents. They wanted us to be happy.'

'I am happy,' she said. 'Weren't you?'

'Yes,' I said. 'I was happy. But I still wanted to know who my birth mother was. I still do. I regret not trying to find out earlier. Now it's too late.'

'Why is it too late?' she said.

'When I started to look for her, I found the home where I was born had been knocked down to build flats. I don't know where the records went. I don't know my birth mother's surname to do a search.'

'Why didn't you try earlier?' she said.

'I didn't want to hurt Mama,' I said. 'I'm sorry you never knew her. I won't be hurt if you want to start looking, you know.'

'I'm not that curious. Really,' she said. 'And I'm not going to get pregnant until I meet a nice man who'll marry me and make you a granny!' She laughed and skipped off. 'I'm not going to get married for ages and ages,' she called back over her shoulder. 'I'm going to have lots of fun, like Alma.'

My eyes had adjusted to the dark. I turned my head on the pillow and looked across at the barely perceptible rise and fall of the duvet around Alma's narrow shoulders.

Alma used to have lots of fun, I thought. When we first met, she would bring a new man every time she came to dinner. For a long time there was no one. Then there was Gerry. I only met him a few times. Once, shortly after they'd met, I arrived deliberately early for a lunch date to catch a glimpse of him. I could tell he sensed my disapproval. Alma was eager to know what I thought of him. 'Too handsome for his own good,' I said.

'You could say the same of Jack,' she replied defensively.

'I trust Jack,' I said.

'And I trust Gerry.'

'How can you trust a man who's cheating on his wife?' I spoke before I could stop myself.

'Because I love him,' she said quietly.

'I'm sorry, Alma,' I said. 'I didn't mean to say what I said.'

'You thought it,' she said. She was hurt. I vowed then to keep my disapproval to myself. I would listen to Alma, and try not to judge her. Hate the sin and love the sinner. Wasn't that what the Church taught us? So for six years I tried to be a true friend. I listened and consoled. And I prayed Alma would forget

Gerry and find someone else. Now I hoped my prayers had been answered. I silently rejoiced that Alma had given up on Gerry. I thought how lucky I was to have Jack, and Mary. And then I fell asleep.

Chapter 13

'Internet? Joe O'Brien in the market square will get you on to the Internet. He'll be open after Mass,' said Michael, when he served us breakfast.

Alma walked into town with me. The road glistened after the rain and the brown river gurgled alongside us for most of a mile until we reached the bridge near the centre of the town. The grey steeple of the church soared above rain-washed rooftops and brightly painted shops and pubs. Cars manoeuvred around the market square. A group of young cyclists in yellow oilskins congregated by the bridge, their heads bent over maps.

Alma was sitting on the bridge when I came out after Mass. She waved with one hand and gestured towards the square with the other. I zigzagged through the dispersing crowd towards her.

'There isn't an Internet café, but I found something else,' she said, jumping down and taking my arm. She pointed towards a single-storey pub, painted salmon pink. Joseph O'Brien was inscribed in black and cream above the opaque plate glass window. A poster in the window said Internet Access.

The bar smelled of Jeyes Fluid and stale beer. A curly-haired young man in shirt-sleeves was sweeping the slate floor with a damp brush.

'I'll see to you in a moment. Hair of the dog, is it?'

'Internet access,' I said.

'You've picked a good time,' he said. 'Most of them wanting the net are young ones travelling around. They go to bed late and get up late. You'll always get a space before one o'clock.' He jerked his head towards a room at the back of the pub. 'It's five punts an hour. Tell me when you log out. Do you know what to do? Or do you need some help?'

'We're OK, thanks,' Alma said.

We went through to the back room. Electronic fish swam slowly across half a dozen computer screens on a shelf that ran round the walls. I took two chairs from the stack in the middle of the room and carried them to where Alma stood tapping on a keyboard. I watched her as she moved the mouse across its rubber pad.

'Right,' she said, adjusting the chair beneath her. 'I think this is the best search engine. Do you want me to do this or do you want to change places?'

'Go ahead,' I said. 'You're more used to the net.'

'I'll put in adoption, Ireland, Saint Joseph's, birth mother.'

For an interminable ten seconds I sat watching her tap in the letters with two fingers.

'I'll do it,' I said. 'I type faster than you.'

She moved over to let me sit in front of the screen. My fingers flew. I pressed return. And waited. And waited. Seconds seemed like ages before *4849 results* flashed up on the screen. The first ten were listed.

'Most of these aren't what I'm looking for,' I said, dismayed.

'The search engine looks for each word separately,' said Alma.

I clicked on the likeliest site: <u>www.reunion-bureau/foreign</u>. Up came an alphabetical list of countries.

Australia: *'I was born 9/19/44. I am looking for my birth mother...'* I scrolled down the alphabet. Bermuda, Canada, Colombia. I had entered a cyberspace filled with lost children and grieving parents. Each country had a variation on the same sad appeal. *'Looking for my birth mother ... looking for my birth parents ... looking for my birth parents and relatives...'* 'Looking for my birth son ... birth daughter...' Occasionally, exclamation marks and bold type flagged a message: *Reunited!!!*

There was only one entry for Ireland. *'Looking for my birth son. Place of birth: Dublin. Adoption: Saint Joseph's Family Association, Chicago.'*

'It's an American website,' said Alma.

This was going to take for ever.

I clicked on the next hyperlink.

Report of the Adoption Board Ireland flashed on to the screen. This was more hopeful. *Enquiries for Adopted Persons*:

'The Board continues to receive enquiries from adopted persons seeking information about their background. The Board is willing to make available to the adoptees such non-identifying information as it has on file and to give any other assistance possible.' Mmm. Nonidentifying. Not so good. *'Regrettably, in many of the earlier cases the amount of information is scant.'*

Damn. Was my adoption of Mary an earlier case? What I needed was an organisation, names of people to contact. Click.

Natural Parents' Internetwork. This was better.

'NPI campaigns against the secrecy of adoption agencies and the State and Church personnel. Secrecy which denies adoptees the right to information about their life history.

113

Register to get in touch with other adoptees and birth parents through our Message Board. Contact us online, or by telephone, or write to us at the above address. All enquiries confidential. If you prefer not to receive a letter at your home you can nominate another address or a PO Box.'

There was a regional office in Limerick!

Alma looked at her watch. 'If we're walking back to meet Donal we need to leave now,' she said.

I wrote down the address and telephone number of the Limerick office. Alma went to tell the bartender we had finished.

'You can use the computers up to closing time,' he said when I paid him. I made my way through the dark bar and emerged into sunshine.

We got back to Atlantic House with ten minutes to spare. I took my mobile outside to get a better signal and dialled the NPI number in Limerick. There was the unmistakable whirr and pause of an answering machine.

'This is Natural Parents' Internetwork, Limerick. The office is open Monday and Wednesday, ten a.m. to twelve noon. If you would like to leave a message, please do so after the tone and we'll call you back.'

I made my decision as I snapped the phone shut. I would go to Limerick in the morning.

Chapter 14

The idea distracted me for the whole of the drive along the coast. I made Alma sit in the front seat of Donal's comfortable Mercedes. I wanted to concentrate on the task I'd set myself, and was only half aware of Donal's running commentary on the landscape. I closed my eyes and thought what a triumph it would be to wave the details of Mary's natural parents in Sister Monica's face! I pictured myself walking up the stairs in Saint Joseph's, the proof – I wasn't sure what kind of document it was – in my hand. She was playing the piano. I was walking towards her. The piano grew louder. A light tenor voice was singing 'The Last Rose of Summer'. Not Donal. The voice was coming from the car radio. It rose to a climax.

'To reflect back her beauty,
And yield sigh for sigh.'

I was back in the present.

'That's a lovely voice,' said Alma, as the music died away.

'Father Frank Devine,' said the announcer, 'ending this edition of Sunday Serenade with an old favourite by Thomas Moore.

Very appropriate for the time of year, too. Keep those requests coming in, I'll be here again...'

Donal switched off the radio.

'I thought so. Father Frank Devine. He was at Saint Finian's with my brother. Great voice. He could have had a career in opera. He could have ended up singing with your Mary,' he called back to me. 'Although he'll not see fifty again.'

'It's a wonderful voice,' I said. 'A real lyric tenor.'

'He's very popular. They call him the singing priest. He's made lots of CDs. We're nearly there,' he said, turning at a sign for Mullaney's Seafood Bar.

We bumped down a narrow road along an estuary, to where the single-storey, white-washed pub stood in a colourful jumble of parked cars, the road ended in rough pasture and the peat-brown river met the sea.

Mullaney's was an old-fashioned bar and grocery. Tins and packets lined the shelves above the optics – baked beans, tomato soup, cereals, sugar, tea, soap powder, shoe polish, toothbrushes and shampoo. Two barmen manoeuvred in the narrow space between the shelves and the counter. There was barely room for half a dozen bar stools and a couple of tables. We squeezed past the crush of customers at the bar and went

116

through to the bright, modern restaurant at the back. Sunlight poured through the glass roof on to the pale wooden floor, and the kitchen was open to view behind a steel counter. A waitress balancing a bowl of mussels on her arm waved us to a table near the glass doors that opened on to a terrace.

Eating oysters and lobsters and crab is gloriously messy and absorbing. I couldn't raise the subject of adoption law with Donal until we had spent a decent interval in silent contemplation of the pile of empty shells on the plates before us, and the view through the window beyond. Little waves sucked the pebbles on the shore and leapt around the grey rocks. A black cormorant perched on a rock pinnacle and spread his wings like Batman.

'I feel like I've slowed to a full stop,' Alma said. 'This is a lovely spot.'

'I'm almost sorry to be going to Limerick tomorrow,' I said. 'If the weather stays like this, it would be nice to be at the seaside. But I've found an organisation that might be able to help me. We looked it up on the web this morning.' I told Donal about Natural Parents' Internetwork.

'They'll know more about it than I do,' he said. 'But I'll tell you roughly how the law stands. There's no legal obligation on the people who arrange adoptions – be they adoption societies or private individuals – to

117

give identifying details about natural parents or adopted children. Were you given any documentation when you adopted your daughter? Did they tell you anything?'

'We got an amended birth certificate giving us the actual date of birth, but with our names instead of the natural parents'. And Sister Monica told us the mother was a talented girl and the father was a very distinguished man. Those were her exact words. I got the impression she was maybe a student and he was a professor, or something like that.'

'That's likely enough,' said Donal. 'There was a girl in the law department in my year who got pregnant. She left and didn't do her finals. We all suspected the father was a lecturer in jurisprudence. Although she never said.'

My heart jumped. 'Did she have the baby adopted, do you know?'

'This was about 1965,' said Donal, 'too early for your case.'

'What information am I legally entitled to?'

'Only general stuff,' he said. 'Age of the mother and father. Maybe their occupations. But nothing that could identify them, or where they live. It's all in the 1952 Adoption Act. There are various groups lobbying for reform. The group you're going to see is probably one of them. They want a contact

118

register and so on. But there are no votes in it so there's no political pay-off for changing things.'

'Oh,' I said, disappointed. 'Thanks anyway, Donal.'

'You'll find out more tomorrow,' he said. 'There could be changes afoot I wouldn't know about.'

There was a sudden rise in the level of background chatter. Scattered clapping preceded a proper round of applause as a waitress came out of the kitchen carrying a chocolate cake decorated with tiny, flickering candles – barely visible in the sunlight. She carried it to a table of ten in the centre of the room. They began singing 'Happy Birthday' and everybody joined in.

I sang as cheerfully as I could. But I never liked birthdays. Especially my own. I always felt sad on my birthday. Sad and guilty. Mum and Dad would take me somewhere special, or organise a party. I knew I should feel happy, and grateful, but all I felt was loss. I would sit watching Mr Magic, or Goofy the Clown, or – when I was old enough – sipping champagne and wonder, 'Is she thinking of me today? If she ever thinks about me, it must be today.' I would concentrate hard and try to send her a telepathic message. It was always the same message. 'I understand. And some day I'll find you.'

Alma said, 'Are you all right, Lena? You look a bit pale. Are you all right?'

Donal had gone to pay the bill, despite our protestations.

'Fine,' I said. 'I'm just thinking of the size of the task I've set myself.'

The atmosphere was flat after the fuss of celebration. Chairs scraped along the floor as people got up to leave.

'All set?' said Donal, coming back to the table. 'I thought we could do some sightseeing. That's if you'd like. We could see a fair bit before it gets dark. Unless, of course, you want to get back.'

'It's four o'clock already,' I said. 'We don't want to take up your entire evening.'

'To tell you the truth,' he said, 'it's lovely to have the company. Especially in the evenings. When you're on your own the days are fine. I play golf. Or if I'm at work, I work. It's the evenings that are hard. It's nice to have a bit of company for a change.'

He drove us up a winding road through the Burren to an ancient dolmen. We walked across the stony field to where the great, sloping capstone rested on craggy limestone stilts.

'*Stony seaboard, far and foreign,*
Stony hills poured over space,
Stony outcrop of the Burren,
Stones in every fertile place,' he quoted.

Alma was delighted. 'More,' she demanded.

'I forget the next few lines,' he said. 'But then it goes,

'Stone-walled cabins thatched with reeds,
Where a Stone Age people breeds
The last of Europe's stone age race.'

He looked at Alma, and then at me. 'Recognise it?'

We shook our heads.

'John Betjeman,' he said. '"Ireland with Emily". It's a perfect description, isn't it?'

I could tell Alma was impressed. She smiled and said, 'The restaurant didn't look very Stone Age people, Stone Age race.'

'That's only the surface,' he said. 'They did some research into blood groups in Ireland. There were people in the west of Ireland who had a different blood group from the rest of the population. Descendants of the original inhabitants, thousands and thousands of years back. Stone Age men. Before the Celts.'

'Are you a Stone Age man?' said Alma.

Donal paused.

'I have Stone Age impulses,' he said.

We were still laughing when we got back to the car. Donal drove us to the Cliffs of Moher as the sun hunkered down on the horizon and the last rays touched the fleecy clouds with pink. A few stragglers from a coach party came down the steep path towards us on their way to the car park. A family of red-haired musicians, dressed in green, finished a reel with a flourish and began to pack their flutes and fiddles into music cases. We stood as near to the edge of the cliffs as we dared. A flock of glossy black birds, with bright red beaks and legs, rode an invisible crest of air to soar above us like hang-gliders, before looping and swooping on the sea again with petulant cries. White lines of surf crawled towards the cliffs and broke over black rocks hundreds of feet below. I looked at Alma and gave myself a pat on the back for persuading her to come with me to Ireland. I had never seen her so relaxed.

'Are you golfing tomorrow?' I asked Donal.

'Are there fish in the sea?'

'Alma was talking last night about taking up golf,' I said. 'Why don't you take her with you and show her what the game's like?'

Before he could reply Alma said, 'I brought some work with me. I need to spend time going over it tomorrow. I absolutely have to get it done.'

She took a cigarette out of her bag, turned her back on us to light it, and began walking down to the car.

After a pause Donal said, 'Walking round a golf course when you don't play isn't much fun. You wouldn't learn much about the game. You need to be able to hit the ball first.'

We walked down to join Alma. She put out her cigarette and got into the back of the car.

'Where to now?' I said.

'There's a pub with good music about ten minutes from here,' Donal said.

I hesitated. Alma said, 'Would you mind driving me back to Atlantic House? I've got a bit of a headache. I think it's all the wine I had earlier.'

'Me too,' I said. 'I think I'll have a bit of a rest.'

'OK,' said Donal. 'There's music every night. I can take you another time.'

As we entered Atlantic House, three silhouettes came giggling down the stairs in the dusk.

'Switch the light on, Noreen, till I check my make-up.'

In the cold electric glare, I saw they were in their late twenties or early thirties, and dressed alike in black miniskirts and silver-spangled tops. Their legs and midriffs were tanned and bare. They dodged and weaved like Balinese dancers in front of the long mirror in the lobby.

'Lend us your comb, Grace.'

'Is this skirt too tight?'

A car horn tooted outside.

'There's our taxi!'

They shimmied around us in a cloud of scent, crying, 'Come with us! We're going to the matchmakers' dance at Lisdoon-varna. Come on. It'll be great crack.'

Two of them grabbed Donal and began to chant 'Oh! Lisdoonvarna. Lisdoon, Lisdoon, Lisdoonvarna!'

He looked back at us helplessly as they waltzed him back outside and we escaped upstairs.

'What's the matter?' I asked Alma when we got back to our room.

She rounded on me. 'Stop trying to manage things, Lena. Life is not a fairy tale. You can't manufacture happy endings.'

'What have I done?' I said. But I knew what she was going to say.

'You're trying to push me towards Donal. It's so crass and obvious. I don't want my life arranged by you. Unsubtle or what. Just stop interfering.'

'I'm sorry,' I said. 'I just want you to find someone nice. Someone available. I thought you liked him. You were flirting with him.'

'You want me to find someone nice? No. You want to feel good. You want to play the fairy fucking godmother. Arrange Mary's life if you want. But leave mine alone.'

'Is that what you think?' I said. 'I'm arranging Mary's life?'

She flopped down on her bed. Her

shoulders collapsed.

'I'm sorry. That's not my business.'

I felt uncomfortable.

'I'm sorry too,' I said. 'I've screwed things up. He said he wanted company.'

'He's a grown man,' Alma said. 'He can run his own life. Anyway, he said he didn't need company during the day. It's in the evening he likes to meet up with people.'

'I've screwed up his evening,' I said miserably. 'And yours.'

'Oh, bugger off,' she said. 'Just leave things alone.'

She gave a short, angry laugh.

'He probably thinks I'm a moody cow. Oh well, it doesn't matter. It's OK.' She shook her head. 'I know you mean well.'

We were both silent for a moment. Alma said, 'Aren't we ridiculous? Two grown women behaving like teenagers at a school dance. And Donal must be fifty, for God's sake.'

'He has his hands full of thirty-year-olds at the minute,' I said. 'Wouldn't you like to give them a run for their money?'

'You don't give up, do you?' She sighed. 'Just promise me you won't try to play the matchmaker.'

'I promise.'

'And Lena,' she added. 'How can you imagine me playing golf? I wouldn't be seen dead in checked trousers.'

Atlantic House didn't do an evening meal on Sundays, so we walked into town and had fish and chips. We were still a little tense with each other. When we got back to the hotel there was no sign of Donal. A party of hikers had arrived and taken over the bar. They looked friendly enough, but we decided against another late night. Alma went up to the room while I took my mobile outside to telephone Jack. The curtains weren't drawn in the bar, and as I waited for Jack to answer, the ruddy, animated faces round the fire made me more conscious of a damp chill in the air.

I pulled my jacket more tightly around me with one hand, while keeping the mobile clamped to my ear. No reply. Then an answering service. Jack's mobile was on divert. It was tomorrow morning in Australia. He was probably driving. I left a message telling him where we were, sending my love. But I was secretly relieved he hadn't answered the phone. When I told him I wasn't going to contact Sister Monica I had meant it, but when we drove past Saint Joseph's it seemed too good an opportunity to pass up. I thought it would be a simple matter of getting a name for Mary. To be honest, if Sister Monica hadn't made such a production of not telling me, if she'd been remotely helpful, I'd have left it at that. It was all too complicated to explain to Jack in a voicemail, I told myself.

Was it too late to call Mary in Frankfurt? What was the time there? Two hours ahead? She always said calls up to midnight were OK, and it was difficult to reach her during the day when she was rehearsing. I scrolled down to her mobile number and pressed the call button. She sounded out of breath when she answered.

'Are you all right?' I said. 'Did I wake you? Is it too late to call? I can ring back tomorrow.'

She laughed, and gasped. 'Oh,' she said. 'I've just been doing exercises.'

'It's after nine here. It must be after eleven with you!'

'It's the only time we get,' she said. 'We've been rehearsing all evening. I need to keep limbered up on this tour. They've brought in a choreographer to add dance steps to "I Got Rhythm"! She sang into the phone, *'I got stardust, I got sweet dreams,'* and burst out laughing. *'I got rhythm, who can ask for anything more?'* she sang. More laughter. 'How's Ireland?' she said. 'Where are you? What's the weather like?'

'In the west. Lovely and sunny this afternoon. A bit cold this evening. I had to come outside to get a signal and I can't see many stars. I think it might rain tomorrow. But the scenery is wonderful. How's Frankfurt?'

'Magic,' she said. I could hear the smile in her voice. 'Pure magic.'

'And the Gershwin songs?'

'Terrific,' she said. 'I'm really enjoying rehearsals. Now, don't stand out in the cold, Mum. Give my love to Alma.' She was in great spirits. 'I'm going back to my exercises!'

Alma was lying on her bed watching television. She pointed the remote control at the set to lower the sound as I came in.

'Leave it on if you like,' I said. 'I wouldn't mind watching a bit of television. Is there anything interesting on?'

'I think this is the guy with the great voice we heard on the radio,' she said, waving the remote at the screen, on a high shelf in the corner. 'He's wearing a dog collar and he's just been singing. Who does he remind you of?'

I looked up as the credits rolled over a professional smile and wave, strong jaw and greying, curly hair.

'He looks a bit like Steve McQueen,' I said. The screen went black for a second. The weather map flashed up. 'Let's see what the weather is going to be like tomorrow.'

We watched black spots denoting rain move across the map of Ireland from the Atlantic.

'Must have been a cracker when he was young,' Alma said. 'What a waste! He's got a new album out or something.' She turned the sound up again. 'Looks like a film's just starting.'

Long lines of minuscule figures streamed from a revolving globe on the screen to converge on a dot on the north coast of Africa. An urgent voice declaimed: *'Paris to Marseille. Across the Mediterranean to Oran. Then by train, or auto or foot across the rim of Africa to Casablanca...'*

We hooted with delight, and settled down to watch our favourite film.

When Humphrey Bogart said 'I think this is the beginning of a beautiful friendship', and the credits rolled, I looked across at Alma and said, 'Friends again?'

'Of course,' she said. 'Never doubt it.'

In the middle of the night, I wakened from a dream in which Sister Monica was saying, 'Be quiet!' to Humphrey Bogart as they boarded a biplane at Heathrow. I lifted my head from the pillow and heard creaking and whispering on the landing outside the bedroom door. There was a loud Sssh! Someone giggled. Feet tiptoed past the door. I wondered if any of them had danced with the man of their dreams in Lisdoonvarna.

Chapter 15

A storm blew in from the Atlantic during the night. I drew the curtains in the morning and saw the trees along the riverbank bounce and sway like dancers in the wind, scattering brown leaves on the sloping lawn.

'Awful day,' Alma said. She examined her face in the mirror above the chest of drawers between the windows. 'I look at myself, crumpled with sleep, flattened hair, eyes tired from too much wine, no make-up, and I see my mother. This is how I'll look when I'm seventy-five, Lena.'

She ran her fingers through her short hair, lifted her chin and stroked her cheeks with the backs of her hands. 'You can't fight gravity and the second law of thermo-dynamics.'

'You look fine, Alma,' I said. I didn't add how lucky she was to know what her mother looked like, but she glanced quickly at me and said, 'I'm sorry, Lena. I wish you could trace your own birth mother instead of Mary's.'

'I've no clues. At least with Mary I know where to begin. Even if I don't get far.'

'Good luck in Limerick,' she said. 'Take

the car. I won't need it. I'm going to sit in that nice, bright conservatory and do some course preparation work, and look out at the rain. You can tell me all about it when you get back.'

'If I'd known you were for going into Limerick, Eileen could have taken you,' said Michael when he asked us about our plans for the day. 'She's only just left.'

The women who had hijacked Donal came down as we were finishing our breakfast. I heard them ask Michael about Donal's whereabouts.

'He can't be golfing in this weather!' one of them exclaimed.

'He's no fair weather golfer,' Michael said. 'I promise you he's out there, battling the elements.'

'If you see him, will you tell him we're going to the afternoon dance in Lisdoon-varna?'

I tried to catch Alma's eye, but she was carefully buttering a slice of toast.

It was still raining when I got to Limerick. I ran from the car to a shopping mall and bought an umbrella. I had walked through Limerick with Jack on a visit to Ireland, not long after we met. When I stepped out from the mall, opening my umbrella, I saw that the town had changed. The dank and grimy streets beside the river Shannon had been replaced by a riverside park and bright, modern buildings. Only the damp remained.

The Natural Parents' Internetwork office was in a grey, Georgian building in a grid of streets back from the river. The ground floor was a newsagent's shop. Entrance to the offices on the floors above was through a side door down a narrow lane. The door badly needed a coat of paint and the fanlight was broken. I peered at a dozen doorbells, most with names or initials on grubby white cards beside them, and pressed the bell for Natural Parents' Internetwork. I heard a buzz and click, and pushed open the heavy, once elegant door. A sign in the hallway directed me to the third floor. There was no lift. Water dripped from my umbrella and the hem of my raincoat as I trudged up the stone staircase, past Tailoring and Alterations and the Women's Advice Centre on the first floor; Limerick Animal Rights and Roger's Radio and TV Repairs on the second floor; and up to Natural Parents' Internetwork, beside Technical Translations, at the top. I was out of breath when I pushed open the door and saw a woman sitting at a desk in the small attic room, tapping the keyboard of a computer. It was Eileen Collins.

I stood for a few moments, still dripping, breathing heavily, incapable of speech.

Eileen swung round from the screen and saw me. I don't know which one of us was the more surprised. Eileen found her voice first.

'Take off that wet coat and sit down,' she said. 'Get your breath back. It's a fierce climb. I'll make you a cup of tea.'

'I had no idea,' I said.

'Why should you?' she said, getting up from the desk and moving to a table by the window. She hefted the electric kettle to test the weight of water before putting it back on the table and flicking the switch. 'We don't go around with signs on our backs saying this woman gave her baby away. I do two mornings a week here. Not many people come in. It's mostly telephone calls and letters. And there's the website. One of our members set it up.' She tapped the filing cabinet beside the table. 'It's nice when I can put a face to a name. Sugar?'

I shook my head. I was still standing just inside the door, conscious of the ceiling only a few feet above me. A big poster occupied most of the wall behind the desk.

The History of a Person Belongs to that Person
NPI Campaigning for Openness in Adoption

'Take one of those chairs and sit down,' Eileen said. 'There's a hook on the back of the door, and you can leave your umbrella outside. There's nobody else up here today.'

The kettle spluttered to a boil. I took a

chair from behind the door and unfolded it to sit down beside the desk. Eileen resumed her seat and pushed a steaming mug of tea towards me. She made no attempt to hide the curiosity in her grey eyes.

'I'll go first, will I?' she said.

She told me the year she had her baby girl. I held my breath and closed my eyes. It was the year I adopted Mary.

I opened my eyes and looked straight at Eileen.

'Where?' I said. 'What month?'

'Eastbourne,' she said. 'January. In the bleak midwinter.'

I let out my breath. My shoulders slumped. Eileen said, gently, 'Wrong place, wrong month?'

I nodded.

'I know how you feel,' she said. 'Whenever someone contacts the office, I think, "Did she adopt my baby?" Every time I see a young woman who looks a bit like me, I think, "Is she my daughter?" Every time I sit here I think, "Maybe she will ring up." It's a hard road,' she said. 'You'll have a lot of disappointments on the way.'

She paused, waiting for me to speak. I was wondering where to begin when she continued in her quick voice, 'Michael is very supportive. He knows all about it, of course. That helps. And my children know they have a half-sister out there somewhere.

What about your husband? Does he know? Is he OK about it?'

'He doesn't know I'm here,' I said. 'It's not straightforward. I'm here for my daughter.'

'When did you give her up?'

'I didn't,' I said. 'I adopted her.'

It was the only time I ever saw Eileen lost for words. They poured out of me to fill the astonished silence.

'I'm adopted,' I said. 'I have an adopted daughter. I want to find Mary's natural parents. For her sake. I know what it's like not to know, not to entirely know who you are. I know she wants to know, but she thinks I'd be hurt. And I wouldn't be hurt, because I felt like that too and I left it too late.'

I heaved a great sigh, dug my hands into my lap, bit my lip and stared at the poster on the wall. When I looked back at Eileen, she was waiting for me continue. Her attention never wavered as I told her how I had adopted Mary, and how I had always wondered about her natural parents because of her voice.

'It's like being entrusted with something special,' I said. 'Jack's musical. We both play the piano and we love music. We sent her to music lessons. But Mary is something else entirely. I don't think she has a great voice because she grew up in a musical household. I think she inherited it. If you heard her sing you'd know what I mean. She says she's not that interested in her birth parents. But I know. I know,' I said earnestly, 'that deep down, she is. I know it because I pretended I didn't care, wasn't interested. When Mama died and I began my search, it was too late. There's a big hole in my life. I don't want that to happen to Mary.'

'You see adoption from both sides,' Eileen said. 'There's not many can do that. How much did you manage to find out about your own birth mother?'

'Not much,' I said. 'Mama died just before I adopted Mary. She told me all she knew, which was almost nothing. She knew the name of the home where I was born. She knew my mother was twenty-four, and her first name was Celia. No surname. And she gave me these.'

I opened my handbag and took out a leather pouch. I showed Eileen the delicate enamelled brooch in the shape of a deer, with tiny silver hooves and amethyst eyes, and the blue knitted teddy bear no bigger than the palm of my hand.

'They were stitched into the hem of my blanket.' Tears pricked my eyes.

Eileen went to the filing cabinet and made a show of riffling through a tray of suspension files. She extracted a sheet of paper. 'It's probably worth while writing down your details. For your own adoption, that is,' she said, coming back to the desk. 'You never know. We have members whose babies were adopted in England. Irish girls have been going to England to have their babies for a long time. That's what I did.'

I took the paper from her. 'Why did you go to England?' I said.

'So nobody would find out. My mother was terrified the whole town would gossip. My father was well known. They couldn't wait to get me out of the country, never mind the town. They sent me to a cousin of my mother's who was a nun in the south of England. I was nineteen. I'd never been out of Ireland before. She arranged for me to stay with a family in Eastbourne until I had my baby. It was the most miserable time of my life.'

Her speech slowed down as she told her story. 'Mammy's cousin never came to visit. Mammy and Daddy were back in Ireland. I had to go to a telephone box to phone them. I was always hanging around in the cold and the conversations were stilted. They never mentioned my being pregnant. The family I was staying with were pleasant enough. It was like being in digs. I wandered around Eastbourne and spent a lot of time in my room. They had a sixteen-year-old daughter, but I hardly exchanged three words with her.'

She gave a short laugh. 'I was there as a

sort of deterrent. That's what will happen to you, my girl, if you step out of line. The wages of sin. I went into labour on Christmas Eve and had my baby in hospital, on Christmas Day. To tell you the truth, it was better than sitting through a Christmas dinner with the family. The nurses were lovely. They could not have been nicer to me. I had no visitors, so they used to sit and chat to me and they brought me flowers. I had such kindness in that hospital. They never mentioned the fact that there was no wedding ring and no man coming to see me. I will always be grateful to those nice English girls for looking after me.'

'Do you have a photograph of your baby?' I said.

'No.' Her eyes glittered with tears. 'It was all done quickly. The adoption agency came to see me in the hospital. Two social workers. They said to me, "Why are you giving up this baby?" They had to ask, because of the adoption rules. I said, "Because I don't want her."'

A tear ran down her cheek. 'I will always regret saying that. I don't know why I said it. It wasn't true.'

'Maybe we should have something stronger than tea,' I said.

'And talk about you for a change,' she said, trying to smile. She sniffed back her tears and groped in the top drawer of the desk for a packet of tissues. 'Do you know you have the right to your original birth certificate?'

'Yes,' I said, 'but I don't have a surname. And when I first went looking, I found the home where I was born had been knocked down. I put my name on an adoption contact register. But I never heard anything. Anyway,' I said, 'I didn't come here about me. I came about Mary.'

'Did you drive here? I could have given you a lift if I'd known,' Eileen said, dabbing her eyes. 'We could go for a drink. Just one. If we have something to eat, we'll be OK for driving back. Don't forget your registration form. You can give it to me any time.' She turned briefly to the screen to log off as I took my coat from the back of the door and collected my umbrella from the landing.

'Let's go,' she said, closing the office door behind her.

We splashed through the noisy centre of Limerick, past blocks of Georgian buildings, and across a bridge to a quayside pub. The lunchtime rush hadn't started and the bar was quiet. We ordered a whiskey each, and I told Eileen about the telephone call.

'Completely out of the blue,' I said.

'And this nun hadn't telephoned before?'

'No.' I said. 'That's what started me on this whole thing. I began to worry that Mary was going to inherit some disease. Or that her natural mother had made some deathbed plea.'

'And it was nothing like that?'

'Nothing. At least I don't think so. I think she was telling the truth. She's retiring. She just wanted to tot up her personal balance sheet. To tell you the truth, if she hadn't stonewalled me so much, hadn't ticked me off like a schoolgirl, I mightn't be here now. She made me more determined than ever to get some information.'

'It's all very strange,' Eileen said. 'I've never heard of an adoption agent getting in touch like that before. Unless they were planning to give some information to the natural mother, or,' she added thoughtfully, 'the father. What was it she said to you? At the time of the adoption, I mean. An important man?'

'A very distinguished man,' I said. 'Her exact words.'

'Maybe he's a politician. Or somebody famous.'

'What difference would that make? And why get in touch after all that time?'

'I don't know. But it's odd. I can see why you're curious.' She shook her head in puzzlement. 'I'll give you our advice sheet on how to trace,' she said. 'You could give it to Mary as well. If she is interested she can search for herself. But it takes a long time. There are no central records, and no right of

140

access. Sister Monica was right about that.'

'I want some clues now,' I said. 'I want to know that if I fall under a bus, I've left something for Mary. So she won't be left wondering, like me.'

'I hope whoever adopted my daughter is like you.'

'And I hope your daughter finds you.' We were silent for a moment.

'At least you know the nun's still alive.' Eileen was brisk again. 'In some cases the people who arranged the adoption are dead, and there's no chance of finding anything out. If the law changes she might have to give you some information. At the moment she doesn't have to.'

'One of the nurses at Saint Joseph's told me Sister Monica wasn't well,' I said. 'God forgive me, but I hope she doesn't die before I can get any more information out of her.'

'Your best bet is to talk to someone who was in that home at the same time,' Eileen said. 'What was it called again?'

'Saint Joseph's, near Tullamore.'

'I'll go through our files when I go back to the office,' she said. 'If I find a name I can contact them and ask if it's all right to put you in touch with them. I'm sure they'll say yes. We're all in the business of piecing bits of information together.'

'They're not likely to be in Limerick, are they?'

'They're as likely to be here as anywhere else. I get calls from all over. Girls usually went away from home to have their babies, so they wouldn't be recognised. Look at me, for example. Sometimes their parents wouldn't know. Or the father wouldn't know. And there would be elaborate arrangements for letters to be forwarded from false addresses. So we could well have a member who went to Saint Joseph's. It's worth a try.' She paused, and contemplated the empty glass in front of her, as though debating whether or not to say what came next.

'Lena,' she said, 'have you thought what you're going to do with any information you get? Suppose you succeed in tracing Mary's birth mother, for example. What are you going to do? You're not considering making an approach yourself, are you?'

'Good God, no.' I truly meant it. 'My plan has always been to keep the information somewhere safe. Probably with my solicitor. It'll be there for Mary. It's for her to decide.'

'Good,' said Eileen. 'We usually advise an approach through an intermediary. A priest, or someone from social services. I'm sure you'll tell Mary that.'

'Of course,' I said. 'Now, how about some lunch?'

Chapter 16

The rain had stopped by the time I got back to the car. I felt around in my handbag for the keys and my hand closed over the leather pouch. My talisman. I rarely showed its contents to anyone. I had shown Jack the brooch and teddy bear after Mama died. He rocked me in his arms and said, 'Oh, Lena. I've neglected you. I've been too busy. Away too much.'

And it was true. When he came to Mama's funeral I felt I hadn't seen him for months. I had been in Surrey a lot, staying with Dada while Mama was in hospital. Jack had been in Ireland on business. After the funeral he said, 'Let's buy a new house. Start afresh.'

That's when we bought Hope House. The house we've just left. The house Mary turned into a home.

I thought about Mama as I drove back to the hotel. I imagined my birth mother saying to her, 'I hope whoever adopted my daughter is like you.'

Mama was a wonderful person.

'Dada will marry again,' she said to me during those last days in the hospital.

'No, Mama! Don't say that!' I cried.

'Listen to me,' she said. 'People marry again because they liked being married. They've had a good experience. Dada and I have been happy together.' She reached out and gripped my hand. 'But you were the centre of my life. Not a day went by but I thanked God and your mother for giving you to me.' She smiled. 'Can you plump up my pillows, please? Don't bother to get the nurse. Just prop me up a bit.'

I did as she asked, as gently as I could.

'There's a tin box in the locker,' she said. 'Will you get it for me? Will you open it for me, please?'

Her hands couldn't grip tightly enough to prise open the lid. I opened the box and gave it back to her. She took out a letter and laid it on one side.

'That was in case I died without being able to talk to you.'

She took out the brooch, and the knitted blue teddy bear.

'She must have thought she was expecting a boy,' she said. 'When I got you, these were in the hem of your blanket. She'd just knitted the back and front for the teddy bear. I could see what it was meant to be, so I finished it. It was my thank-you to her. I didn't give you the brooch either. I was afraid you would lose it,' she said. 'Maybe I was a bit jealous as well. I'm sorry.'

144

'It's all right, Mama,' I said.

'Your adoption papers are in there too. You might want to look for your other mother,' she said. 'It's all right. Everybody wants to know who they really are. It doesn't affect how they love people. I know that. Remember that.'

I was too choked to speak.

'We've been a lovely family,' she said. 'I've had a good life, Lena. You'll have a good life too. Jack's an exciting man.' She leaned towards me a little and dropped her voice. 'He reminds me of Ronnie Drysdale. My first boyfriend. Your grandparents didn't approve of him. He had no money. He married Joan Butler and they went to Canada. I heard years later they got divorced over there.' She sighed. 'Funny how things turn out.'

She smiled, and settled back on her pillows. 'Give my love to Jack. Tell him from me to look after you well. I'll be watching from wherever I am.'

I held her hand until she fell asleep and the nurses came in and busied themselves. Dada was with her when she died that night. Two years later he met and married Catherine and moved to France.

When the sun came out I stopped to consult the map, and decided on a route that would take me back along the coast. A few miles from Atlantic House, a patch of bright pink and a flash of steel caught my eye. I slowed down as I passed the sign, Pitch and Putt. 9 Holes, and scanned the miniature golf course that lay between the coast road and the sea. Two figures stood on a smooth and irregular sward of green overlooking the beach. Donal's long back was bent over a ball on the putting surface. Alma was holding the flag.

'I decided to walk into town and buy some postcards,' Alma told me when she got back. 'I got a lot of work done. I stopped when the sun came out. I thought it was a pity to stay inside.'

'So you sat in the sun and wrote postcards?'

'Yes.'

'You must have got a good few written,' I said.

She went as pink as her jacket.

'Actually,' she said, 'I got cornered by Donal. He came back to get changed. He got a soaking on the golf course.'

'You had a chat?'

'I couldn't avoid it without seeming rude,' she said. 'He came into the conservatory looking like a wet duck. I made the obvious comment.'

I tilted my head in enquiry. 'You said?'

'You look like a wet duck.'

'So what did you do for the rest of the day?'

'Tell me about Limerick first,' she said. 'I'm dying to know how you got on.'

'There was a nice woman in the office,' I said. 'She's going to see if they have any members who were in Saint Joseph's around the time Mary was born. It's a start. And I might post something on the bulletin board on the website.'

When we went in to dinner I saw Eileen had laid a table for three, and a much bigger table for one of the groups.

'Oh, is Donal joining us?' I said.

Alma still hadn't mentioned her outing to the pitch and putt. But her diffidence was offset by Donal's bouncing into the dining room saying, 'Well? Has she told you she's a natural? Great swing!'

I pretended surprise. 'Alma! Have you been playing golf?'

'We went to a pitch and putt,' she said. 'I must admit it was great fun.'

'She's a natural,' Donal said. 'Ex-hockey player. If I get her out on a proper course, she'll probably hit the ball miles.'

Alma smiled her pleasure at the compliment, but changed the subject. 'Donal was asking how you got on in Limerick.'

I quickly retold the story of my trip, conscious that Eileen Collins was about to appear with the first course. She caught my eye a few times as she came and went with fresh crab, lamb chops, and broad beans from her garden. I thought she was signalling a warning not to tell my companions the secret she hid so well.

The hikers streamed into the dining room as we were scoffing our second helpings of Eileen's gooseberry tart. When we got up to go to the bar, I hung back and allowed a burly hiker to come between me and Donal and Alma. I hovered by the sideboard as Eileen opened bottles of wine. She brushed off my whispered assurances.

'Ah,' she said softly, 'I don't mind if Donal and Alma know. She's not likely to be talking to anyone I know, and Donal is the soul of discretion. But I was looking for a chance to talk to you. I have a name.'

I gripped the sideboard to keep myself steady. She said in a louder voice, 'I'll see to that for you, Lena. Come into the kitchen when you've had your coffee and I'll sort it out.' The cork came out of the bottle with a satisfying pop. She gave me a wink, and whirled away.

Alma looked up when I came into the bar.

'Are you all right, Lena?' she said. 'What's happened?'

We had the room to ourselves. I tripped over my words as I rushed to explain Eileen's connection to the Natural Parents'

148

Internetwork, and her promise of a name.

'She's found someone who was in Saint Joseph's around the time Mary was born,' I said. 'I might be able to go and see her. She might remember something.'

'That's great,' Donal said. 'A witness.'

'I don't know where she is, or if she'll see me,' I said. 'But thanks, fingers crossed.'

I downed my coffee and made my way to the kitchen.

'Is this an OK time?'

'Fine, fine,' Eileen said, arranging the last of the dinner plates in the dishwasher. 'Sit down.' She pulled out a chair from the kitchen table and cleared a space for me. 'Here!' she said, extracting a Post-it message pad from the pocket of her apron. 'I found one name in the files. Teresa Flanigan. I spoke to her this afternoon. She doesn't mind talking to you.'

She peeled the note from its pad and stuck it on the table in front of me. 'She sounded nice on the phone. Give her a ring. I told her a bit of background. Who you're trying to trace, the year, and so on. I hope you don't mind.'

'Not at all,' I said, transfixed by the yellow square with words and numbers scrawled across it. 'I don't know how to thank you. This is marvellous, Eileen.' I looked at the address. 'How far away is that?'

'Ninety miles? Maybe more. It's at least two

and a half hours each way. You'd be driving nearly to the east coast. But there's a main road a good part of the way. You'd get there and back in a day. Use the phone in here,' she said. 'I'm just going to serve the pudding.'

She drew a plate of gooseberry tart towards her and began cutting slices and sliding them on to plates. 'Go on,' she urged. 'Ring her now. The phone is on the wall.' She beamed encouragement as she picked up her tray and backed through the door to the dining room.

My hand tightened on the receiver as I dialled the number and waited for an answer.

'Flanigans,' said a man's voice.

'Can I speak to Teresa Flanigan, please?' I said.

'Hold on a minute,' he said. I heard him call, 'Teresa!'

There was a clatter as she picked up the handset.

'Hello?'

'This is Lena Molloy,' I said. 'Eileen Collins gave me your number. Is this a good time to call?'

'Any time's a good time for a good cause,' she said. 'Eileen told me about you. She said you might ring. I was in Saint Joseph's for nearly three months before my daughter was born.' She paused. 'I've been trying to trace her.'

'What day was she born?' I felt my lungs contract.

'The first of August.'

My breath escaped in a whoosh. 'Mary was born on the tenth.'

'Oh.' I could hear disappointment even in that one syllable.

'I'm sorry.'

'It's all right,' she said. 'I'm used to disappointment by now. How long have you been searching?'

'I've only just begun.'

'I don't know how much help I can be,' she said. 'But I have some photographs. And maybe I overlapped with the girl you're looking for.'

My heart squeezed tight like a spring.

'You stayed three months?' I said. 'Did most girls stay three months?'

'It varied. They came and went. Some stayed a year before their babies were adopted. The photographs might be some help. If you can get here you can have a look at them. And maybe I'll remember something that will help. I don't often go to Limerick. We have a chemist's shop here in the town. I can't be away for a whole day, but I can take an afternoon off.'

'Could I come tomorrow?' I said, crossing my fingers. 'I'm here on holiday and I don't want to waste any time.'

'We've all wasted too much time already,'

she said. 'Look for the County Pharmacy when you get to the town. We're on the main street. Just come in and ask for me and I'll take you up to the house. I'll show you what I've got. But don't build your hopes up too much. You're in for a long slog. And there'll be a lot of disappointment on the way.'

It seemed to me I had already heard that warning a few times, and would hear it again before my search was over.

Alma offered to come with me and share the driving, but I told her I'd rather go on my own. She didn't press me. She could see I really meant it and wasn't pushing her into spending time with Donal.

'If you're sure,' she said. 'I still have plenty of work to do. I've wasted a lot of time trying to hit a ball into a hole.'

Alma came out to the car with me the next morning.

'Good luck,' she said, giving me a quick hug.

Donal came down the steps waving a map.

'I've marked the route for you,' he cried. 'You'll go straight past the Rock of Cashel. It's a great sight to behold.'

I paused at the end of the driveway, twisting round in my seat in a last gesture of farewell. Donal took off his tweed cap and waved it in the air. Alma had already gone inside.

Chapter 17

At traffic lights on the far side of Limerick, I
changed cassettes from Beethoven's Pastoral
to Schubert's great C major symphony. I like
gloriously dramatic, orchestral music. Beethoven, Tchaikovsky, Schubert, Mahler; and
of course nineteenth- and early twentieth-
century operas by Verdi, Bellini, Puccini,
Richard Strauss. I was sure Mary would star
in them.

When Jack discovered my taste in music,
he told me I liked drama and emotion
because I am organised and orderly in my
approach to life. Music let me express my
wild side. It was my escape from routine. I
soon learned Jack was the opposite. He'd let
paper work pile up on top of him. Then he'd
spend hours in the office catching up. He
wasn't good at managing time. That's why
he played Bach and Scarlatti in the
evenings. He was soothed by their clarity
and precision.

I drove through a broad, flat valley of
green pastures, creamy cattle and brown
horses. The sky was a pearly grey; there was
almost no wind. Haws, rosehips and
blackberries spotted the hedgerows purple,

orange and red. I pressed a button on the car door and the window slithered down, letting in the smell of burning leaves from an autumn bonfire, and the cawing of crows circling above a stand of chestnut trees.

Just before midday, I rounded a bend and saw, rising from the green plain, the Round Tower, High Cross and vaulted chapels of the Rock of Cashel, silhouetted against the sky. The Schubert hurtled to its grand finale. I had a sense of events moving fast. My life rushing ahead of me. I felt suddenly shaken and apprehensive. I stopped the car in a lay-by, turned off the music, and calmed myself in contemplation of the great outcrop of rock, crowned with the broken ruins of mediaeval Ireland. I hunted through the stack of cassettes for something ordered and serene. I selected Mary singing *Arias from the Baroque Era.* That was better. By the time I parked near the County Pharmacy, I was composed.

The young man in a white coat behind the counter asked me to wait for a moment and disappeared around the back of some shelves. A dark-haired woman in a well-cut linen suit of periwinkle blue came out, lifted the flap of the counter and joined me on the other side.

'Hello, Lena,' she said, sizing me up with shrewd eyes that matched her suit, as she shook my hand. 'You've arrived at a good time. I'm Teresa. The car's parked outside. I'll drive ahead of you up to the house. We can have a bite of lunch.'

She lived in an ivy-covered Georgian house by a crossroads about two miles from the town. There was a swing in the front garden and a basketball net on the wall of the garage. 'My youngest is ten,' she said. 'I have two other boys aged fifteen and twelve. I haven't told them they have a half-sister. My husband thinks I should wait until they're older.'

She led me down the hallway to the kitchen. The back of the house had been extended, and the kitchen was roomy with an unimpeded view of purple mountains rising in the distance. She sat me at the long pine table by the window.

'Soup and bread and cheese all right?' she said. 'I made the soup last night.'

'Lovely,' I said.

'How long did it take you to track down Saint Joseph's?' she asked, putting a loaf of home-made soda bread on the table.

'I always knew it was where Mary was born,' I said. 'To be honest, although I suppose the idea was at the back of my mind for a long time, I didn't try to find out anything more until the nun who arranged Mary's adoption got in touch with me a couple of weeks ago.'

'What!' said Teresa. 'She actually got in

touch? Which nun?'

'Sister Monica,' I said. 'Do you remember her?'

Teresa scraped a saucepan across the hotplate of the cooker. 'The old tartar,' she said, moving across the kitchen. The cupboard door banged as she took out two bowls and two side plates. 'Men can't control themselves, that was her big thing.'

She stood holding the plates and mimicked Sister Monica's arch manner of speaking. 'It's up to girls to be modest and avoid provocation.' She rolled her eyes and continued her impersonation. 'It's easy to spell contraception. Two letters. N.O.' She put the plates on the table and opened a drawer for knives and spoons. 'We all loathed her. She had a degree in sarcasm.'

'She gave me a lesson in it,' I said. I told her about the telephone call from Sister Monica, my impulsive visit to Saint Joseph's and my humiliation.

'That's her all right.'

'Of course it's made me all the more determined to get some solid information.'

'I'm amazed she got in touch with you at all. I wrote to Saint Joseph's and got absolutely nowhere.'

'Join the club,' I said. 'That's why I'm here. She absolutely refused to tell me anything.'

'So why did she get in touch?'

156

'Search me,' I said. 'I have no idea.'

'What did she say when she called?'

'She said she was going to retire soon, and she wanted to find out what had happened to all the babies she'd found homes for.'

For the first time in my life I actually saw a jaw drop.

'What!' Teresa stood frozen in the act of ladling soup into a bowl. She gave her head a quick shake. 'I don't believe it. Are you sure there wasn't more to it than that? Had she ever rung you before?'

'Never. That's what started me out on all this. It made me think maybe there was something wrong. That's why I went to see her at Saint Joseph's.'

'And you asked her about Mary's birth mother, if there was anything wrong, any message from her?'

'Yes,' I said. 'And she showed me the door.'

'How much do you know about Mary's birth mother? What were you told at the time?'

'Not much. When Sister Monica first approached me, I got the impression there'd been another couple lined up to adopt the baby, but something went wrong at the last minute and the mother couldn't stay in Saint Joseph's, and this would be better for the baby, and hence the rush.'

'Did she actually tell you all that?'

'Not in so many words. It was just the impression I got. Oh,' I added, 'she told me the father was a very distinguished man.'

'Sounds as if the father was the important one,' said Teresa. 'Maybe he was the one who fixed everything.'

'What do you mean?'

'Fixed for the girl to go to Saint Joseph's,' said Teresa. 'We'd better eat our soup before it gets cold.'

We ate our soup in silence for a few minutes. I digested what Teresa had just said.

'It still doesn't explain why Sister Monica rang me out of the blue,' I said.

'Maybe she was trying to find something out for the father.'

'Eileen thought it sounded like he was a politician, or someone famous.'

'Or someone rich,' said Teresa. She set down her spoon, rested her chin on her hand, and gazed out of the window, deep in thought. 'They've changed the law on illegitimacy here. I don't know precisely what the difference is, but I think illegitimate children are entitled to a share of the estate. I wonder if that applies to children who are adopted?'

I stared at her. 'I have no idea. The thought never occurred to me.' I thought about Donal. 'But I know someone I could ask.'

'It's just a thought,' she said. 'I've probably got it all wrong. Was the adoption straight-forward? Apart from happening quickly.'

'Yes,' I said. 'The documents were explained to us by the solicitor when we got Mary. We had them checked by our own solicitor when we got back. We paid an adoption fee, and the solicitor's fees in Ireland. I suppose the only strange thing was that Mary was handed over in the solicitor's office. We never went to the home. Although I had an idea where it was. It's an old people's home now.'

'An old people's home,' Teresa mused. 'Changed times, huh? I lie awake some-times and think, if only I'd been born just a few years later I could have kept my baby. Things changed so fast.' She looked sad and lost in thought for a few moments. 'You're a Catholic?'

I nodded.

'I don't know if it was the same in England. But Ireland changed quickly. I just got caught a bit too soon,' she said sadly. 'A few years later, when I met my husband, when I first slept with him, before we were married, I thought it was a sin. But the priest only said, "Do you love this man?" I said I did. He said, "Then you should pray he marries you. Three Hail Marys."'

'I think a lot of things changed after the 1960s.'

'The 1960s didn't happen here until the 1970s,' Teresa laughed, suddenly bright again. 'By the end of the '70s it was OK to keep your baby. It wasn't shameful any more. You didn't have to be invisible. Now nearly everybody keeps their baby, or goes to England to have an abortion.'

'But that wasn't a choice for you?'

'No,' she said. 'I never considered it. I was muddled and unhappy about a lot of things, but I never considered an abortion. I just got pregnant at the wrong time. At the end of an old era, instead of the start of a new one.'

'I can't imagine you ever being muddled,' I said. 'You seem so confident and calm.'

'I was a real mess,' she said. 'Eighteen, in my first year at college. Straight out of convent school. Totally naïve.' She gave a wry laugh. 'The father was a really romantic figure at college. Wore a velvet jacket and a bow tie. He was engaged to somebody else. He didn't tell me. I was just a fling to him. I had no sense at all. Do you know what he said to me after we, you know, for the first time?'

I shook my head.

'See you around. Not original. But I didn't know it was the oldest brush-off line in the book. So I trotted around for days in a happy dream until another girl marked my card. Told me he was engaged. I felt sick.

Then I discovered I was pregnant. When I tracked him down and told him, he begged me not to tell his fiancée. He was terrified she would find out. He was so anxious to avoid me, he moved out of his flat. I still can't believe I was so naïve,' she said. 'I felt shunned.'

'We were all naïve.'

'We didn't all get caught,' she said. 'My mother nearly went out of her mind when I told her. My father didn't want to know. He left it all to her to sort out and she organised for me to go to Saint Joseph's. I had to keep well away from the town. The college was fine about it. So I went to lectures until I was six months pregnant. Then I went to the home.'

'What was it like?'

'Boring, mostly. Bum-shiftingly boring. Awful. We only went out to go to Mass on Sundays. The rest of the time we were sewing or cleaning. Or just sitting around going out of our minds with anxiety. They didn't try to allay your fears, or prepare you much for what was ahead. We had a portable record player and a transistor radio, but we only got to listen for about half an hour in the evenings. Sometimes one of the nuns would play the piano. But it was always stuff we weren't interested in. Old fashioned waltzes. Parlour songs. Thomas Moore. We wanted David Bowie and Don

161

McLean. On Sunday nights we had to listen to Tommy's Choice on the radio. It was a record request programme,' she explained. 'It ran for years. And for years after Saint Joseph's I couldn't bear to listen to it. Sister Monica wouldn't miss it. There was nearly always a request for her brother.'

'Why was he always getting requests played for him?' Curiosity diverted me.

'No,' she said. 'Not for him. By him. He was a well-known singer. There was a request for him nearly every week. He specialised in what you might call the religious light classical. "Ave Maria" and "Panis Angelicus" and that kind of thing.'

'What was he called?' I said, almost idly.

'The singing priest,' she said. 'Father Frank Devine, the singing priest. Have you ever heard of him? He's still well known.'

'I saw him on television the other night!' I exclaimed. 'Did he ever come to Saint Joseph's?'

'Not that I know of,' Teresa said. 'We were only subjected to him on the radio. She would sit there all puffed up with pride. We all knew if we wanted any favours, that was the time to ask. I still can't bear to listen to him.'

She got up and went to the pine dresser that stood against the back wall of the kitchen and took a flat, rectangular box from the wide drawer below the shelves glowing with old china. It was a chocolate box, with a picture of a fluffy Persian cat on the lid. I hadn't seen anything like it since I was a child. She read my expression and smiled.

'I've had this box since I was about ten,' she said. 'They don't make them like this any more, do they? I haven't opened it in twenty years. I brought it down from the attic this morning. I used to keep all sorts of things in it.'

She lifted the lid with her two hands and laid it to one side. 'You say you're going to keep in touch with people. But it's all too painful. And you don't. I know some people just want to forget. But I didn't. Every moment I was there I was saying to myself, remember this.'

She lifted out a folded square of tissue paper and unwrapped it.

'It's like losing part of your body,' she said. 'You'd remember if you left your leg somewhere. Or a piece of your heart. You'd remember how and why it happened. I never wanted to let the memory go.'

Inside lay a scrap of white ribbon and a tiny wisp of dark hair.

'That's all I have of her,' she said quietly.

She shook two Polaroid colour snaps out of a large brown envelope. Each was about three inches square, the colour faded and unreal. 'One of the other girls took these.

163

She sent them to me after she left. Imelda. She had a boy. Our babies were born in the same week.'

My reading glasses were in my handbag. I fished for them before picking up a photograph of two brunettes in near-identical blue and white patterned tent dresses and navy shoes, framed by a doorway.

'That's Imelda and me,' Teresa said. 'Tent dresses were all the rage that year, thank God. Sister Monica hated us wearing platform shoes. She made us wear slippers. We put our shoes on for the photograph.'

I picked up the second photograph. 'Do you still have names and addresses?' I asked, studying three girls, arms linked, sitting on a low whitewashed wall. Imelda, with a blonde and a smaller brunette.

'The names are on the back,' she said. 'I've lost the addresses. Sorry.'

I peered more closely at the blonde girl in the middle. I thought I saw a definite resemblance to Mary. I turned the photograph over and read the names, written neatly from left to right. Imelda Murphy, Maggie Kane, Patsy Malone.

'Imelda had a boy? Is that right?'

She nodded.

'Maggie Kane,' I said, showing Teresa the photograph. 'The one in the middle? Do you know when she was in the home?' I tried to keep my voice neutral. 'She looks a bit like Mary.'

I put the Polaroid back on the table and took a folding leather photo-frame, about the size of a postcard, from my handbag. Four photographs unfolded like a concertina. Mary, aged nine months sitting on a piano stool; Mary last year, with Jack, taken by me at our house in La Colline; Mary meeting the Pope after a private concert at the Vatican; Mary in a bronze silk dress with a bouquet of yellow roses.

'Her publicity photograph. Taken last year. She's an opera singer,' I said. 'A mezzo-soprano. She's going to sing in the National Concert Hall in Dublin next Monday.'

'Mary Molloy!' said Teresa. 'I think I've read about her in the *Irish Times*. And she's met the Pope! She's beautiful. She looks just like your husband and you.'

'Everybody says that. It's the hair and the eyes.' I laid Mary's photograph beside the photograph of Maggie Kane. 'Same hair, same shape of face,' I said.

'Yeah. That's Maggie,' said Teresa. 'Do you think...?'

I shrugged, and held up crossed fingers.

'What do you know about her?' I said.

'She was a nice girl, Maggie,' said Teresa. 'She arrived a few weeks before I left. She was a teacher. Lucky she didn't show until the summer term was over so she was able to keep things quiet. She was giving her baby up for adoption too. I remember we talked about it. She was planning to go back to her job.'

'Do you know where she taught?'

'Some school in County Sligo. I don't remember the name. Sorry.'

'What did she teach?'

'Music,' said Teresa.

There was a sudden frenzied barking and scraping. Teresa got up and opened a door into the back porch. A wire-haired fox terrier was spinning round in circles like a demented dog on wheels.

'Joey's on his way home from school,' Teresa called to me. 'Pepper gets excited. I'll let him out.'

A brown and beige woolly bundle shot into the garden and began bouncing up and down as though on the end of a string. It hurled itself at the small figure in a blazer and grey flannels coming through the gate at the bottom of the garden.

'That's Joey,' said Teresa. 'My youngest.'

I watched the boy swinging his satchel round and round as the terrier circled him, jumping up to lick his face at every turn.

The time for confidences was over. I could sense Teresa changing gear. Getting ready for the after-school routine of tea and homework.

'I'll go now,' I said. 'Do you think I could

take the photograph of Maggie Kane? I'll post it back to you, I promise.'

'Sure,' she said. She took a plain white envelope out of the drawer of the dresser and rooted around for a pen. She slipped the photograph into the envelope and wrote her address on the front.

'It's not that I ever take it out and look at it,' she said. 'But I hang on to these things because, well, you know, it might be a lead to somebody or something, some day.'

She handed me the envelope. 'I hope your answer's here. Let me know what happens. I'd be interested, really. Even if, well, even if it's not what you think. What you hope. Let me know what you find out anyway. Every little scrap of information helps.'

She took me back through the hallway to the front of the house and my car. She clasped my hand in both of hers.

'I wish you all the best in your search,' she said. 'I hope you find what you are looking for.'

'I hope we all do,' I said.

Chapter 18

On the way back to Atlantic House, I kept glancing at the white envelope on the seat beside me. I tried to suppress the urge to stop and examine the photograph again. But the tantalising possibility, the amazing possibility that I had found the person I was looking for, kept bobbing to the surface of my mind. I wanted to explore the faces of the girls sitting on the wall, and trace the detail of one face in particular.

The sun made a late appearance as I crossed the Shannon into the west. I had denied my urge long enough. I pulled into a layby at the top of a broad hill, parked so the sunlight streamed through the driver's window, and extracted the photograph from its white envelope. I held it sideways to the light and slowly studied the features of Maggie Kane. She had a wide forehead, shoulder-length blonde hair like Mary, and a dreamy expression. I had seen that same, faraway look in Mary's eyes. The look of a mind focused elsewhere. In Mary's case, probably on her first big break. In Maggie's case, dreaming perhaps about the man who wouldn't, or couldn't, marry her.

I sighed, slid the photograph into its envelope, put the car into gear, and swung back on to the road. I had surfed enough emotions in the last three days to last me a lifetime. Now I wanted dinner and a good rest before deciding what to do next.

As I drove past the Cliffs of Moher and the purple outline of the Aran islands beyond, the fading light grew cold and deepened to darkest grey. A damp blanket of air settled on the land. I was glad to see the welcoming lamp on the desk at Atlantic House.

Alma was in the bathroom applying lipstick with a brush. 'Not a word,' she said through tight lips folded wide over her even teeth. 'Not a single, solitary word.' She finished with a few strokes on her lower lip. 'I do use a lip brush occasionally,' she added defensively, in response to my raised eyebrow. 'Tell me how you got on.'

'Later,' I said, retreating. 'There's a lot to tell. But just now I'm shattered. I'll tell you over dinner.'

I lay down on my bed and closed my eyes. I sensed Alma float past me in a delicate cloud of lemony scent to retrieve her bag from the bedside table.

'Dinner in half an hour,' she said. 'Are you going to join us in the bar first?'

'Not sure.' I could feel the dregs of my energy seeping into the bed. 'Come and wake me if I'm not down in half an hour,' I said, and promptly fell asleep.

I awoke with a nervous jump and glanced at my bedside clock. Questions poured into my mind. Would Eileen have an address for Maggie Kane? Unlikely. Otherwise she would have produced her name from the files along with Teresa's. So how was I going to track her down? And if I found her, should I try to speak to her? Should I approach her for information? Could I find her before Mary arrived in Dublin? The concert was a week away. With a sense of relief I redirected my thoughts from Maggie Kane to a more practical problem. Booking a hotel in Dublin.

There was just time to speak to Mary before dinner, if I was quick. I padded to the bathroom and splashed cold water on my face until it tingled. I changed into a pale yellow shirt, pulled a light brown cardigan round my shoulders, and slipped outside to telephone.

I heard the insistent, low ring; then a pause, followed by 'This call is being transferred'. When I heard the message tone I said, 'Hello, darling! I hope it's all going well. I just thought I should ring about the arrangements for Dublin. Let me know where you're staying and I'll try to book the same hotel. I assume you're taking care of my ticket for the concert. Lots of love, darling. Alma sends love too. Bye!'

Through the window of the bar, I could see Donal and Alma, side by side at the turf fire, heads inclined towards each other. They looked up briefly and turned their heads towards the window as I mounted the steps to the door. But they were looking from light into dark and I knew all they could see was their own reflected closeness as the night made a mirror of the glass.

As I walked across the bar to join them, I caught the tail end of a sentence.

'...charming, of course,' Alma was saying. 'Positively exudes sex. He turns women's heads. But not always there for you when you need him.'

Good, I thought. She's having a proper conversation with Donal. Telling him about Gerry. Although I thought the bit about positively exuding sex was a bit over the top. Alma went bright red when she saw me.

'Hello, you two,' I said. 'Did you have a nice day?'

Over dinner, I told them about Maggie Kane. Between the goat's cheese soufflé and the beef braised in Guinness, I produced the photograph from my handbag and passed it to Alma.

'Mmmn,' said Alma. 'I can see a resemblance. Same forehead.'

'I'd really like to talk to her,' I said. 'But where do I begin to find her?'

'Eileen?' suggested Donal.

'Teresa was the only one she found who'd been in Saint Joseph's that year,' I said, adding doubtfully, 'I suppose I could ask her to have another look.'

'She was a teacher, you said? What about going through the Teachers' Union?' said Donal.

'They probably have a website,' said Alma. 'You might be able to leave a message.'

I was suddenly energised. 'We can get online in the pub until closing time. I could try to leave a message tonight,' I said.

'A bit of a walk after dinner will do us good,' said Donal. 'It's not raining. We can walk to O'Brien's for a drink.'

We went upstairs to get jackets and coats. Being tall, I almost always wear flat shoes, or shoes with a tiny heel. My loafers would carry me comfortably into town. Alma kicked off her high heels and took from a plastic bag a pair of stout, brown and white leather brogues, with a soft fringed tongue hanging outside the shoe.

'You've bought a pair of shoes!'

I looked more closely as she eased them on to her shapely feet. The soles were dotted with little black plastic claws.

'They're golf shoes,' she said, proud and embarrassed. 'I thought I could wear them into town. They have soft spikes. They're comfortable.'

I raised an eyebrow.

'OK,' she said. 'Donal spent the afternoon teaching me how to swing a club, and putt. I really enjoyed it. I'm going to have golf lessons when I get back.'

I raised my other eyebrow.

'I bought a few second-hand clubs as well,' she said. 'They're in the boot of Donal's car.'

'It'll be checked trousers next,' I said.

She laughed. 'The thing is, I've really taken to golf.'

'And Donal?' I said.

Her shoulders lifted. She shook her head. 'He's not really my type.' Her shoulders dropped. 'But I like him, Lena. He's a nice person. He's interesting. He's patient. I like his mind. In my head I really like him.' She paused, and looked away. 'My heart may take a while.'

Chapter 19

The night was clear and cold and lit with a million stars. A few clouds drifted across the bright half-circle of the moon. An aeroplane slowly winked across the sky.

'On its way to Shannon, I suppose,'

Donal said.

The distant growl of the aeroplane died away. The river babbled beyond the black shapes of the bushes and the willows that bent down to the road. Back home in Oxfordshire, streetlights drained the beauty of the night sky. I had forgotten the wonder of it. We walked for a while in companionable near-silence, with only the occasional expression of delight in the glittering stars.

Donal said, 'What does your husband think about all your detective work?'

'I haven't told him about it,' I said.

'Are you keeping it secret from him?'

'No,' I said defensively. 'I'll tell him when I get the chance for a proper chat. Mostly we've been leaving messages on each other's mobiles, because of the time difference.'

'So it's a temporary secret,' Donal said.

'You don't approve of secrets between partners?' said Alma.

'Nooo,' he said mildly. 'Some secrets are necessary.'

'What kind of secrets?' Alma demanded.

'Well. A man might want to keep secret the fact that he clipped his nose hair,' said Donal. 'Whether he could actually fool anybody or not is beside the point. He might want to keep it a secret. A woman might want to keep secret the fact that she's not as blonde as she used to be.'

174

'Jack knows I cover up a few grey hairs,' I said.

'What about affairs?' said Alma. 'Should they be kept secret, or should a man confess his affairs to his wife?'

'Or vice versa,' Donal said.

'Whichever. Should affairs be confessed?'

'I note the plural,' he said. 'Do you think if a man has one affair he's likely to do it again?'

'Yes,' I said, before Alma could reply. 'Once a taboo is broken, it doesn't have the same power.'

'People have affairs because there's something missing in their marriage,' Alma said.

'Do you think so?' said Donal. 'You don't think it's possible to give in to a fleeting temptation? And regret it. And never do it again.'

Alma considered this. 'It's possible, I suppose. But whether it's a fleeting temptation, a one-night stand or a full-blown affair,' she said, 'my question was, should a man confess it to his wife?'

'I think confession can be selfish,' Donal said. 'If a man isn't going to break up his marriage, why cause pain? He's only confessing to make himself feel better. Why should the wife carry the cross of her husband's guilt?'

'Marriage should be based on trust,' I said. 'I don't like secrets.' A sick, guilty feeling rose like bile. I was keeping a secret from Jack. I cleared my throat and added, 'As a rule.'

'Too much trust isn't good,' Donal said. 'A small homoeopathic dose of suspicion is no bad thing. Keeps you on your toes.'

Alma softly intoned,
'We dance around in a ring and suppose,
But the secret sits in the middle and knows.'

'What?' said Donal.

'It's a poem by Robert Frost.'

'How does it go again?' he said.
'We dance around in a ring and suppose,
But the secret sits in the middle and knows.'

'What does it mean?'

'Whatever you think it means,' said Alma.

'So what do you think it means?' said Donal.

'I think it's about what I am trying to explain,' Alma said. 'The poem knows itself. Neither the poet nor the reader can be entirely sure what its meaning is. What do you think it's about, Donal?'

'I think it's about the unknowability of things. Life, other people...' He looked sideways at Alma.

'That's two different answers so far,' she said. 'What do you think, Lena?'

'I think those lines are smug,' I said. 'And people who keep secrets are horribly smug too.'

'There you are, Donal,' said Alma. 'A two-

176

line poem, three people, three different interpretations. What is it you lawyers say? I rest my case?'

We had reached the comparative brightness of the town. The streetlights cast an orange glow on the houses. Here and there a shaft of white light from the open doorway of a pub fell across the pavement and the dark surface of the road.

'Donal,' I said, 'do you mind if I ask you something? What does the law say about the rights of illegitimate children to inherit? And what if they've been adopted? Teresa thought there must be some secret reason for Sister Monica to get in touch after all this time. She thought it might be something to do with an inheritance. Could she be right?'

'I have no idea,' he said. 'You need a specialist in family law to answer that question. I know there was a change in the law a few years back. I can give you a few names if you like.'

I thanked him and added, 'I might take you up on that. First, I'd like to go back and see if I can get any more out of Sister Monica. I'd like to drive over to Saint Joseph's tomorrow. If that's all right with you, Alma?'

'Sure,' she said. 'I still have a lot of work to do.'

'And that's just on her swing,' Donal said.

Music flowed out of O'Brien's as we crossed the empty square: fiddles, a concertina and the rumble of a goatskin drum beating a hornpipe. The pub was packed. The musicians sat squashed together on a bench by the curtained window. The fiddlers slid their bows over the strings in neat economical movements, arms close to their sides. The music swirled above the din of the crowd. Donal pointed to the bar, raised an imaginary glass and cocked his head enquiringly. I mouthed 'Whiskey', and pushed my way through the nodding, smiling, foot-tapping throng to the computer room at the back.

Three backpackers, pints at their elbows, were hunched over separate keyboards along the back wall. They looked round briefly when I opened the door and returned to their screens. I dragged a chair to the nearest free computer, logged on, and tapped in the web address for the Natural Parents' Internetwork. The page came up. I clicked the icon for the bulletin board. It was just a matter of leaving a message for Maggie Kane, in the hope she had a computer, access to the Internet and the address of the Natural Parents' Internetwork site.

The Teachers' Union website was easy to find. But there was nowhere to post messages. No way of contacting individual teachers. I took down the address and telephone number, thinking I could write and ask to be put in touch with Maggie Kane, assuming that was still her name, she was still teaching, and she was still in Ireland. I was about to log off, sagging with disappointment, when I had a brainwave. I remembered a popular website that reunited old school friends in Britain. Maybe there was a similar site in Irish cyberspace? I typed 'find a friend website ireland' into the search engine. A heartbeat. Up it came. www.blastfromthepast.ie

Across the top, a montage of smiling boys and girls in school uniforms, interspersed with nuns and priests pointing to blackboards. ***Thousands Registered! Find a Friend! Register Now! Free Search! Message Boards!*** *Home. Help. About Us. Search by School. Search by Name.*

I said a prayer and selected *Search by Name*. My fingers trembled as I typed Maggie Kane into the blank box and clicked *'Search Now'*.

Six names flashed on to the screen. My eyes raced down the page. No addresses. Just the schools they'd been to and the years they left. None in County Sligo. But even if Maggie Kane taught in County Sligo it didn't mean she'd been to school there. I would have to contact all six schools. Would they have records going back that far? How would I know which of these Maggie Kanes

179

became a music teacher? It would take for ever!

I sank my head in my hands. Hot tears stung my eyes. I fumbled in my handbag for a clean tissue, sensing the backpackers eyeing my incongruity. A middle-aged woman in cardigan and pearls, crying in front of a computer screen. I blinked at the screen and saw through the mist, on the left hand side of the screen, *Message Board*. I pushed the mouse wearily across the pad and clicked.

First Ten Messages. Use Arrow to Search Further Back.

'*Does anyone know where Terri Murphy is? She worked for Daintywear, Carlow 1990-1994.*'

The air tasted sweet as I sucked it into my lungs and sat back, refreshed, to read through the messages.

'*Trying to find Sheila Corrigan. She used to work with me in Kelly Plastics in the 1980s. We lost touch. If you read this, Sheila, or if you know where Sheila is now, please contact me.*'

Some messages gave a mobile telephone number as well as an email address. I was suddenly filled with hope. 'Thank you, God!' I cried.

I glanced over my shoulder and saw three faces grinning back at me. I smiled, sniffed, turned back to the screen and typed: '*I am trying to contact Maggie Kane. She was a music teacher in County Sligo. I would like her help with a personal matter concerning Saint Joseph's.'* I gave my mobile number. She would know what I meant. I sent a prayer into cyberspace with my message, straightened my shoulders, blew my nose, waved at the backpackers, opened the door to the pub and wriggled my way through the crowd in search of Alma and Donal and my much-needed drink.

I spotted Alma's pink jacket in an alcove near the door. She had put it on a stool to reserve it for me. Donal was alone, nursing his drink. He was gazing at the musicians, but seemed to be hearing other, sadder music in his head. He didn't see me working my way towards him. I arrived at the table as the fiddlers bowed a final flourish to end a reel. There was a brief moment of quiet before the background chatter increased to a roar. I had to lean towards Donal to hear his answer to my old cliché, 'Penny for your thoughts?'

He set his glass down and tapped it lightly on the table.

'I was thinking of something Proust wrote,' he said, looking into the empty glass with a wry smile. 'There is nothing like desire for preventing the things we say from having any resemblance to the things in our minds.'

'I can see why Alma likes you,' I said.

He started with grateful surprise. 'My technique's a bit rusty,' he said. 'I haven't done this for years.'

Then his anxious attention was caught by something. I turned in the direction of his gaze and saw Alma's slender figure weaving through the crowd towards us. I took my seat and watched Donal's eyes grow wide and bright at her approach.

I thought of how Jack had turned to look at me as I walked down the aisle on Dada's arm. His brown eyes widened and darkened. As I took my place beside him he whispered in my ear, 'You are more beautiful today than you have ever been. I am the luckiest man alive.'

I was hardly aware of the girl's voice at first. Then, as the cry of Sssh, Sssh was passed around the pub, I heard a sweet treble soar above the residual murmur.

'I have seen the lark soar high at dawn
Till he sang up in the blue.
I have heard the blackbird pipe his notes,
The thrush and the linnet too.
But there's none of them can sing so sweet
My singing bird, as you.'

The crowd lilted a chorus that rose hopefully but fell away on a note of yearning. Donal said it was a popular Irish folk song. The tune hummed in my head all the way back up the dark road.

Chapter 20

'Don't wait for me,' I told Alma as we made our way downstairs to breakfast the next morning. 'I'm going outside to telephone Jack.'

We met Donal in the lobby.

'What have you two planned for today?' I asked. It seemed right to address them as a couple. At any rate, I got no embarrassed or angry glances from Alma. She seemed relaxed.

'Golf,' she said, beaming from ear to ear.

I sat on the garden seat beside the stone cupid on the lawn and dialled his number. Success this time. He answered immediately.

'Hello, darling! How's the Emerald Isle?'

'Green,' I said. 'And alive with match-making.'

'What?' he said.

I told him about the matchmaking festival in Lisdoonvarna.

'Oh, I've been there,' he said. 'There's a smokehouse there. We've had some of their salmon. How's the weather?'

'Changeable,' I said. 'Fine on Sunday. Dull yesterday, dull today. The sun came out in time to set.' I looked up at the milky sky. No trace of blue. Grey cloud was descending on the distant black bulk of the Burren. 'We'll be lucky if it doesn't rain today.'

I told him about Donal and Alma. 'He's completely smitten,' I said.

'I know the feeling,' he said.

'Do you remember when we first met?'

'Of course,' he said. 'You appeared at the party like a blonde goddess. Shiny and golden. I had to carry you off before anyone else did.'

'More shy than shiny,' I said.

'All part of your appeal,' he said. 'I loved your solemnity. Where are you going to stay in Dublin?'

'I don't know yet. I don't know where Mary's staying. I went out last night with Donal and Alma and didn't take my mobile. I forgot to check for messages.'

'You'll enjoy the concert,' he said. 'Mary will be terrific. How are you filling your time? Are you playing gooseberry a lot?'

'Not really. I've done plenty of sightseeing.' It was only a white lie.

'What are you doing today?'

'I thought I'd go somewhere in the car,' I said casually. 'Donal is taking Alma to play golf.'

'That'll be interesting,' he said. 'I'd like to be a grasshopper on the course. Alma doesn't look hearty enough to play golf. She's tiny.'

'And he's tall,' I said. 'But Donal says there's an old Irish saying – "They are not always standing up."'

Jack was still laughing when he rang off.

Before going inside I checked my voice-mail. There was a message from Mary.

'Hello Mum. We're booked into the Conrad Hotel on Sunday and Monday night. It's across the road from the concert hall. Looking forward to seeing you! Must dash. Lots of love. Talk to you soon!'

'Where are you going to play?' I asked Alma and Donal at the breakfast table.

'There's a nine-hole links along the coast,' Donal said. 'Never crowded, great fun. I used to play it when we came to visit our relatives. It's ideal for a beginner.'

'I hope the day stays dry for you,' I said.

'We're not just fair weather golfers,' Alma said, with mock indignation.

'She's got the bug,' Donal said. 'She's raring to go. There'll be no stopping her now.'

As they left the dining room, Eileen emerged from the kitchen. I was still enjoying my breakfast of grilled, home-cured bacon and eggs and toasted soda bread.

'It's nice to see Donal smiling again,' Eileen said, clearing the empty plates from the table. 'He has a real spring in his step.' She lowered her voice, but the only other occupants of the dining room – three of the

185

hikers – were engrossed in the Ordnance Survey map spread over their table. 'I think he's quite interested in your friend.'

'I think so too,' I said.

'I didn't get a chance to talk to you last night,' Eileen continued softly. 'How did you get on with Teresa?'

'I've got the name of a girl who was in Saint Joseph's at the same time,' I said. 'And a photograph. She was a music teacher. Maggie Kane.'

Eileen put the plates back on the table and sank on to the recently vacated chair opposite me.

'That's terrific.'

'But no address.'

'Maggie Kane,' she repeated. 'I'm going into Limerick. I'll have another look through the files, although I had a good look on Monday. So I don't hold out too much hope.'

'Don't worry,' I said. 'I went to O'Brien's last night to use the Internet. I found a website www.blastfromthepast.ie. It puts old friends in touch with each other. I've posted a message there.'

'That's a good one,' she said. 'Blast from the past. Isn't the Internet a marvellous thing altogether? Sure it only seems like yesterday I was making calls on a wind-up telephone with Agnes Murphy in the post office listening to every word.'

186

She was starting to rise from her chair when I said, 'Eileen, do you know a singer called Father Frank Devine?'

'The singing priest?' she said. 'Everybody knows him. He's been around for years.'

'He's Sister Monica's brother.'

Eileen sat down again. 'I never knew that,' she said. 'He's still popular. Highly thought of.'

'Mary's birth mother called her Frances,' I said.

Eileen looked out the window reflectively. A stout speckled thrush flew out of the hedge by the river and settled on the lawn below the sill. It cocked its head to one side, took two bounds across the grass and cocked its head again. Eileen's bright eyes darted back to me.

'Are you thinking what I'm thinking?' I said.

'I'd been thinking more along the lines of a bishop.'

'Eileen!' I said, half-laughing, half-shocked, trying to keep my voice down.

'Well,' she said. 'It's crossed both our minds. We've had a lot of scandal with the clergy recently. Mostly small boys. Nasty stuff. It's almost a relief to remember some of the more normal affairs, so to speak. I'm thinking of Bishop Casey and his American divorcee and their son. The bishop kept that quiet for twenty years.'

'And there was that Scottish bishop too.'

'It would explain why the nun was so anxious to have the baby adopted quickly,' Eileen said.

'It still doesn't explain why she rang up after all these years. Teresa thought maybe it was something to do with inheritance.'

Eileen said, 'I suppose he's made a lot of money over the years. I don't know if it all has to go to the church.'

'Donal said he'd give me the names of some solicitors who know about adoption and inheritance. I might just ask. It would be interesting to know. Although I can't imagine Mary wanting to make a claim.'

'I was thinking about that. Maybe it's the other way round. You can leave your money to whomever you like. I could leave money to you, for example. He might be the one wanting to leave money. Maybe he's been in touch with his sister.'

We were both silent for a moment. I finished buttering the last slice of toast.

'I'm going to Saint Joseph's today,' I said. 'I haven't said I'm coming.'

'I'll be interested to hear how you get on,' Eileen said. 'You've done remarkably well so far.' She shook her head. 'What a tale. You couldn't make it up.' She gathered up the plates. 'Would you like some fresh tea?'

'No thanks,' I said. 'I'll be off as soon as I finish my toast.'

Donal and Alma were waiting for me outside.

'You don't mind going alone?' Alma said. 'Are you sure you don't want some moral support?' She glanced at Donal. 'I could come with you.'

'We could both come,' Donal said. 'I'd be interested to see Sister Battleaxe for myself.'

'No,' I protested. 'I'll be fine on my own. I know what I'm going to say. I'm not expecting great revelations. I'll just ask her about Maggie Kane. Her reaction alone will be interesting. I'll make a point of mentioning her brother as well.'

'Whose brother?' said Alma, startled. 'Maggie Kane's?'

'Sister Monica's brother. I forgot to tell you last night. Sister Monica's brother is that priest we saw singing on television.'

'Frank Devine?' said Donal. 'Is he her brother?' He gave a low whistle. 'And you think...?'

'I'm not sure what I think,' I said, 'but I know I have a musical daughter.'

'Wow!' said Alma.

And we stood for a moment taking in the implications of what I had just said.

'You know the road?' Donal asked.

'I'll go the way we came. I'll be back in time for dinner. Or maybe earlier.'

He told me how to find the golf course, in

189

case they were still there when I got back. He opened the passenger door of his car for Alma. She hugged me before getting in.

'Calmness and confidence equals composure,' she whispered in my ear. 'That's what I tell my students before an exam or a viva. Stand up to her!'

Donal said, 'Is it advice she's giving you to stare down Sister Battleaxe?'

I smiled and nodded at him over Alma's shoulder.

'I always think it's good advice to imagine a person on the lavatory,' he said. 'It helps to bring things down to earth. They're only poor, fallible humans like us.'

Alma laughed, and eased herself on to the passenger seat. Donal closed her door, put a long arm round my shoulders and gave me a quick squeeze.

'Good luck,' he said.

I waved goodbye as they crunched down the short driveway and made for the coast. Then I slid behind the wheel of the car, chose *The Marriage of Figaro* to accompany my journey – I like happy endings – and set off for Saint Joseph's.

Chapter 21

The cloud came down to meet me as I drove up into the Burren. Damp sheep stood stoically against the grey dry-stone walls that lined the road. Black cattle bent their heads to munch invisible grass between the flat grey flagstones in the fields beyond. The mid-summer music filling the car was a glorious contrast to the monochrome landscape outside.

'Porgi amor...' sang Adela Contini, as the countess, lamenting the count's infidelity. Only Mozart could have written a comedy about jealousy, I thought.

The square shape of Lemaneagh Castle loomed above me. I peered through the windscreen at the mullioned windows and imagined a man's body falling through the mist. Was I lucky or unlucky never to have felt sick with sexual jealousy? The kind of jealousy that drives people to quarrel and hurt, and set fire to stage curtains.

I had suppressed the occasional pang when Jack mentioned having dinner with a female client when he was away. I trusted him. When he travelled alone, he always came back laden with flowers and gifts and stories about the new suppliers and products. Stories about bankers who left the city and bought vineyards in France – 'He woke up one day and thought I don't want to do this for the rest of my life. He lost his first harvest. Then he met the widow of a small champagne house.' I would listen entranced – Jack is a great storyteller – and imagine other, more reckless lives than mine. 'She used to be a teacher. Swapped the inner city for a herd of sheep. She sells wool as well as making cheese.'

I would say, 'Is she attractive?'

'You're the one I love,' he'd say. 'I think about you all the time I'm away.'

When Mary left home, I was able to travel with him again. We'd been together to Sicily and Morocco. I might have gone with him to Australia and New Zealand if we hadn't been moving house.

A pale sun appeared in the sky when the road descended below the clouds to a flat, watery plain and I could see for miles instead of yards. I drove faster, anxious to get to Saint Joseph's by midday, when Sister Monica would most likely be playing the piano for her captive audience. I would not announce my arrival to the office. I would make my way upstairs, to the piano on the landing. I would wait, unnoticed, until she was leafing through her music, choosing what to play next. I would applaud, softly clapping my hands, and say, as I moved to where I could see her face, 'Music runs in your family, Sister. I didn't realise your brother was Father Frank Devine. I've come to ask you about another musical person as it happens. Maggie Kane. She was a music teacher when she came here about the time my daughter was born. Do you know where she is now by any chance?' I pressed harder on the accelerator.

Hope and nervous expectation sped me to the entrance of Saint Joseph's. The doors slid open, detecting my approach. But the sound that met me was the dull, tinny thud of pop music playing on a radio somewhere off the lobby. A nurse came out of the office, head down, pulling on a navy blue cardigan and clutching a packet of cigarettes and a box of matches. She shook herself into the cardigan and I saw it was Maureen. She stopped when she saw me.

'Hello,' she said. 'I know you, don't I? Who have you come to see?'

'I met you last Saturday,' I said. 'I was here with my friend. We spoke in the car park. I was visiting Sister Monica.'

'Yeah,' she said. 'I remember now. Are you looking for her again? She's not here today. Sister Pauline's on duty. She's in the office.' She jerked her head towards the half-open door further down the lobby and resumed her walk towards the glass doors and the freedom to smoke. I followed her outside, dismayed.

'It's Sister Monica I need to see,' I said. 'Will she be back at all today?'

'I don't think so,' Maureen said. She took a cigarette out of the packet and paused to light it. She took a long drag, exhaled smoke with a contented air and waved her cigarette in the air. 'First one today. I'm down to five. No, she'll not be here today. She's gone for her chemo. She usually stays a few days in the convent in Dublin to recover.'

'Chemotherapy?' I said. 'For cancer?'

'Yeah,' Maureen said. 'Terrible, isn't it? No cigarettes, no drink, no sex, plenty of fresh air and she gets cancer. Makes you wonder about God, doesn't it? Sally O'Connor told me. Still, she's a good age, I suppose.'

'It's hard to face at any age,' I said. 'Makes you realise it's all mapped out in our genes. We can't escape them.'

We were both silent for a moment.

'Maybe Sister Pauline could help you?' Maureen suggested. 'Or somebody else. Can I help you?'

'I wanted to ask about someone who was here before it became an old people's home,' I said.

'Ah,' she said. 'You mean when it was the home for unmarried mothers. The orphanage?' She shook her head. 'All the staff's new since then. Except Sister Monica.'

'And you're too young to remember,' I said bleakly.

'My mother isn't,' she said. 'Would she be any help to you? She worked here years ago. Before I was born.'

I did a quick calculation in my head. Maureen looked about twenty-two. Her mother could have worked in Saint Joseph's at the right time.

'What's her name?' I said.

'Dolan. Same as me. Only she's Orla.'

'Could I talk to her?'

'Twenty-three, Monagh Cottages,' she said. 'They're the first houses you come to after the Esso garage about five mile down the road. Turn right out of the drive and go straight over the crossroads. You can't miss it. She'll be there now. Tell her I told you to call.'

I repeated the directions and held out my hand. 'I can't thank you enough, Maureen,' I said. 'This is a great piece of luck. I thought I'd be going away disappointed, after coming all this way.'

She looked at me in a kindly, puzzled way. I guessed she was trying to work out why an English woman had left her illegitimate child in a home in the middle of Ireland.

'Don't mention it,' she said, giving my hand a warm squeeze. 'I hope Mammy will be able to help you now.'

Monagh Cottages was a misnomer. It was a small development of breeze-block built bungalows, adorned, but not rendered more beautiful, by stone cladding along the bottom half of the front walls in various shades of brown. A line of leylandii, planted as a wind break, added to the overall effect of bleakness, softened only by the ascending puffs of smoke from a dozen chimneys, including the one on number twenty-three, at the end of a cul-de-sac.

The woman who answered the door had the enduringly youthful look of the genuine redhead. Only the crinkles round the eyes and mouth betrayed her age. She was carrying a toddler who had the same bright russet curls, and a baby's bottle.

'Mrs Dolan?' I began, hesitantly. 'I'm Lena Molloy. I met your daughter Maureen at Saint Joseph's. She said it would be all right to call. She thinks you might be able to help me.'

'Come in,' she said. 'Sorry I can't shake hands because of this handful.' She kissed the tight red curls. 'My grandson.'

'Maureen's?' I ventured.

'No,' she laughed. 'Maureen has no intention of getting married yet. She has more sense. This is my son's child. They're both working, so I mind him and the baby during the day. The baby's asleep upstairs. Come in.'

I followed her to the kitchen. Chairs and table had been pushed against the wall to make space for a playpen. A sofa sat snugly under the window. A plastic drying rack draped with baby clothes occupied most of the remaining floor space in front of the cream enamel cooker, which radiated heat and filled the room with the pungent smell of peat. A wisp of steam rose from the spout of a kettle half-sitting on the hot plate.

'I'm Orla. This is young Seamus. Sit down,' she said, indicating the sofa with a nod of her head. 'What can I do for you?'

'Maureen says you worked in Saint Joseph's when it was a home for unmarried mothers,' I said.

'I did,' she said. 'Did you have a baby there?' She was straightforward and un-embarrassed.

'No,' I said. 'It's more complicated than that.'

She sat on a chair against the wall and bounced her grandson on her knee while I told her I was trying to trace the natural mother of my adopted daughter. I kept my story simple. To be honest, I gave the distinct impression I was searching with Mary's blessing. I was tired of offering my own background as an explanation. I had come to see Sister Monica. She wasn't there. I was disappointed. Could Orla help?

She lifted Seamus over the side of the

playpen to sit among a pile of red and yellow plastic bricks before moving to the cooker to centre the kettle on the hot plate.

'I'll make you a cup of tea,' she said. 'Would you like something to eat? I'm making something for Seamus and myself.' She took butter from the fridge, a sandwich loaf from a large, square, white enamel tin, and a banana from a bowl on the table.

'This is what I did in Saint Joseph's,' she said. 'Make sandwiches for the tea.'

'When were you there?'

'I went there from school,' she said, as she buttered slices of bread. 'I stayed about three years. Then I got a job in the canteen at the power station.'

'Do you remember Sister Monica?'

'Could anybody forget? I remember when she came over from the home in England to take charge. Changed all the routines. Ran the place like a military camp. She terrified the daylights out of me. She terrified the daylights out of everybody.'

'What about the girls who came?'

'To have their babies? I didn't see much of them. I was on the nuns' side of the building. I never really got a chance to talk to them. Everything was secret in those days.'

'Did you ever come across a girl called Maggie Kane?'

She shook her head.

'She was a music teacher.'

'I never really knew anything about them. Their parents never even knew they were there in some cases.' She laughed and added, 'I think Mammy got me the job there as a deterrent. Look what'll happen to you, girl, if you don't behave yourself. And it worked, I can tell you. I didn't want to end up in a place like that.'

'Did you see the babies?'

'I remember going into the nursery a few times. Bringing tea and sandwiches to people who'd come to choose a baby.' She spread mashed banana on a finger of bread and stooped to give it to the toddler.

'I used to feel sorry for the babies who had to wait to be adopted. They were always the ones who cried.'

Memory came at me in a rush. The day Mama and Dada told me I was adopted, Mama said, 'We picked you out immediately. You smiled at us. You were the only baby in the nursery who wasn't crying. We wanted to take you home with us there and then.' They told me the afternoon I ran home in tears. The afternoon Louise Jenkins shouted, 'You haven't got a real mummy and daddy. You're adopted.' I ran all the way home. Down the long avenue of chestnut trees, along South Park Road, up Market Hill, round the back of the surgery and in through the back porch. I tripped over the mat and banged my head on the door. Mama flew downstairs in a panic. Dada had seen me hurtle past his window and came into the hall from the surgery. I was crying and shouting, 'Louise Jenkins says I'm adopted.'

Dada said, 'She must have overheard Ivor and Gillian talking.'

Mama was stroking my hair. 'You're special. We picked you. You were the best baby in the world. Far nicer than Louise Jenkins.'

Seamus threw his bread out of the playpen and laughed up at me. Orla opened the fridge and took out a block of cheese and some tomatoes. 'Would you like chutney or mayonnaise on your sandwich?' she said.

I swallowed the lump in my throat that had come with the memory, and said, 'Chutney, please. How long did the mothers stay?'

'I think some stayed until their babies were adopted. There were some babies there a long time. More than six months anyway. Isn't that terrible? To have your baby for that length of time and then give him up.'

She picked up the bread from the floor and gave the child another piece of bread and banana. 'Sister Dervla said it was easier on them if the baby was taken away immediately. Although that sounds hard. Thank God times is changed. They all keep their babies these days.'

'Sister Dervla!' I cried. 'I met her. She handed Mary over to me at the solicitor's. Is she still in Saint Joseph's? Do you know where she is?'

'She's not a nun any more. She left the convent. About the same time I was leaving.'

'Do you know where she went?'

'Somebody told me she went to university. She wasn't from around here. I think she was from Connemara originally.'

She put two mugs of tea and a plate of cheese and tomato sandwiches on a tray and placed it on the floor in front of the sofa before settling herself beside me.

'Sister Dervla was nice,' she said. 'She was a lot younger than the others.'

We ate our sandwiches in companionable silence. Orla said, 'There's not much more I can tell you. You need to speak to Sister Monica again.'

'Unfortunately, yes,' I said grimly.

'I shouldn't be too hard on her. She can be cutting. But she's kind.'

I looked at her in amazement. 'Kind?'

'Jim's mother is in Saint Joseph's,' Orla said. 'I couldn't cope with her any more. She used to wander out of the house and on to the road. No more sense than a child. Threw her food on the floor. One time I went to visit her, Sister Monica was feeding her. She didn't see me watching her. She had the patience of a saint. The food would go on the floor. She would stroke her arms, and just start again. Sally O'Connor says she feeds a difficult patient every teatime. And she plays the piano for them at dinner time as well.'

'"Count your blessings",' I said dryly.

A thin wail came from upstairs.

'That's one of my blessings waking up,' Orla said. 'I'll bring her down.'

'I must go,' I said, getting to my feet as well.

In the narrow hallway, Orla handed me her three-month-old granddaughter, wrapped in a pink shawl.

'You take her while I get the door open,' she said.

I felt the baby's warm breath against my throat, and inhaled the sweet scent of milk and baby powder. When I handed her back, Orla said, 'Maybe your daughter will make you a granny someday. I can recommend it. Good luck, now. Call in if you come back to see Sister Monica. I'm sorry I couldn't be more help.'

Chapter 22

I drove away from Monagh Cottages, smiling at Orla's parting words, 'Your daughter will make you a granny someday.' Except for Alma, all my friends and former neighbours are grannies. The first ten minutes of every book club meeting for the last five years have been devoted to granny competition. Alma says they've taken it to Olympic standards. I have a dim memory of Dada's mother. Mama's parents died before I was adopted.

I'd like a grandchild, I thought, as I drove west across the bog. But Mary showed no sign of getting married. There had always been boyfriends, of course. One or two had looked promising. But it's hard to maintain a relationship when one partner is constantly flying backwards and forwards between continents.

I stopped the car beside a lake to check my route. I was on a secondary road, empty of traffic. I sat staring at the brown, ruffled surface of the water. I was exhausted. Emotionally and physically spent. I felt as though I had lived another, second lifetime since setting foot in Ireland. I had become driven, compulsive, obsessed. I had a sudden urge to ground myself in the details of a life familiar to me. Mary might be on a break. She might have her mobile switched on. She was. She had.

'Mum!' she said. 'Did you get my message about the Conrad?'

'Yes,' I said. 'I tried to book, but they're full. I've got a room in the Shelbourne. It's not far away.'

'That's great,' she said.

'When does your flight get in?'

'Don't bother coming to the airport, Mum. I'll see you at the hotel.'

'I'm going there anyway to drop off the car. I won't need it in Dublin. We can share a taxi.'

'We might be late. You'd have to hang around.'

'It must be difficult moving a whole orchestra.'

There was a pause. Mary said, 'I'm not travelling with the orchestra, Mum. I'm travelling with a friend.'

'A friend?'

'A man,' she said. 'He's nice. More than nice. Pretty amazing, really.'

'A boyfriend?'

'Sort of. He's important to me. He could be very important to me.'

I gave a silent cheer. My mental search engine called up hotel suites with double beds, champagne, engagement rings and a suitable outfit for the mother-of-the-bride in .03 of a second.

'I'd like you to meet him. I'm sorry Dad's not going to be there. I'd like Dad to meet him too.'

Children. Grandchildren. My brain was in overdrive.

'What's his name?'

'Rick,' she said.

Rick. That sounded American. I hoped Mary wasn't going to live in America.

'He's wonderful, Mum. Intellectual, which is a bit of a challenge. But good for me. He has me reading lots of books. You'll like him.'

'I'm sure I will,' I said. 'That's wonderful news, darling.' News I had wanted to hear for a long time. The long-imagined, hoped-for, hopefully-a-husband had a name and a reality. Mary would have children, I was sure. I'd read how adopted children became more curious about their birth parents when they had children of their own. More than ever I longed to present her with the true history of her origins. Lost in my imaginings, I was only just aware Mary was still speaking.

'Mum, are you there? Are you listening? You've been awfully dreamy when I've called you recently. How's your holiday?'

'Oh, fine,' I said. 'I'm having a really interesting time. Alma has met a really nice man too.'

'That's fantastic. I really like Alma. I hope he's good enough for her.'

'I hope Rick is good enough for you,' I said.

'He's changed my life,' she said. 'I'm so glad you're pleased, Mum. I'll tell you all the rest when I see you.'

I heard her turn away from the phone to call out, *'J'arrive,* I'm coming, *vengo!'*

'Bye, Mary darling.'

'It's the Tower of Babel here! Must go. I won't have time to talk properly until Dublin but I'll leave messages. Lots of love!'

'What's your flight number?'

But she was gone. I pictured her running up imagined theatre steps, glowing and breathless, blonde hair flying in the wind, laughing. How could anyone resist her? Light of my life.

From their vantage point atop a giant sand dune, Donal and Alma saw me drive into the car park between the golf course and the sea. Donal caught my attention with a wind-piercing whistle and beckoned to me to join them. I walked along the fairway and scrambled up through fine sand and coarse marram grass to arrive at the edge of the handkerchief-sized green.

'Mary has a serious boyfriend,' I said breathlessly.

Alma studied the line of her putt, holding

her putter like a plumb line to gauge the slope of the green. The flag snapped in the salty wind.

'That's great. When are you going to meet him?'

She looked professional and sounded preoccupied.

Donal said, 'Marvellous. You'll have to tell us all about it. And about your day.' He lifted the flag smartly out of the way as Alma's ball rolled across the green and dropped into the hole.

'She's got a great eye,' he said to me, and winked.

I felt the slight chill of exclusion. How strange to be excluded by love, I thought. First Mary, now Alma. I longed for Jack and quiet evenings at home.

'I'll go back down and wait for you in the car park,' I said, turning to stumble back down the dune.

'If you wait until we tee off, we can all go down together.' Alma called after me. I waved an arm in response and pointed to the car park.

Halfway down the dune, I paused to watch first one, then a second ball soar skywards before dropping on the grass and rolling forward to a stop. The sea danced towards the strand in lines of spume-tipped waves. Pink clouds sailed across the sky. The wind stung my cheeks and made my eyes water. I hurried across the fairway and through the gate into the car park and the privacy of the car.

Seven o'clock. Dusk in Ireland. Dawn in Australia. Too early to telephone Jack. I rolled down the window, held my face to the fine spray blowing off the sea and hauled the ozone into my lungs. I closed the window, leaned back against the headrest and closed my eyes. I was startled out of sleep by Alma gently shaking my shoulder.

'Move over,' she said. 'I'm driving us back. You're exhausted. You need a day off. Or a least a day when you're not driving hundreds of miles.'

I was too tired to argue. I eased myself over the gear lever and into the passenger seat. 'Thanks, Alma. You're a star.' I closed my eyes. A car horn tooted. I heard Alma switch on the ignition, put the car into gear and release the handbrake to follow Donal out of the car park and along the coast road to Atlantic House.

Chapter 23

'I'm worried about you,' Alma said, after I had dragged myself upstairs to our room and collapsed again on the bed. 'You're supposed to be on holiday, Lena. All this can wait. It's intriguing. Compelling even. But the story isn't going to go away. Leave it. You can come back to Ireland another time. Or let Mary finish what you've started.'

'I'm all right,' I said. 'Thanks for looking after me.'

'Hey, you've looked after me too. It's payback time.'

I sat up on the bed. 'I'm fine, Alma. Really. I must be tired. But in a funny way I'm energised too. All I need is a shower, dinner and a good night's sleep.'

'Tell me about Mary's boyfriend,' she said. 'Sounds interesting.'

'She's bringing him to Dublin,' I said. 'I'm going to meet him! All I know so far is, his name's Rick. I think he's American. He must be recent. This is the first I've heard of him.'

'Lucky man,' said Alma. 'Mary's so lovely she must have dozens of men chasing after her.'

'She moves around so much it's been difficult to keep relationships going,' I said. 'The men she meets are always on the move as well. One partner needs to be a fixed point. Like me with Jack.'

Alma said, 'Do you mind if I shower first? You can rest a bit longer and follow me down. I can hear all the rest of your news at dinner.'

When I came down to the dining room I saw some regrouping of the guests had taken place. The Lisdoonvarna Ladies, as I mentally categorised them, had detached three men from the group of hikers. They now occupied a separate table from the rest. There was a lot of teasing between these tables, about the relative merits of dancing, walking and other kinds of exercise.

'Love is in the air,' I hummed, as I joined Donal and Alma at our table.

'So Mary's in love,' Donal said. 'It takes you back, doesn't it, when your children fall in love. They, of course, think we're all past it.'

'And we're not?' Alma said.

'Speak for yourself,' said Donal. 'I still have a spring in my step.'

'It almost makes me wish I was twenty again,' I said.

'You're never too old for love,' Donal said. 'The older the fiddle the sweeter the tune.

210

Did you see that story in the paper this morning? Two men in an old people's home somewhere in England. Ninety the pair of them. Fighting over an eighty-eight-year-old woman. The staff had to separate them. They were as bad as that opera singer I've been reading about as well. Set fire to La Scala and slashed the tyres of her husband's Maserati because he was having an affair. She wouldn't tear in the plucking either. I saw her at Covent Garden last year. In *Aida*.'

Alma said, 'That's a terrible expression, Donal. Tear in the plucking. Would you say that of a man? She's the same age as me.'

'I would say it of myself,' he said. 'I'm no spring chicken. But you are a much younger bird. I stand rebuked.'

'Adela Contini?' I said, ignoring the banter. 'It wasn't La Scala. It was San Francisco. Mary was there. She was going to sing with her in *Suor Angelica* before she was offered the concert tour.'

'Good God,' said Donal.

'I told you. She leads an exciting life,' said Alma.

Donal said, 'I often wonder what makes singers and actors choose one engagement over another? I would have thought–' He was interrupted by Eileen's arrival at the table to recite the menu.

'Nearly all fish tonight but I have steaks

and lamb chops if you don't fancy the salmon. Mussels or tomato and red pepper soup to start. Salmon with sorrel sauce, plum clafoutis. That's a fancy name for a light sponge with poached plums in it. And cream, of course. Wine?'

Donal looked at us. 'The Sancerre?'

We nodded agreement.

Eileen smiled at me, dropped her voice a tone and added, 'I hope you had a good day.'

'She wasn't there,' I said. 'I'm no further on.'

'What did I tell you,' she said, clucking sympathetically. 'It's a long slog with many disappointments on the way. But you've done awfully well to get this far. Hasn't she?' she said to Donal and Alma.

We took only seconds to decide on the mussels before the salmon. Eileen whisked away to the big jolly table by the window.

Alma said. 'Oh, Lena. I'm sorry. What a disappointment. So you had a wasted journey?'

'I don't know about that,' I said. 'I learned Sister Monica has cancer. She was away having treatment. I think that explains why she telephoned. Whatever her interest in Mary, time's running out for her, God help her.'

Donal said, 'Maybe it's just as she said. She knows she's dying. She's doing her accounts for Saint Peter at the pearly gates. It could just be as simple as that.'

'Then why won't she tell me anything?'

'It's the culture,' he said. 'The culture of control. The religious orders ran everything in Ireland for years. Schools, hospitals, orphanages, old people's homes. It's a mind-set. Hard to give up.'

'You think her brother, that singer, the priest, is involved, don't you?' Alma said to me.

'His name has cropped up a few times,' I said. 'I bet he knew Maggie Kane.'

'Maybe the nun was phoning you on his behalf,' Alma said.

'The whole thing's intriguing,' Donal said. 'Do you remember the Australian book that was made into a television series? It was popular in Ireland. That actor who played Dr Kildare was in it. I'm showing my age.' He smiled at Alma.

'Richard Chamberlain?' I said. 'I remember it. He played a priest who had an affair.'

'*The Thorn Birds*,' Alma said. 'The book was by Colleen McCullough.'

'You've a great memory, Alma,' I said.

'Bits of useless information stick to my mind like fluff,' she said. 'But I can't remember where I put the car keys. The Richard Chamberlain character becomes a cardinal. Then he has a son, although he doesn't know it.'

We sat for a moment in awestruck speculation.

'Do you think...?' Alma said.

'What would Mary think?' Donal said.

'She takes things in her stride,' I said. 'The opera world's as rococo as anything in Mozart – including cross-dressing and a harem. According to Mary.'

'I suppose setting fire to an opera house is pretty rococo,' Donal said.

'All the same,' said Alma. 'A cardinal would be something else again. Very ... baroque.'

I had a sudden thought.

'You were at school with him, weren't you?' I said to Donal.

'He was in my brother's year. Two years ahead of me. We all knew who he was, of course, because he was always picked out to sing at school concerts or whenever anybody important came to visit.'

'Take a look at Mary's photograph, please. See if there's a likeness.'

'To Father Thorn Bird?' said Alma. 'That's a good idea.'

'My brother thought he was a bit of a cissy,' said Donal. 'Amazing how people turn out.'

'That's another terrible expression!' Alma said.

Donal looked sheepish. 'I'm sorry, Alma.

But that's what boys said in those dark pre-feminist days. You know what I mean. He was a bit of a...' He searched for the word. 'Hairdresser,' he pronounced. 'And,' raising a hand to stop her interjection, 'before you berate me, I'm quoting an American feminist who says all men are either men, boys or hairdressers. And,' he raised his hand again before rushing to the end of the sentence, 'all women are either women, girls or men.'

Alma laughed. 'I read that too,' she said. 'And hairdresser doesn't have a sexual connotation. It just means he's fussy.'

'I admit to being a bit of a hairdresser myself,' Donal said.

'I see what you mean for men,' I said. 'But how does it work for women?'

'Well,' he said. 'For example, Elizabeth Taylor is a girl. Grace Kelly is a girl. Mrs Thatcher is a man. Katharine Hepburn is a man.'

'What women are women?' I said.

'They're nearly all French,' he said. 'Jeanne Moreau, Simone Signoret. But Joan of Arc was a man.'

'What am I?'

He thought for a moment. 'You're a girl, Lena. And you still look like one.'

Alma said, 'And what am I, Donal?'

'You might be small,' he said, 'but you're all man.'

Alma is not often lost for words.

When we had stopped laughing, I took the leather folder out of my handbag and opened it out on the table.

'This is Mary,' I said. 'Can you see a likeness? I only saw him for a few minutes on television.'

Donal extracted a pair of reading glasses from the top pocket of his tweed jacket and settled them on the bridge of his nose.

'So, I'm looking for a likeness to Father Thorn Bird?' he said, smiling at Alma over the top of his spectacles.

He studied the photographs, looked at me, and back at the photographs.

'Is she like him?' I said.

'I can't really tell,' said Donal. 'I've not seen him at close quarters for thirty-five years. Except on television.'

He scanned the photographs again. 'She's a stunner,' he said, 'almost as beautiful as you.'

'She's a darker blonde than me,' I said. 'But people think we're her real parents.'

'I can see why,' he said. 'You've seen these?' he said to Alma, pushing the photographs towards her.

'Of course.'

'Look closely,' he said. 'What do you think?'

'I only saw him for a few moments as well,' she said. She folded the photographs and

216

handed them back to me.

'I see a bowl of mussels steaming towards us,' he said. 'Let's eat.'

I hid my disappointment, and all through dinner chatted with every appearance of interest about golf, the weather and how much Ireland had changed since my first visits with Jack thirty years ago. What I really wanted to do, despite my lingering exhaustion, was check for a message from Maggie Kane.

After dinner I said, 'Excuse me while I pop outside to make a call. I'll see you in the bar.'

I knew it would be cold, so I went upstairs to get my coat. On my way back down the stairs, at the turn of the landing, I saw Donal and Alma directly below me in the hallway. Donal had his hand on Alma's arm.

'You know I could be right. I see it in your eyes,' he said.

'No,' she said. 'No. Please. No. I don't want to hear this.'

'Will you at least consider it?'

'I need a drink,' Alma said.

Donal sighed. 'We could both do with a drink.'

I signalled my presence by beginning to hum, 'Love is in the Air' again. They looked up and saw me. Alma caught her breath. Donal released her arm. I flitted downstairs, calling out, 'Will you get me a whiskey, please? I'll only be a minute,' before slipping past them, embarrassed, into the night.

I stood at the edge of the lawn and switched on my mobile. The light from the bar fanned out across the gravel towards my feet. When the screen lit up I saw I had a message. It was Mary saying she was flying into Dublin at two o'clock on Sunday afternoon and going straight to rehearsals. She didn't need to be met. I saved her message and dropped the mobile back into my bag. I thought about driving into town to check www.blastfromthepast.ie. But I was tired. The turf fire beckoned from the bar.

Alma blew a smoke ring and said, 'I think you and I should go off somewhere tomorrow on our own and do some gentle sightseeing. You've done enough driving. I'll drive for a change. You can sit back and pretend you're in a pram. I want to see Ireland beyond the eighteenth tee. I want to swim in the wide Atlantic.'

'Swim?' I said. 'In the Atlantic? In autumn?'

'It's not cold,' Donal said. 'Not *really* cold.'

'Compared to what? The Antarctic?'

'Compared to Frinton in the summer,' Alma said. We had both spent childhood holidays on the east coast, and swum in the icy waters of the North Sea.

'We get the effect of the Gulf Stream,' Donal said.

'Are you going to swim?' I asked him.

Alma kicked my foot under the table. 'Just you and me,' she said.

There was an awkward pause. Donal said, 'Another whiskey?'

'Why did you kick me?' I asked Alma when Donal got up to get the drinks. She stubbed out her cigarette.

'I'm not ready for a new relationship,' she said. 'I need some time to think.'

'I want you to enjoy yourself,' I said. 'I'm sorry I've been neglecting you.'

'I'm having a great time, Lena. He's good sparring practice.'

'At least you're boxing at your own weight.'

'I'd like a day out of the ring,' she said. 'You and I are supposed to be on holiday together. *On holiday,*' she emphasised. 'Be happy with what you've found out. Let Mary take it up if she wants to. Let's spend some time together. What do you think?'

Alma was right. Nothing would go away. There was little I could do until I'd traced Maggie Kane. I was whizzing back and forth across Ireland, seeing little, chasing disappointment. I was neglecting my best friend. I made a quick calculation. Alma was leaving on Saturday. Mary's concert was on Monday night. There was still time to see Maggie Kane if she contacted me.

'All right,' I said. 'I'll take a day off. Where do you want to go?'

Chapter 24

I woke to the smell of coffee and the sound of rain. I had no memory of dreaming. Just the sensation of opening my eyes and turning my head to the bright window spotted with blowsy raindrops, and a tray on the bedside table. I sat up.

'Alma! You angel!'

'You were sleeping so soundly I didn't want to wake you. I've had my breakfast. I've brought you coffee and rolls, and a bowl of blackberries. Picked yesterday, Eileen said.' She presented the blue and white china bowl, its sides stained with the purple juice of the fruit. 'And cream. If you want bacon and eggs she says you can still have them when you go down.'

'This is a feast,' I said. 'I won't want anything else. What time is it?'

'Nine thirty.'

'Oh, Alma. We'll be late setting out. I'm sorry.'

'We're on holiday, Lena,' she said. 'You're supposed to take things easy. Anyway we're not going far. And the rain's clearing.'

A cloud moved sideways to let a patch of yellow sunlight fall across the bed.

'There, you see?' she said. 'The sun's out. I'll get my swimsuit and wait for you downstairs.'

I tried to think of the last time I had breakfasted in bed. Our wedding anniversary. Jack appearing round the door with a tray and a bottle of champagne and freshly squeezed orange juice. He had begun that tradition just after we bought Hope House. Not that he hadn't made a special effort on anniversaries before that. If he was away, he always sent roses. If he was at home, we always went out to dinner as well. But I liked breakfast in bed best. Jack would get back into bed and have breakfast with me. We'd finish the bottle of champagne. Jack would take the morning off work. Once, when he was away, I opened the front door to find a waiter with a tray – coffee, croissants, strawberries, champagne and orange juice. 'I arranged it with Victor before I went away,' Jack said. Victor was the manager of a rather good hotel a few miles from us. Jack sometimes took clients there.

I bit into the buttery softness of a croissant and poured hot milk into my coffee. Thinking about Jack revived my guilt about keeping secrets from him. Maybe I should just mention casually to Mary that I'd met an organiser of the Natural Parents' Internetwork. Let her show an interest. Give her the website address. Tell her about Maggie

Kane and leave the rest to her. When Jack got back from New Zealand, I would pick my moment carefully and confess all.

I poured thick cream over the blackberries and spooned them greedily into my mouth. For the first time in days I felt I was on holiday. I could devote the day, and the rest of the week, to relaxation.

The sun came and went as white clouds drifted across the blue sky, but the wind was from the warm southwest and the air was mild. Alma and I took a road that spiralled up into the Burren, and followed signs for the complex of caves beneath the stony slopes. By unspoken agreement we avoided talking about my stalled search.

For a few hours I swear I almost never thought about it. We browsed contentedly in the craft shops at the entrance to the caves. We took the group tour through the dank corridors of the cave system. Water seeped and plopped from the knobbled grey-green walls. Curious shapes coiled from the ground, and hung from the roof – a bunch of carrots; a wasp's nest; calcified hands, palms together, pointed in prayer.

I found myself thinking, 'Please God, make Maggie Kane telephone.' Feeling guilty for breaking my resolve to leave things as they were.

We emerged from the caves into an Indian summer's day. The sky seemed brighter.

Ravens floated on currents of air, high above the hillside. My spirits lifted. Alma pointed to the distant sparkle of the sea.

'Are you brave enough to swim?'

'If you're sure it's warmer than Frinton,' I said.

Beyond the Cliffs of Moher, the shoreline curved into a wide bay and the land descended to the ocean in terraces of wide, black rocks. We sat in the shelter of a curve in the rocks and watched the incoming tide wash against giant boulders on the pebbled floor of the bay. Alma said, 'Gerry telephoned this morning.'

I sat up. 'What did he say?'

'I didn't speak to him. He left a message asking me to call him.'

'And will you?'

'I don't know.'

We sat for a while in easy silence. Alma smoked a cigarette. The incoming tide whooshed over the flat rocks at the land's edge and drained on to the wrinkled surface of the sea.

I said, 'I'm sorry, Alma. I've been so wrapped up in my own obsession I haven't bothered to ask how you are.'

'I'm fine,' she said. 'I'm more worried about you. You're wearing yourself out. I think you've got enough information now.'

'I'd just like to speak to Maggie Kane.'

'You think she's Mary's birth mother. In

which case, is it a good idea? Shouldn't Mary be the one to approach her?'

'I've already left messages for her. She knows my name and my telephone number now. What am I supposed to say if she gets in touch?'

'I don't know,' Alma said. 'I just think it may be a bad idea to take this thing any further.'

'Why are you suddenly saying this now?'

'I'm not. You know I've had reservations all along.'

'You haven't said much until now. You've been happy enough to speculate.'

'Yes. But I've been thinking about it. We shouldn't get carried away. It's interesting to speculate, but there's not much to go on. Just the fact that this priest is Sister Monica's brother. And Donal says...' She trailed off, and turned her head away.

I stood up and moved round the rock to face her.

'What does Donal say?' I demanded.

'He doesn't think it's wise. These things can be difficult and emotional,' she began. 'Sometimes it's better to leave well enough alone.'

'What!' I exclaimed. 'You have the nerve, the absolute nerve to accuse me of pushing you two together, and you parrot his opinions back to me! And you accuse *me* of interfering?'

'Calm down, Lena.' Alma paused to steady her voice. 'Donal has dealt with some adoption cases. He knows how difficult they can be.'

'He told me he didn't know much about it,' I snapped.

'He's been thinking about it.'

'And when did all this thinking go on? Was he thinking maybe about protecting his old school friend? Father bloody...' I searched for the name. '...Songbird,' I finished angrily.

'It's not like that,' Alma said. 'We're only thinking of you.'

'We! Suddenly it's *we*. I thought you wanted to put some distance between you.'

'I do,' she said miserably. 'But I respect his opinions too.'

'Well I don't.'

I walked away from her to calm down. A flock of oystercatchers flew low over the waves, dipping their black wings, turning white undersides to the air, like a flying chequerboard. Beyond the flat rocks was a strip of golden sand. Bobbing, bright grey birds chased the retreating surf and raced back over the wet sand inches ahead of the incoming waves.

I sensed Alma come up behind me.

'Please don't be angry,' she said. 'I don't want to fight with you. I'm just worried you're walking into a highly emotional situation. And you don't know what's going to happen. Just think about it.'

'She hasn't contacted me anyway,' I said. The sanderlings turned and ran from the wave rolling over the sand. 'I thought you were going to swim.' I heard her sigh and walk away.

I stood looking out to sea until I heard the splash of Alma's entry into the water. I walked back towards the pink jacket covering the pile of clothes in the shelter of a rock. I was watching Alma treading water, her shoulders rising and falling with the soft swell of the sea, feeling awkward, thinking I should join her and make peace, when I became aware of a long, low trill. Then another. I realised it was the mobile vibrating in the depths of my handbag. I don't know why I had my mobile switched on. Perhaps part of me was constantly on watch. Scanning the horizon of possibility.

'Is that Lena Molloy?' The voice was hesitant. Out of the corner of my eye I saw Alma slither on to the flat top of a boulder, stand upright, and angle herself for a dive.

'Yes,' I said.

'I'm Maggie Kane,' she said. 'Are you my daughter?'

The question hit me like a punch. Stupidly, I had not thought of this. Of course she would think I was her daughter.

'Hello?' Still hesitant.

'No,' I said. 'I'm not your daughter. But I may have adopted your daughter.'

She let her breath out slowly, in time with mine. 'My neighbour saw your message on a website,' she said. 'Where are you? Where do you live? How did you get my name?'

'I got your name from Teresa Flanigan. I don't know her maiden name.'

'Teresa,' she repeated slowly.

'She was in Saint Joseph's home at the same time as you.'

'I think I remember Teresa.'

'I live in England,' I said. 'But I'm on holiday in Ireland. In County Clare. Near Lisdoonvarna.'

A quick intake of breath.

'Oh, my God,' she said. 'You're only an hour and a half away. Can I come and see you?'

'Of course,' I said. 'Or I can come to you. Where do you live?'

'Near Oughterard. We could split the difference. Meet halfway.'

'OK,' I said. 'When?'

'This evening?'

Slow down, I thought. Slow down.

'Shouldn't we check some dates first?'

'August 1973,' she cut in.

'What date?'

'I can't remember. I have no idea of the time or the date. I couldn't think straight.' Excitement turned to distress. 'I had to give her up. I had no money. They had to take me to hospital. Toxaemia.'

I couldn't think of anything to say.

'I blanked it from my mind,' she continued. 'I can't even remember signing the consent form. God, I can't believe this. Have you any photographs? Will you bring them?'

'Of course,' I said. 'And I have a photograph of you too.'

'What!'

'Teresa gave it to me.'

'How did you track down Teresa?'

'The Internet.'

'I'll have to get a computer,' she said. 'Can you make this evening?'

I looked at my watch. Ten past three.

'What time.'

'Half past five?'

'Fine.' If Alma wanted to keep the car, there would be time enough time to go back to Atlantic House. I could take a taxi. 'Where?'

'There's a seafood pub near Kinvara. Mullaney's.'

'I know it,' I said. 'I've been there. How will I know you?'

'I'll be wearing a light green jacket. I'm driving a grey BMW. I'll wait in the car. If I'm going to be late I'll ring your mobile. Five thirty, Mullaney's. See you there.'

Alma seemed to be walking on the water. I realised she was standing on a submerged boulder. She waved tentatively. I checked that no one else was watching before stripping off my clothes and wriggling into my swimsuit. I padded, shivering, to the edge of the ocean and dived in, breaking through the shimmering surface. I shook the water out of my eyes and swam towards Alma, standing ankle deep on the rock. She squatted to give me a hand on to the slippery surface.

'I saw you on the phone,' she said, teeth beginning to chatter.

'Maggie Kane. She's meeting me tonight in that seafood bar we went to. You can take the car. I'll get a taxi. This is a stupid place to have an argument.'

Alma said, 'I don't want to argue.' She rubbed her hands on her upper arms to warm herself. 'Will you at least take me with you? You might be glad of the support.'

I saw the concern in her eyes. I thought she was probably torn between liking Donal and being loyal to me. I tried to smile.

'It's beyond bracing,' I said. 'It's down-right cold. I'll race you in.'

Chapter 25

We didn't talk much on the drive along the coast to Mullaney's until Alma said, 'Half five. Let's say you talk for an hour at least. Half six, seven. We might not be back in time for dinner. If it looks as though we're going to be late, I'll slip out and warn Eileen.'

Four cars sat outside Mullaney's. One of them was a grey BMW. As Alma pulled in beside it, I leaned forward to look across her at Maggie Kane. There was a man in the driving seat beside her. His hands gripped the wheel. He stared straight ahead at the estuary. Maggie Kane lifted her hand in a hesitant greeting and turned to say something to him.

'She's brought someone with her,' I said. I got out of the car and hurried round to introduce myself in case Maggie Kane mistook Alma for me. 'Hello,' I said breathlessly. 'I'm Lena. You must be Maggie. Thank you for coming.'

I took a quick audit. My first, mean-spirited, thought was that Mary had not inherited those ankles. Maggie had long, straight legs with no visible curves, pale blue, almost colourless eyes, slightly curling beige blonde hair and fair skin with a faint dusting of freckles.

'Thank you for meeting me,' she said. 'I've come with my husband.' I turned to greet him.

'Jimmy, this is Lena,' she said.

He shook my hand and muttered a conventional greeting. He was tall and tweedy. His dark moustache was streaked with grey. Alma came to stand beside me.

'My friend, Alma,' I said. 'We're on holiday together.'

There was an uncomfortable moment. Maggie's husband said, 'Well, let's not stand about. Shouldn't we go inside?'

The front bar of Mullaney's was empty. Soft swirls of dust spiralled in the shafts of sun filtering through the frosted glass of the bay window. Behind the bar, a door to the yard lay open. We could hear the metallic bump and rattle of a beer barrel being rolled along the ground. We moved in silent consensus to a table at the window.

'Shouldn't we get down to business?' Maggie's husband said. 'My wife's upset by all this.' He took her hand.

'You're not sure of the dates,' I said to her gently. 'The date on my daughter's birth certificate' – she flinched, he squeezed her hand – 'that is, on the certificate given to me when I adopted her,' I amended. 'The date is the tenth of August. But sometimes dates were changed. I never saw the original birth certificate.'

'They're difficult to get hold of,' Maggie said. 'They put so many obstacles in the way.'

'She doesn't remember the exact date,' her husband said, and then to her, 'You've tried, haven't you?'

'I think it was a Thursday.' She drew the words out slowly as she sat, head tilted, as though listening to a voice far away. 'I remember a woman saying, "Thursday's child has far to go."' Her pale eyes glistened. 'And a man said, "It's not a great start."'

'We could work out the dates of all the Thursdays in August that year,' I said.

'I've done that,' she said.

'We've been through all this before,' her husband said. 'A girl rang up. It was the wrong year. But Maggie insisted on seeing her.'

'Because I'm not sure of anything,' she said. 'They rushed me to hospital. I was seriously ill. The baby nearly died. I nearly died. That's why I don't remember much. I must have signed a consent form. But I don't remember.'

Her husband got up. 'I can't hear all this again,' he said. 'I'll find the barman and get us some drinks. What will you have?' To Maggie he said, 'I'll get you a brandy.'

Alma jumped up as well. 'I'll come with

232

you,' she said. 'Whiskey for you, Lena?'

Maggie said, 'Jimmy gets worked up. It's good of him to come with me. I have to see people. Just in case. Can I see a photograph of her?'

I unfolded the photographs on the table. 'She's an opera singer,' I said. Her eyes widened. She fixed them on the photographs.

'I was a music teacher,' she said.

'I know.'

I added the faded Polaroid from Saint Joseph's to the spread on the table.

'I was lucky to keep my job,' she said. 'Thank God for tent dresses. I didn't really show until the end of term. Then I went to Saint Joseph's. I remember going there. And the first few weeks. Then I got this terrible headache, and dizziness. I couldn't see properly. I remember the ambulance, and the bumpy road. After that it's a bit of a blur.'

Her husband placed two drinks in the middle of the table. 'Classic pre-eclampsia,' he said. 'Happens in about five per cent of first pregnancies.' He stood looking over Maggie's shoulder as she studied the photographs.

'She hasn't the same colour of hair,' he pronounced. I looked at him in surprise.

'Dyed,' he said, ruffling his wife's hair.

'I have so much grey I had to go blonde,' she said.

'Classic Irish beauty,' said her husband. 'Dark hair, blue eyes, pale skin.'

'But you're a blonde in the photograph!' I said.

Alma pushed a glass of whiskey towards me and sat down. Maggie's husband hunted in the inside pocket of his tweed jacket with one hand and picked up the folder of photographs with the other. He put on a pair of spectacles and appraised Mary's features, moving the photograph to catch the best light.

'Eyes the colour of turf,' he commented. 'Beautiful girl.'

Maggie examined the photograph of her younger self. 'I bleached my hair. I had this stupid notion someone would recognise me. Even though I was miles away from home. Ireland is a small country.'

Her husband put the folder back on the table and sat down. 'What colour of eyes did he have, Maggie?'

'What?'

'What colour of eyes did he have?'

She froze. She closed her eyes.

'I can't remember,' she said in a panicky voice.

'Come on,' he said. 'Think.'

A pulse beat at the side of her pale forehead. She clasped her head in her hands, elbows on the table.

'It wasn't a one-night stand,' he said. 'You

must have looked into his eyes.'

Alma said calmly, 'It can be really difficult to remember these things sometimes. I have to think hard to remember what colour of eyes my father had.'

Maggie raised her head, looked at the ceiling, then at her husband, and said, 'Blue. Same as yours.'

'Do we have a brown-eyed child?' he said. 'No. Because two blue-eyed people can't have a brown-eyed child.' He rapped the table. 'Ergo this is not your daughter.' Her shoulders crumpled. He put his arm around them.

'I'm a pathologist,' he said. 'I'm sorry. You've had a wasted journey.'

'You too,' I said.

'Doesn't it sometimes happen?' Alma said. 'Blue eyes, brown eyes?'

'Chance in a million,' he said. 'If she had blue eyes, I'd say it was worth doing a DNA test. But frankly, I don't think it's worth it.'

'DNA?' I said. 'A blood test? Can that be done privately?'

'Sure,' he said. He was relaxed now. 'There are private clinics. You don't need a blood test. A single hair pulled from your head would be enough.'

I turned to Maggie. 'Can you remember anyone else who was in Saint Joseph's around the same time as you? Apart from Teresa.'

'I wasn't there long before I went to the hospital.'

'What about the other girls in the photograph?'

'I don't remember their names. I don't even remember it being taken.'

'The names are on the back.' I turned the photograph over. She sat forward to read.

'Imelda Murphy. Patsy Malone.' She closed her eyes in concentration.

'Patsy Malone,' said her husband. 'There used to be a showband with a singer called Patsy Malone. The Four Kings. Some name like that. They played at dances when I was at college.'

'That's right,' Maggie said. 'Yes. That's right. I remember now. She was with a showband.'

'She's small,' I said. 'And she has dark hair.'

'She had red hair, actually,' Maggie said.

'The Patsy Malone I'm thinking of had red hair,' said her husband. 'She could have a blonde baby. Blonde is more dominant than red.'

He picked up the folder of photographs and studied Mary's features again.

'She has a dimple,' he said. 'Dimples are dominant.'

He stared at me for a second and barked, 'Smile!'

I looked blankly at him.

236

'I think you have a dimple,' he said. 'At least one of your parents probably had a dimple.'

I beamed my wonderment and gratitude. The afternoon wasn't wasted after all.

'Thought so,' he said. 'A dimple.'

He picked up the Polaroid. 'Patsy Malone is the one on the left?'

'Yes,' I said. 'And I know the one on the right had a boy.'

'I can't see whether or not she has a dimple,' he said, peering at the photograph. 'Can't see the ear lobes. Can't tell the eye colour either.'

'Jimmy's interested in genetics,' Maggie said.

'Genes don't lie,' he said. 'I tell Maggie she would save herself a lot of unnecessary pain if she would just ask a few simple questions before rushing to meet people. Eye colour, hair colour, ear lobes.'

'Ear lobes?' Alma said incredulously.

'Oh, yes,' he said. 'Unattached ear lobes are dominant. Attached ear lobes are recessive.'

'What about height?' I said. 'Patsy Malone looks tiny, compared to Maggie. And you're what?' I said to her. 'About five feet nine? Same as me?'

'Tall is dominant,' he said. 'Only one parent needs to be tall to have a tall child. Two small people will have a small child.'

'Do you know when Patsy's baby was born?' I said to Maggie. 'Was it a boy or a girl?'

She shook her head. 'I was in the hospital for weeks. I hardly knew what was happening to me, much less anybody else.'

'You're lucky to be alive,' her husband said. 'You had kidney failure.' He stood up. 'We'd better get back. We left the boys getting their own supper. I'll just...' he nodded in the direction of the door marked 'Toilets'.

Maggie said, 'We have four boys. The oldest is at university. The others are still at home.' She hunted in her handbag. I thought she was going to show me a photograph. Instead, she produced a pair of nail scissors and a biro. 'Quick,' she said, giving me the scissors. 'He was tall. The baby's father. Cut a piece of my hair. Just in case, you know.' She offered me the back of her head, where her hair curled on to the collar of her jacket.

I took the scissors and snipped a curl. Alma handed me a clean tissue. I wrapped the curl and zipped it into the inner pocket of my bag. We heard the flush of the lavatory and the buzz of a hand drier. Maggie scribbled her telephone number on the back of a beer mat and gave it to me.

'He's all right about it, really,' she said. 'He knows I'll never give up. I just want to know

238

for certain that I did the right thing. You'll tell me if...'

'Of course,' I said. 'One last thing. Do you remember Sister Monica?'

'She came to visit me in hospital.'

'Did she ever talk about her brother?'

'Her brother? I don't think so. Why would she talk to me about her brother?'

'He's well known,' I said. 'Father Frank Devine, the singing priest.'

'I never knew that,' Maggie said. 'She just used to sit by my bed and say the rosary. I don't remember her talking to me at all. There was one nice nun who used to sit and talk. She came to see me when I was a bit better. I can't think of her name. She was really nice. She used to chat, and read the newspapers to me.'

'Sister Dervla?' I said.

'That's the name! Yes. Dervla.' She struggled for a moment with her memory. 'She told me her surname,' she said. 'She had the same surname as my mother. I remember asking if they could be distantly related. I don't think they were.'

Her husband fidgeted beside us. Alma stood up and offered her hand to him in farewell, moving him towards the door.

'What was the name?' I said quickly to Maggie.

'Jagoe,' she said. 'It's unusual. That's why I remembered.'

'Spelt?'

'J A G O E.' A smile lit up her face. 'It's great to remember something, anything,' she said. 'Thank you.' She looked over at her husband. 'I'm coming, Jimmy. I'll just say goodbye.'

She embraced me and Alma in turn. Her husband shook my hand. He was ushering Maggie out, when she stopped and said, 'I'll call you if I remember anything else. Good luck!'

'Come on, Maggie,' said her husband.

The door swung shut behind them. We heard the car start up and drive away. I sank on to a stool.

'I have a parent with a dimple,' I said.

'*On the baby's knuckle, on the baby's knee, where will the baby's dimple be?*' I sang on the way back, bouncing with happiness.

Alma was driving. 'I've not heard that before.'

'You're too young to remember. Mama used to sing it to me.

'Baby's cheek, or baby's chin,
Seems to me it'll be a sin,
If it's always covered by the safety pin!
Where will the dimple be?'

'I feel I'm nearly there,' I said. 'Patsy Malone and Father Songbird. Makes sense, doesn't it? It was worth the journey.' I paused, before adding, 'Thanks for coming with me, Alma.'

'He wasn't so bad,' she said. 'Once he got on to his favourite subject.'

'Do you ever get something flash into your mind and disappear?' I said. 'I have this feeling he said something, and I thought something, and then he said something else and I forgot what it was I thought. It's hovering on the edge of my mind, but when I try to pounce, it floats away.'

'Happens to me all the time,' she said cheerfully. 'What kind of important thought? Give me a clue.'

'I haven't got one. I just have this feeling. It's probably nothing. Something he said. Or maybe a question I was going to ask and then he answered it anyway.'

'If you try not to think about it, it will come back to you. Relax. You can afford to relax now. When is Mary coming over?'

'I'm meeting her on Sunday night,' I said. 'And it can't come too soon.'

Chapter 26

When we got back, there was just time to tell Eileen my news before sitting down to dinner. She waved me to a seat in the kitchen, while she cut brown bread for smoked salmon.

'I didn't know that,' she said after my excited explanation of dimples, ears and eyes.

'Two blue-eyed parents can't have a brown-eyed child,' I said. 'Apparently it's really rare. A chance in a million. I wonder what colour eyes...'

'How should I know?' She was suddenly off-hand. 'You can look on a CD cover to find out. There's a music shop in the town.'

'I'm sorry. I'm keeping you back.' I got up to go.

She continued slicing the loaf. Without looking at me she said, 'I could hate you, you know.' She put the knife down and turned to face me. 'It's not fair. I've been searching for years. I set up the Limerick branch of NPI. I write letters to district health boards and religious orders. I trawl through birth records. I get nowhere. And you come here and in a few days you find out everything you need to know. Why do you get all the luck? And she isn't even your child!' She began to cry.

'Eileen,' I said helplessly. 'I'm sorry. I didn't think...'

Michael came in from the dining room.

'I'd better order some more Rioja,' he began, before taking in the scene. In two steps he was between us, motioning to me to leave, rocking Eileen in his arms.

I backed out of the kitchen and stumbled

242

upstairs. Alma wasn't in the room. I sat down on the bed, shaking. How could I have been so insensitive? Crowing my triumphs night after night. Oblivious of Eileen's pain.

Memories boomed around my brain. Friends from secretarial school, after I got my first job with the bank. 'We always knew they'd pick you, Lena.' Daphne, who took me to the party where I met Jack. 'You don't even try, and you win every time.' I hadn't realised she was in love with Jack. She came to our wedding, but didn't keep in touch.

There was a rap on the door. 'Lena?' Eileen's voice. I didn't move. She rapped again. 'Lena? Please. I need to say something.'

When I opened the door she said, 'I'm sorry, I should be glad for you. I am glad for you. And it was really interesting. What you found out. About blue eyes and dimples.'

It was my turn to cry. 'Eileen, forgive me.' I reached out for her. We hugged each other.

'We're a right pair,' she said. 'Now, come down for your dinner. And we'll say no more about it.'

Alma and Donal seemed to have resumed friendly relations. When I joined them at our usual table they were chatting as though there had never been any tension between them. If they noticed my red eyes, they said nothing. We were the only people in the dining room.

'They all checked out this morning,' Donal said. 'There were a lot of fond farewells outside. I think the Matchmaking worked for a couple of them anyway.'

'We'll be saying our fond farewells on Saturday morning,' I said. 'And hasn't the time flown!'

Alma was about to say something when Eileen whisked in, looking like her normal, affable self. She made a point of patting my shoulder when she took our order. Smoked salmon, roast shoulder of lamb with boiled potatoes, carrots and leeks, and apple tart. I smiled my gratitude before she bustled back to the kitchen.

'I was telling Donal about Maggie and her husband,' Alma said, 'and Patsy Malone.'

'She used to sing with a band. Do you know her?' I said.

'What was the band called?'

'The Four ... somethings? Playing cards. Aces, Kings something like that?'

'I'd stopped going to dances by that time,' Donal said. 'A baby was the only thing keeping me up at night.'

'I'm sure Mary will be able to find her,' I said. They both looked at me. 'I think I've got enough now,' I added. 'Wouldn't you agree?'

'I'm delighted,' Donal said warmly. 'To tell you the truth, I think it's better to be a bit cautious. Especially with your man, the singing priest. We got a bit carried away speculating the other night. We'd had a few drinks, and it was all good fun. But really, there's no hard evidence to connect him. We could be slandering the poor chap.'

'There's the voice,' I said. 'Or do you think great talent just pops up out of nowhere?'

'Well,' he said mildly. 'The only person who knows for sure is Mary's birth mother.'

Alma said, 'Reward yourself now. Is there anywhere you'd like to go?'

'I hadn't thought about it. There's only tomorrow before we have to go back to Dublin.'

'The concert isn't until Monday,' Alma said.

'What about you? You have to fly back on Saturday. We need to get you to the airport.'

'Donal has offered to take me,' she said, trying to sound casual, but ruining the effect by blushing. 'He's going home on Saturday. He says he can drop me off. You can stay here. Or go somewhere else.'

There came into my head the vision of a rough field sloping to the sea, a stream with irises growing along its banks, a stone wall and a shrine.

'I'd like to go to County Mayo,' I said. 'The scenery is beautiful. I could drive up there on Saturday. It shouldn't be difficult to find a hotel or a bed and breakfast at this time of year.'

That night I dreamed an old, familiar dream. I was walking along the avenue towards the convent, looking up at a light blue sky, with fluffy clouds. But this time there was only one Madonna and child floating in the sky above the chestnut trees. The white veil of the Madonna hid her face. The larger-than-life infant smiled in his sleep. He had a dimple.

When I woke, Alma was dressed and about to go downstairs. I refused her offer of breakfast in bed. It was a day for a cooked breakfast of bacon, eggs, mushrooms and hot toast.

'Even I wouldn't play golf today,' Donal said, looking at the black veil of rain sweeping in from the Atlantic. Eileen lit a fire in the residents' lounge – a comfortable, high-ceilinged room with chintz-covered armchairs, an upright piano, sporting prints, a big brass fender and a long window looking out on the lawn sloping to the damp shrubbery and the river beyond. We spent an agreeable morning browsing through the newspapers, with occasional bursts of chat.

'There's a bit about the concert in the arts section,' Donal said, from behind his broadsheet. I had a map spread out on the table, devising a route for the following day.

'Does it mention Mary?'

'Mmmn. There's a bit here.' He read aloud: *'Dawn Upshaw is replaced by Mary Molloy. The up-and-coming mezzo-soprano, whose paternal grandfather was from County Mayo, fled operatic storms in San Francisco to make her Irish debut. "It was a difficult time," she said, referring to dramatic incidents in which Adela Contini, the world-famous soprano, set fire to stage curtains at San Francisco Opera House, slashed the tyres of her husband's car and fired blanks from a stage pistol at the woman she accused of being her husband's mistress.'*

He stopped reading.

'I wonder who that is,' I said. 'I suppose they can't name her.'

Donal lowered the paper and looked at me over the top of his half-moon spectacles. He paused before saying in a tone of mild wonderment, 'It's a baroque world, all right.' He set the paper aside. 'Does anybody fancy a walk in the wind and the rain and a bowl of hot soup somewhere warm and dry?'

'I do,' Alma said.

'I think I'll stay here,' I said. 'I bought a bit of light fiction at the airport. The kind of book that has silver writing on the front. I haven't even opened it.'

I put more turf on the fire, settled myself into a comfortable armchair and tried to absorb myself in the story of a fashion designer whose ideas are stolen by an employer who then tries to kill her. I couldn't concentrate.

The door opened. I heard a chink and rattle before turning round to see Eileen carrying a tray with a bowl of soup and a plate of scones.

'I'm glad you stayed behind,' she said. 'I wanted a chat before you leave. I have a party of Germans checking in later but I have a bit of time before then. The soup is leek and potato.'

'Oh, Eileen,' I said. 'I'm so sorry.'

She stopped me with her hand. 'It's all right,' she said. 'We won't mention my little tantrum again. I'm the one who should be saying sorry. Now.' She put the tray on a side table by my armchair and took the armchair opposite. 'I want to hear properly about yesterday and what you managed to find out.'

She interrupted a few times to say, 'Don't let your soup get cold!' and 'Eat your scones!' but otherwise listened intently. When I'd finished, she said, 'All that stuff about eyes and ears is interesting, and useful to know. And you have another name to follow up. I can't say I've ever heard of her. I'll have another look through the files.' She paused and added, 'Of course, this nun might have arranged the adoption without the mother ever having been in Saint

Joseph's. She might have had the baby somewhere else. Anywhere.'

'I never thought of that,' I said, dismayed.

'What did I tell you?' she said. 'It's a long road with many disappointments on the way. I'll take your tray now.'

She left me skewered by uncertainty. My mouth tasted sour. I couldn't settle back down to read. Why had I assumed Mary was born in Saint Joseph's? Through the rain-streaked window I could see the bonnet and radiator of the car, parked by the side of the house. Whoever the mother, Sister Monica had arranged a swift, private adoption for 'a very distinguished man'. Who else but her brother? What else could explain her tele-phone call? I remembered Eileen's offhand comment, 'You can look on a CD cover. There's a music shop in the town.' It was time for a visit to the music shop. Action jogged my memory. As I stood up, I remembered Sister Dervla. Of course! She would know if Mary had been born in Saint Joseph's. She had left the convent, but I knew her surname. Maggie had told me. Jagoe. Dervla Jagoe.

Chapter 27

Rain water raced along the gutters in the town and swelled the river, roaring under the bridge and almost drowning the melancholy air on a tin whistle emanating from the open door of the music shop. The tune asserted itself, became more familiar as I approached.

'That's a nice, sad tune, if it's not a contradiction in terms,' I said, as I stooped to enter through the low door. Inside, there was barely enough room to walk around the rack of CDs and cassettes in the middle of the floor.

The youth behind the counter said, 'I know what you mean. I like a sad song myself. It's called "The Singing Bird". It's a popular tune. There are dozens of versions – flute, fiddle, harp, voice accompanied, the voice unaccompanied. What version would you like?'

'I was looking for a CD of Father Frank Devine,' I said.

'I don't think he's recorded it,' the young man said. He had a smooth, round face and a neat ponytail. 'Folk music isn't really his thing. He's more into religious stuff and opera.'

'Do you have any of his CDs?' I said.

'You'd have to go into Ennis or Limerick for that,' he said. 'I only carry folk music and a bit of crossover. Van Morrison, some country music, that kind of thing.'

'Have you got a singer called Patsy Malone?'

'Not in stock. I'll see what's available.' He tapped into the computer by the till and gazed intently at the screen.

'She sang with a showband in the seventies. Did a lot of country music. Then she went solo as a folk artist. She's a big name in Germany.'

'Germany?' I said.

'Oh, yes,' he said. 'Irish music is popular over there. They can't really play their own traditional music. It's a bit, you know,' he lowered his voice, 'Third Reich. Hitler was fond of it apparently. Then there's a thing called Volksmusik which has nothing to do with folk music at all. So they play Irish music instead.'

'Very Irish.'

'Or very German,' he said. 'Depending on where you're coming from.'

'I'm English,' I said.

'I can tell.'

The music died. I tried to get the conversation back on track. 'Patsy Malone?'

He peered at the screen. 'She has a couple

251

of CDs on an independent label. I could order them for you.'

'No, it's all right,' I said. Embarrassment made me add, 'I'd like a CD or cassette with "The Singing Bird" on it.'

'Voice accompanied, unaccompanied, or instrumental?'

'Voice,' I said.

'Accompanied?'

'Unaccompanied.'

'Male or female?'

I hesitated.

'You can read the words either way,' he said. 'But I think it's a man's song.' He opened his throat and sang in a slightly nasal tenor,

'I have seen the lark soar high at morn
Till he sang up in the blue
I have heard the blackbird pipe his note
The thrush and the linnet too
But there's none of them can sing so sweet
My singing bird as you,
La la la la la, la la la la la,
My singing bird, as you.

'They say the man who collected the song from an old woman in the west couldn't write the words down fast enough,' he said.

'He just wrote down *la la la* for the second line of the chorus. When he went back to get the right words she'd died. So it's been *la la la* ever since.'

He launched into a second verse.

'If I could lure my singing bird
From her own cosy nest
If I could catch my singing bird
I would warm her on my breast
And it's on my heart my singing bird
Would sing herself to rest
La la la la la, la la la la la,
Would sing herself to rest.'
'Whoever you recommend,' I said.

I left the shop with *Irish Folk Favourites: Various Artistes,* and the thought that I, for once, would be the one to come home with a musical reminder of my trip. The rain had stopped and the sun was attempting a breakout when I crossed the square to O'Brien's and made my way through to the back.

Chapter 28

The home page for Father Frank Devine flashed up in an instant. Across the top, *Ireland's Singing Priest* in gold, Celtic lettering on a broad green band. On the right hand side, a younger version of the face I had seen on television. Dark hair, dark eyes above a clerical collar. Impossible to tell the eye colour. Down the left hand side, four CD covers – *Father Frank's Christmas*

Favourites; *A Tribute to Count John Mc-Cormack*; *There is a Flower that Bloometh*; *Bless This House*. Impossible to see the face clearly.

Picture-Gallery. Click. 'With Pope John Paul II.' Hmmph. I wondered what the Pope would say if he knew about Father Songbird's extra-curricular activities. The exterior of a modern church – white-rendered brick and abstract stained glass windows. *'When not on tour, Father Devine fulfils his duties as P.P Holy Family Church, Rathkeeran, North Dublin.'* A black and white first communion photograph. *'Aged 8, with his sister Monica, 20.'* A young nun with a solemn expression clutched the hand of a boy in jacket and short trousers. A lock of dark hair fell over his eyes. He grinned engagingly at the camera. In his other hand he held a prayer book and rosary beads. There were no photographs of parents. Were Sister Monica and her brother orphans? I still couldn't see the colour of his eyes.

If Patsy Malone was Mary's birth mother, Mary would want to hear her voice as well. She might have a website. There might be a picture. I typed Patsy Malone into a search engine and scrolled through links to an actress, a palmist, and several high schools in America before finding a German website. I recognised the words *musik* and *produktion* and *independent label aus Frankfurt*. No photographs or CD covers. I forwarded the link to my email address and returned to Search. I had remembered Sister Dervla and her unusual surname. I typed in *Dervla Jagoe*. Bingo! A link flashed on to the screen.

Dr Dervla Jagoe. Research Interests: Ideology and Discourse in post-feminist criticism; Faith and Feminism in Literature; 20th-Century Attitudes to gender-swapping in Shakespeare. www.may.ie/feedback Click.

National University of Ireland: Maynooth. English Department. Staff Telephone Directory. Scroll down.

Dr Dervla Jagoe. I wrote down the telephone number and logged off.

As I drove back to Atlantic House, an unfamiliar emotion made my nerves tingle. Guilty pleasure. The search had become exciting in itself. Sister Dervla would know if Mary had been born in Saint Joseph's. A phrase came into my head and I spoke it out loud. 'Knowledge is power.' That was it. I felt powerful. I accelerated past an elderly Vauxhall. Vroom. The car raced up the hill towards the hotel.

Vroom. Would I go back and confront Sister Monica? The gravel crunched gratifyingly under the wheels as I braked to a halt.

I sat for a few minutes indulging my dream of triumph and revenge, before settling for magnanimity. Why torment a dying woman? I could afford to be generous. I might never know why she telephoned, but did it matter? She had set me on the road to the precious knowledge I would keep for Mary. In my mind's eye I saw the envelope – 'To Mary, all my love, Mum.' I had no need for a confrontation with Sister Monica. Indeed, I felt almost sorry for her. Nuns and priests were no longer held in the highest regard in Ireland. It was a hard row to hoe.

Chapter 29

Overall, I felt satisfied as I lay in the bath, occasionally pushing the tap lever with my toe to top up the hot water. I thought we might have a bottle of champagne with our dinner, in celebration and farewell.

Donal beat me to it. 'Shall we have a bottle of fizz? What do you say?' Michael appeared at the table with a chilled bottle of champagne and three flutes, a white linen napkin over his arm. Alma clapped her hands in delight. The party of Germans at the big table in the window turned their heads to watch. Michael placed the glasses in front of us, flicked open the napkin, wrapped it deftly round the bottle and turned the bottle slowly.

'The ear's gain is the palate's loss,' he said, as the cork slid out with a low plop.

'*Prost!*' the Germans chorused. 'Cheers!'

'To you, ladies, for making my holiday special.' Donal raised his glass to us both, but his eyes lingered on Alma.

She raised her glass. 'To Lena, for taking me to Ireland. Donal, for introducing me to golf.'

'To happy endings,' I said, raising my glass in turn.

'Happy endings,' they echoed.

It sometimes happens that two groups of people, meeting by accident, with nothing obvious in common, can blend harmoniously for an evening and part without a second glance. Our fellow diners were intent on enjoying themselves. In conversations exchanged from time to time between our small table and the big table in the window, it transpired they were on a music tour of Ireland and two of them had brought guitars. From there, it was a short step to a proposal for a singsong after dinner. We had followed the champagne with a couple of glasses of a decent cognac, and happily agreed.

It was after midnight, the fire growing cold in the hearth, when I heard Pieter and

Marianne, the young German couple on the sofa beside me, say, 'Patsy Malone?'

'*Ja, Dienstag abend.*'

'Excuse me,' I said. 'Are you talking about Patsy Malone, the singer?'

'Do you know her?'

'I've heard about her. She sings country music?'

'Some country music. Some folk. She sings often in Germany. We go to a concert where she will sing in Dublin.'

'When?' I said.

'Next week.'

At the other side of the room Donal got to his feet,

'Time for *The Parting Glass*,' he said. We all clapped. Alma's eyes followed him to the piano.

'Where's the concert?' I said softly.

'In Dublin Castle. The Coach House. Eight o'clock. Tuesday night. It is possible you will come?'

I was booked to fly back on Tuesday morning. I smiled and shook my head, before settling back on the sofa for the last verse of the evening. Donal sat down at the piano and, with a few accompanying chords, sang in a light baritone,

> *'Oh all the money that e'er I had, I spent it in good company*
> *And all the harm that e'er I've done, alas, it was to none but me*

258

And all I've done for want of wit to memory
   now I can't recall,
So fill for me the parting glass, good night and
   joy be with you all.'

I blew a goodnight kiss to Donal and Alma before slipping upstairs to mull over my plans. Should I telephone Dervla Jagoe? I took my suitcase from the bottom of the wardrobe and began to lay my clothes out on the bed, ready for packing. My thoughts arranged themselves as my hands smoothed and folded.

What did I have to lose? If she wasn't there, or wasn't my Sister Dervla, or didn't want to meet me, my position was unchanged. I could still drive to Mayo and be back in Dublin for Mary's concert on Monday. Decision taken.

Next decision. Should I go to Patsy Malone's concert? That would depend on what Sister Dervla told me. I didn't need to decide straight away. Decision deferred.

I finished packing, switched off the overhead light and got into bed.

If I decided to drive to Dublin instead of Mayo would I tell Alma? No. She might feel obliged to come with me. It wouldn't be fair to put her in the position of having to choose between Donal and me.

I switched off the bedside light and waited for sleep. There was a faint rumble of speech from downstairs. An occasional burst of laughter. Tired footsteps on the stairs. The impromptu party winding down. Not enough noise to irritate. I've never liked counting sheep. I made a mental list of the capital cities of Europe. Then all the counties in England. Then I began to assign furniture to each room in our new house.

The door handle rattled softly. I heard a whisper, a click as the door was shut, a bump as Alma failed to negotiate the space between the door and the bathroom. Blue light framed the bathroom door. The lavatory flushed. Water splashed into the basin, then gurgled and swooshed down the plughole. The light went out. Alma patted her way along the duvet to the pillow.

'It's all right,' I said. 'I'm not asleep. You can put on the light.'

'Sorry.' she said. 'I stayed up talking to Donal.'

Decision confirmed.

Chapter 30

It was all a bit of a rush in the morning. Donal and Alma were already checking out when I came down to breakfast. They had decided to leave early and stop at Donal's house on the way to the airport. In the distance, the sky was blue above the horizon of the sea. The clouds above me were moving resolutely to the east. It was going to be a fine Saturday in the west, in Mayo.

'Enjoy Mayo,' Alma said. 'Give my love to Mary. Ring me with your return flight and I'll meet you at the airport.'

Donal gave me his card. 'I'm looking forward to the concert,' he said. 'Will we meet at the box office? It's on the left, as you go in through the main door. About half an hour before the concert? If there's any problem, give me a call.'

Eileen stood beside me on the steps as we waved them goodbye. 'She's a lucky woman,' she said. 'Donal is a lovely man.'

'He's the lucky one.'

'Maybe I'll see them both back next year.' She looked straight ahead and said, 'I'm jealous of your success. It's as simple as that.'

'Eileen,' I said, not looking at her either. 'If you hadn't given me Teresa's name, I'd be no further on. I'm grateful. I hope and pray you find your daughter.' I grasped her arm and turned to look her in the eyes. 'I know from in here, that she wants to find you.' I pressed my other hand against my heart. 'And some day she will. Now, will you give me some breakfast?'

Before setting off, I telephoned Dervla

Jagoe's office number and left a simple message. 'I am trying to contact a Dervla Jagoe who used to be in Saint Joseph's, near Tullamore. If I have contacted the wrong person, I apologise.' I gave my mobile number. 'If you are the same person, I would be grateful if you could call me.'

When Jack couldn't decide on a course of action, he would toss a coin. 'Whatever I call, heads or tails, there's always a slight feeling of elation or disappointment at the result, so I know what I really want to do,' he told me. 'That's how I decided to propose to you. Only joking!'

I turned a silver twenty pence coin over in my fingers. On one side the Irish harp, on the other a horse. 'Harp for Dublin,' I said to myself. The coin landed with a clink on the gravel, horse side up for Mayo. Ten minutes later I was on the road to Dublin. Jack was right.

Mary's voice accompanied me. *Arias from the Baroque Era.* The final notes of *Che Faro* had died away, ending side one of the cassette, when my mobile rang. It was Dervla Jagoe.

'I've just got your message,' she said. 'But I don't know who you are.'

'I may have got the wrong person,' I said. 'But I think we met twenty-seven years ago in a solicitor's office in Tullamore.'

There was a worrying pause.

'A baby girl?' I prompted. 'Frances Mary Dervla Molloy.'

'Hello, Frances Mary Dervla,' she said. 'I often wondered what became of you.'

'I grew up in England and became a professional singer,' I said, before I could stop myself. 'I've often wondered if my parents were singers too.' My heart hammered against my ribs. My mouth was dry.

'Can you come and see me?' she said. 'Where are you?'

I tried to moisten my mouth.

'Frankfurt,' I said. 'I'm rehearsing for a concert tour. Please, I just need to know.' I was floundering.

'It would be better if you could come and see me,' she said. 'It's hard to discuss these things over the telephone. Are you likely to be in Ireland in the near future?'

'No,' I said. This was getting worse. Not only was I lying as myself, I was also lying as the person I was pretending to be. I could hear my breath coming in short gasps.

'Are you all right?' she said. 'You sound distressed.'

'My mother – my adoptive mother has traced Patsy Malone for me,' I said. 'I haven't spoken to her yet. I don't want to approach her without knowing. Please, tell me if you know. Is she my mother?'

'Yes,' said Sister Dervla.

I tried to keep my voice steady. 'And my

father,' I said. 'My father. Please. Is he Father Frank Devine?'

The name seemed to hang in a black void between us. Seconds passed. Then, 'I don't know,' she said.

'But there is a connection? I know it,' I said.

'It would be better if you came to see me, or wrote to me,' she said. 'These things are difficult over the phone.'

I heard myself say, 'My adoptive mother is in Ireland on holiday. Will you see her for me? Can she call to see you? She's in Ireland today and tomorrow and Monday. Please. Her name is Lena Molloy. You can tell her anything.'

Eventually she said, 'Whereabouts is she in Ireland?'

'I'm not sure,' I said. That at least was true. 'Somewhere near Dublin.'

'I live and teach in Maynooth, in County Kildare,' she said. 'About thirty minutes from Dublin, three-quarters of an hour to an hour if the traffic's bad. Does she have a car?'

'Yes,' I said.

'I'll be teaching all day Monday. But I'm at home this evening, and tomorrow evening. I'll give you my home telephone number. You can tell her to call.'

Oh no! I didn't want to speak to her on the telephone again. She might recognise my voice.

'Hold on, hold on. I'll get a pen,' I said.

I wrote down the telephone number, calmed my breathing, and said, 'And the address?'

'Thirty-one Carton Street, Maynooth,' she said. 'Tell her I'll be in from about five thirty. It was nice talking to you, Frances Mary Dervla.'

I dropped the mobile on to my lap, closed my eyes and leaned back against the headrest until my pulse rate slowed down. I felt sick. I had always thought of myself as a truthful person. I had been brought up to abhor lying. I had brought Mary up the same way. But a lie had just popped effortlessly out of my mouth. Not an evasion. Not a little white lie. A big black lie.

I concentrated on breathing slowly and evenly. I tried to think calmly.

If I confessed my deception to Dervla Jagoe, I would feel better. But she might refuse to tell me anything. In which case, I could give her telephone number and address to Mary. In which case, I didn't need to contact Dervla Jagoe again at all.

But I was so near! So near to Dervla Jagoe. So near to the secret I had set out to uncover.

Supposing I went to see her, with the genuine intention of coming clean? If necessary. At any rate, no more lies, I said to myself. No more lies.

My hands were steady when I lifted them to the steering wheel. A glass of water. That was what I needed. And food. At the next service station I filled up the car and bought a bottle of mineral water and a Mars bar. Nearly there, I told myself. Nearly there.

Chapter 31

I checked into a hotel on the outskirts of Maynooth. The well-groomed girl at the reception desk drew me directions to Carton Street.

'You could walk there in twenty minutes,' she said. 'Will you be wanting dinner?'

I was about to ask if I could have it in my room. Ridiculous, I told myself. If I could prove that Ireland's favourite priest had fathered an illegitimate child, and face down Sister Monica, I could eat alone in a hotel dining room.

'What time do you finish serving?'

'Nine o'clock.'

'A table for one at eight thirty,' I said.

I crossed the hotel courtyard and took the footpath to town. The path ran along a stone wall guarding a demesne. At the entrance to the town was a Norman keep. Next to the keep, the tall university buildings, Georgian

266

and Victorian gothic, dominated the smaller Georgian houses near the university gates.

I knew Maynooth College had once been the largest seminary in the British Isles, and wondered if Father Songbird had walked these lawns and quadrangles reading from his breviary. A group of girls, books bunched under their arms, came chattering through the gates, backlit by the last rays of the evening sun. Maynooth was no longer a male-only preserve. It was part of the National University. And Sister Dervla taught here now.

She welcomed me into the two-storey redbrick terraced house in a side street at the other end of the wide main road through the town. She wore a pale blue long-sleeved sweatshirt, blue jeans and sneakers. Her short dark hair was speckled with grey. Her brown eyes were bright and inquisitive as a bird's.

'The last time you saw me I was all black serge, veil and wimple,' she said. 'But you hardly look a day older.'

'A few more wrinkles,' I said. We stood at the bottom of the stairs for a moment, sizing each other up. The house smelled of dog.

'We'll go upstairs to the study,' she said. 'I'll make some tea. Or would you rather have a gin and tonic?'

'Gin and tonic, please.'

'Did you drive out from Dublin?'

'Er, no,' I said. I tried to reduce deception to a minimum. 'I got the message when I was on my way to Dublin. It was easy to stop off.'

Dervla led the way upstairs to a room overlooking the paved back yard. Bookshelves lined the walls. Books and papers covered the desk, and much of the floor. There was a faint hum from the computer.

She lifted a pile of manuscripts from an armchair.

'Sit down,' she said. 'Sorry about the mess. I'll nip down and get the drinks.'

I heard a door open downstairs, an excited yelp, scampering feet on carpet. A pekinese shuffled through the door with Dervla. She handed me my gin and tonic and scooped up the dog with her free hand. 'Come on, old girl,' she said, taking the swivel chair at the computer and settling the dog on her lap.

'Meet Rover,' she said.

'Hello, Rover,' I said. 'You have an unusual name.'

'Useful for explaining irony and gender when I take her to college.' Dervla raised her glass. '*Sláinte.*'

'Your good health,' I said. 'I don't suppose you had many of these in Saint Joseph's.'

'Drink wasn't the only thing I discovered when I left the convent,' she said, her eyes glinting with mischief. 'But that's a long time ago. I've spent more of my life out of it than in it.' I glanced at her left hand. There was no ring.

'Why did you leave?' I said. 'I'm sorry. None of my business.'

'It's all right. Nobody has asked me that for a long time. I thought I was running towards God, but I was really running away from a small farm in the west. It's a bleak place I grew up in. Beautiful. But bleak. There's a saying in Irish about that area – they're powerful fond of the rope. It's the isolation.' She looked out of the window as though seeing not red brick and slate, but black bog, grey rock and the wild sea. 'It's all different now – grants, tourism, and an airport. But when I was growing up there was damn all.' The faint profanity sounded strange coming from someone I had last seen in the habit of a nun. 'Monica saw that. She changed the narrative. She told me to leave and go to university. She got me a place at UGD.'

'Sister Monica?' I asked, incredulous.

Dervla nodded. 'She has her faults, God knows. But lack of imagination isn't one of them.' She stroked Rover and regarded me thoughtfully.

'Your daughter told me you were helping her trace her birth mother.'

'Patsy Malone,' I said.

'How did you find her? I can't believe Monica told you.'

'She didn't,' I said. 'She sent me away with a flea in my ear.'

'So tell me the story.'

I began with Sister Monica's telephone call. 'Completely out of the blue,' I said. 'I don't know why she called. Then I spoke to Mary. And she thought it was a good idea for me to come to Ireland.' I chose my words carefully, conscious of a flush creeping up my neck.

'She wanted you to search for her birth mother?'

I took a deep gulp of gin and tonic. 'I'm adopted myself. I understand the need to know.'

Her eyes never left my face as I told her about the Natural Parents' Internetwork. How Eileen Collins had put me in touch with Teresa. How Teresa had mentioned Father Devine. The fact that he was Sister Monica's brother, and a singer.

'From that moment I felt sure he was involved,' I said.

I told her about the photograph, and how I thought Mary looked a bit like Maggie Kane.

'She was blonde in the photograph,' I said. 'And she's tall, like Mary.' Then I described finding www.blastfromthepast.ie and Maggie Kane.

'Marvellous,' said Dervla, clapping her hands.

'But she had dyed her hair. In case someone would recognise her. And Maggie has blue eyes, and her baby's father had blue eyes. Two blue-eyed people can't have a brown-eyed child. Maggie's husband explained it all.'

Dervla took her gaze from me while she thought for a moment. Then she nodded. 'My mother had blue eyes. But my father's eyes were brown.'

'Brown's dominant,' I said.

'Go on.'

'Well,' I said, 'I had the photograph with the three names on the back. I could rule out the one who had a boy. That left Patsy Malone. I hadn't considered her because she was small and had dark hair. But Maggie's husband recognised the name. He said she was a singer. A singer! And she had red hair. It just looked dark in the photograph. Maggie didn't really remember her. She didn't remember much at all.'

'I remember Maggie Kane,' said Dervla. 'I'm not surprised she can't remember much. She nearly died on us.'

'She remembered you. And your surname. It was the same as her mother's. So I did an Internet search for Dervla Jagoe. And that's how I found you. On the university website.'

She clapped her hands again. 'Marvellous. Picaresque.' Rover stirred in her lap.

'And you told Mary?'

I took another slug of my drink. 'I think it's better for Mary to make contact.'

'She sounded excited on the telephone,' Dervla said. 'An opera singer. Wonderful.'

'Yes,' I said. 'She's coming to Ireland next week to sing in the National Concert Hall.'

'She told me she wouldn't be in Ireland in the near future.' Dervla said.

I felt the blood rise from my neck to my face.

'I suppose she couldn't wait. It's understandable.' Dervla paused. 'An opera singer,' she repeated, slowly shaking her head. 'Well, well.'

'Like Father Frank Devine,' I said.

There. The name was out. It seemed to electrify the space between us. Seconds passed. Neither of us spoke.

Dervla sat up straighter. Rover shifted, slid off her lap and pattered to the door. Dervla got up and opened the door for the dog. I could hear Rover flopping downstairs. Dervla resumed her seat.

'I'll tell you what I remember.'

My hand gripped the glass so tightly I was afraid it might break.

'Father Frank,' she said. 'The singing priest. Monica practically brought him up, you know. There was just the two of them. The parents died when Frank was a baby. The grandparents sent them away to school. Paid for music lessons and so on. But the emotional bond was with each other. She talked about him all the time. Proud as anything about him.' She paused. 'He brought Patsy Malone to Saint Joseph's.'

Every nerve in my body sprang to attention.

'Patsy was distraught. She wanted to keep the baby. She knew she couldn't. There were no social security payments for single mothers then. She sang with a showband. I can't remember the name. The Melody somethings. She was on the road most of the time, playing in dance halls, staying in hotels. There was no way she could bring up a child on her own.'

I felt a surge of sympathy for Patsy. 'What age was she?'

'About twenty-four, I think,' Dervla said. 'Anyway, Monica was sympathetic and kind to her. Any friend of her brother, and so on. Patsy was in Saint Joseph's for about ten weeks before the baby was born. Father Frank – that's how Monica always referred to him – telephoned quite a few times to speak to Patsy. I remember one time Sister Genevieve called her to the telephone in the lobby. Then she turned to me and said something like, "Hmmph. More than a friend if you ask me."'

'Did you think that too?'

'Not at first. Genevieve was a gossipy sort of person. You couldn't believe half the things she told you. But she put the idea in my mind.'

'Did Monica think it?'

'I don't think it occurred to Monica until the day Patsy's baby was born. I was outside the office when she took a call from Father Frank. "A baby girl," I heard her say. Then he must have said something and she said, "You're that concerned, you'd think you were the father yourself!" Or words to that effect. Then she saw me and put the phone down. She went white. Then red.'

Dervla closed her eyes for a moment in concentration. The room was still. 'I think she must have brooded all night. Two days later I heard Monica shouting and Patsy crying.'

'Good God!' I said.

Dervla paused to switch on the lamp beside the computer.

'There was a couple in Dublin who'd been waiting to adopt. We all thought they would adopt Patsy's baby. The day after the row with Patsy, I was sent off with one of the nuns who had a sick relative. We always had to travel in pairs, you know. Like atoms. Anyway, when I got back to Saint Joseph's, Patsy was gone. I was given the baby to take to you in Tullamore. She was about a week old. A lovely baby. But Monica couldn't wait to get her out of Saint Joseph's. Out of the country, in fact.'

It all made sense.

'It was a shocking thing, back then,' Dervla said.

'Did she tell him she knew?'

'I doubt it. She never said a word to anybody. But I think it knocked the stuffing out of her. She completely withdrew into herself.'

'She's got cancer,' I said. 'One of the nurses at Saint Joseph's told me.'

'Poor Monica.' She was silent for a moment. 'Maybe she called you because she wanted to check your address. To leave it for her brother. In case...'

'In case he ever wanted to trace his daughter,' I finished, conscious of the irony. I swallowed the last of my drink.

'I have the story now,' I said. 'Enough to give to Mary anyway.'

'Will you stay and have something to eat?'

She lives alone, I thought. She would welcome the company. I was just about to say yes, thinking I could telephone the hotel and cancel my dinner reservation, when Rover scampered upstairs, yapping excitedly. Dervla said, 'She always knows when Noreen's coming up the street.'

The front door opened. A woman's voice called, 'Hi Dervla! Rover! I'm home!'

I said, 'Thank you, but I need to get back to the hotel. It's been really nice meeting you again.'

We followed Rover's high-speed descent to the hallway. A youngish, blonde woman was hanging up her coat. 'It's getting cold in the evenings,' she said. Rover nuzzled her ankles. She turned round. 'You must be Mary's mother. Dervla said you might call. Hello. Are you staying for something to eat?'

The warmth and domesticity made me feel homesick.

'Thanks for the invitation, but I booked dinner at the hotel,' I said. 'And I need to make a few phone calls.'

Dervla handed me my coat. 'Good luck and God bless. Maybe I'll get to meet Mary some time.'

'Thank you,' I said. 'You've been terrific.'

I looked back at the three of them, backlit in the doorway of their terraced house, Dervla, Noreen and Rover.

Chapter 32

Why had I assumed Dervla lived alone? She wasn't a nun any longer. She had a friend to share her life, a dog to fuss over, and a fulfilling job. I had misread her situation and felt sorry for her. I felt foolish, and guilty at having deceived her.

Yellow streetlamps lit the path back to the

hotel. Cars swooshed past, their headlights raking angled light across the verge and up the wall. I was nervous and walked quickly. It occurred to me that, outside home, I was not used to being alone.

'What will you fill your time with when Mary goes to London?' Alma had said, other friends had said. What had I filled my time with these last ten years? Running the office, organising Jack, one evening a week at bridge, one evening a month at the book group, four hours' charity work a week, lunch with Alma on Fridays. My life was meticulously planned, months in advance. I filled my time. But I felt bringing up Mary had been the best, most satisfying job of all.

Plop. A small green grenade fell at my feet and split open. The half-exposed chestnut winked in a pool of yellow light. Plop. Louise Jenkins and I pushing our feet into fallen leaves beneath the chestnut trees along the avenue leading to the convent. Looking for conkers to give to my cousin Johnny, staying with us at half term. Louise had a crush on him. I found the biggest, smoothest, shiniest conker I had ever seen.

Louise said, 'He's not your real cousin, you know. You're adopted.' She looked smug and defiant. I wanted to hit her.

'It's not true,'

'It is true. Everybody knows. You haven't

got a real mummy and daddy. You're adopted.'

Dropping the conker. Turning to run. Running down the avenue, along South Park Road, up Market Hill, round the back of the house, past the surgery window, tripping on the mat in the back porch. My tidy world overturned.

I stopped and picked up the chestnut, still half-encased in its spiny green jacket. Dervla had confirmed what I suspected about Father Songbird and Patsy Malone, yet I felt rattled and uneasy. I tossed the green grenade over the wall, along with the memory of Louise Jenkins, and hurried towards the hotel.

My face in the bathroom mirror looked tired and crumpled. Grey skin, greying hair beginning to show at the temples, dull eyes. Was this the face my birth mother saw in the mirror every day?

'Pull yourself together,' I said sharply to my reflection. 'Stop feeling sorry for yourself.'

I went to work with foundation, blusher, eye shadow, mascara and lipstick. I put on my favourite tomato-red cashmere jumper, my triple strand of pearls – one for each decade of our marriage – and the pearl earrings Jack had given me for my fiftieth birthday. I slipped my feet into low-heeled, red shoes. They raised my spirits. I squared my shoulders and lifted my chin, determined to enjoy my first ever dinner alone in a public place.

The maitre d' showed me to a table half-hidden by a fake Grecian pillar. Good. I could survey the room without being seen by too many people. There were at least three men eating alone. Why should I be noticed any more than they were? Couples, or groups of friends enjoying a Saturday night out, occupied the rest of the tables. Their chatter drowned the faint plink-plonk of harp music drifting from loudspeakers in the ceiling. What did Jack do when he was on the road, alone? He entertained customers and suppliers, that's what. And travelling alone was easier for men. But why should it be? What did Alma do on holiday, alone? What would she do in my situation?

I summoned the wine waiter, a rotund, friendly-faced man. 'Do you have any half-bottles of champagne, please?' I asked quietly.

'We do,' he said, handing me the wine list. He dropped his voice to a whisper. 'May I ask if it's a birthday you're celebrating?'

'No,' I whispered back. 'I'm just not used to dining alone, and my friend says champagne is a cure for everything.'

'The best medicine,' he agreed.

I ate carefully, trying not to look around,

focusing my attention on the unexciting but competent sole meunière. 'Nobody's looking at you. Most of them can't see you,' I told myself. I waved away the pudding menu and knocked over my champagne glass. My face went as red as my jumper. I imagined every head swivelling towards me.

The wine waiter was at my side in seconds, mopping up the spill. He removed my glass, and the almost empty bottle. I looked around. No one was looking disapprovingly in my direction. But I felt uncomfortable.

A clean champagne flute materialised in front of me, a cork popped at my ear. I looked up in astonishment. The wine waiter put a finger to his lips. He smiled and set another half-bottle down in front of me.

'It's a cure for everything,' he said, and tapped his nose conspiratorially. After two more glasses, I felt cheerful enough to change my mind and have pudding after all.

I sailed out of the dining room, with a wave and a smile of thanks to the genial wine waiter. Back in my room, I kicked off my shoes, lay down on the bed and dialled Jack's mobile.

'Lena. I was just going to ring you. You've heard Mary's news?'

'Isn't it great,' I said. 'He's coming to Dublin. I'll meet him. Isn't that terrific?'

'You sound in great form,' he said. 'I

thought you'd be shocked.'

'Just surprised,' I was slurring the words slightly.

'You're not upset?'

'Why does everybody think I want her tied to my apron strings?' I said crossly.

'Lena, are you a bit drunk?'

'I had some champagne with my dinner,' I said, enunciating carefully. 'About three-quarters of a bottle, actually.'

'I didn't think you'd be celebrating,' he said.

'Not celebrating. Drowning my sorrows. I miss you.'

'I miss you too, angel.'

I felt sleepy. 'When are you coming home, Jack?'

'In nine days' time.'

'I don't want Mary to go and live in America.'

'I don't think there's any question of that,' he said, 'although I don't think she'll stay in Stuttgart. I'm glad you'll be in Dublin to give her some support. You can tell me what he's like when you meet him.'

'When are you going to New Zealand, Jack?'

'In an hour's time. I'll call you from Gisborne. Love you,'

'Me too,' I said. And promptly fell asleep.

I woke with the sensation that I had just

spoken out loud. A sentence was running around my brain. I spoke it into the dimly lit room. 'The Singing Bird is the best restaurant in Dublin. Try the poached sole.' The curious thing was, I knew, even in my sleep-dazed state, that I had dreamed a riddle. Was it poached as in cooked or stolen? And sole as in fish or soul?

My throat was dry. No headache, thank God. I brushed my teeth and drank a tumbler of water. My watch showed a few minutes past midnight. I undressed properly, switched off the light, got back into bed and slept for eight hours.

Next morning, I felt more relaxed than I had been for days. I got out of bed, stretched like a cat, and padded towards the chrome electric kettle and tea tray on the reproduction cabinet that concealed the television. A selection of tourist brochures fanned out from the faux-leather folder of hotel literature beside the tray. I browsed through them as I waited for the kettle to boil. The National Stud and Japanese Gardens in Kildare, Castletown House. Nothing in Dublin. I leafed through the hotel literature – restaurants, room service, baby-sitting, local shops, religious services ... times of Masses. I realised it was Sunday. My next thought came almost immediately. I could go to Mass in Father Songbird's church. What could be more natural? I carried my cup of tea back to bed and planned my day.

Chapter 33

Rathkeeran was a housing estate on the north fringe of Dublin. Holy Family Church stood square in the middle of a giant car park, bordered by a strip of grass on which leggy roses had shed the last of their petals. Its white bulk stood out against the dull brick municipal houses, the untidy parade of shops and the drab industrial units that ran between the estate and the main road into the city. A brisk wind bowled empty crisp packets and polystyrene fast-food containers along the road.

I took a copy of the parish newsletter and a Mass book from a table at the back of the church, made my way down the main aisle leading to the altar, and found a seat in a pew on the same side as the lectern. Soft murmurs, coughs, the rustle of paper filled the church. I glanced at the newsletter.

'Cead Mile Failte to all our parishioners and visitors. If you are a newcomer or a visitor to the parish please say Hello to Father Devine after Mass. Newcomers please take a parish

283

registration sheet from the box in the porch and return it to the parish office.'

The bell tolled. Behind and above me, the organ sounded the opening notes of the processional hymn. The congregation rose to its feet. The choir and congregation began to sing,

'Be Thou my vision, O Lord of my heart
Naught be all else to me save that thou art...'

Then, out of the tuneful clamour, rose a strong, sweet tenor, soaring effortlessly above the chorus like the hero of an opera, pulling choir and congregation into harmonious unity.

'Thou my best thought by day or by night
Waking or sleeping thy presence my light.'

I leaned forward slightly and looked sideways past the other occupants of the pew as the procession approached the altar. He was smaller and leaner than he looked on television or the website and he walked with a springing step. The hymn ended as he ascended the altar.

He turned to face us.

'As we begin this celebration of the Eucharist let us call to mind our sins...'

What age would he have been when Mary was born? Twenty-five? Twenty-six? Such a long time ago and it still felt like yesterday.

I bowed my head and joined in the confessional prayer.

'I confess to Almighty God, and to you my

brothers and sisters, that I have sinned ... in what I have done, and in what I have failed to do...' I thought about my sins of omission. I had avoided the lie direct, but my intention had been to deceive Jack. I had impersonated Mary to Sister Dervla. God forgive me.

I longed to be able to tell Jack the whole story. But I wasn't sorry I had ignored his advice. I will tell him when he gets home, I said to myself. He will forgive me too.

'...and I ask the Blessed Mary ever Virgin, all the angels and saints and you my brothers and sisters to pray for me to the Lord our God.'

I made myself concentrate on the Mass and not on the priest. Mostly I succeeded. Only during the sermon did I allow myself to study the face of the man I called Father Songbird.

He spoke briefly and fluently about what he called the Benedictine pause. The extra rest, halfway through a couplet of Gregorian chant. How, as a young seminarian, he had rushed in at first and found himself out of time with the other singers. How he had learned the vital pause that kept the measure of the music. He said we should apply that pause to our daily lives, and think carefully about what we had just done, and what we were about to do.

Do I wish I had followed this advice? Taken a Benedictine pause? Left the church without meeting Father Devine, and spent the day sightseeing on my leisurely way to Dublin? Of course, I would still have had shocks. But would I be sitting here, my life turned upside down?

Or was everything ordained from the moment Sister Monica lifted the telephone to call me? Not ordained in the sense that some unseen hand was guiding events – though it was chance that led me to the gates of St Joseph's; but predetermined, rather, because of the personalities involved. And who or what creates our personalities? Was Sister Monica protective of her brother because they were orphans, or because of her genes? Did I set out to thwart her because a long time ago Louise Jenkins knew more about my life than I did, and I vowed that would never happen again? Or because I am the product of the parents I never met?

I only know I could no more stop myself waiting to meet Father Songbird than I could stop breathing. After Mass, I hung back in the vestibule of the church, pretending to read the notice board, one eye on the queue of well-wishers on the steps, wanting to be the last to greet him.

I couldn't hear the exchanges over the chatter of the dispersing crowd, the revving of engines and banging of car doors. But I noted the firm handshake, the good eye contact. Like a politician, I thought.

I came face to face with him as the last car backed away from the rosebeds and turned to drive out through the wrought-iron gates. Father Songbird smiled, held out his hand to me, but said nothing. I heard myself say, 'Hello, Father. I know all the titles of your CDs.' That at least was true.

'I hope you enjoyed them,' he said, shaking my hand. 'Mrs...?'

'Molloy,' I said. I felt my face redden. 'My daughter's an opera singer,' I blurted out.

'Molloy,' he said. 'Would that by any chance be Mary Molloy?'

I nodded. I couldn't speak.

He grasped both my hands, leaned towards me and said, 'That's wonderful. I'm delighted to meet you. You're in Dublin for her concert? Will you tell Mary I'm a great fan of hers? Well, well, well.' He dropped my hands and stood back, still holding my gaze. Still smiling. 'You know we sang at the same concert for the Pope?' he said. 'I remember she sang Schubert. *Mein Gott, der ist mein Hirt.* The Lord is my shepherd. Great. His Holiness loved it. She's recorded it, I hope?'

I managed to swallow the frog in my throat.

'It's going to be on her next CD,' I said.

'Fantastic,' he said. 'I'll be first in the queue. Tell me, did she get her great voice from you?'

'No,' I said. 'Mary is my adopted daughter.'

A brief pause. 'You nurtured a great talent,' he said. 'A voice like that is a gift from God.'

'You'd know all about that,' I said.

'Oh, I'm not in the same league.'

'Did you meet Mary at the concert in Rome?'

'Only a brief encounter at the reception afterwards,' he said. 'She was swept away by an admirer. She's beautiful.' Pause. 'Like you, if I may say so.'

I wondered if he was flirting with me. But his expression was serious. There was no give-away gleam in his – I suddenly realised – blue eyes. So Patsy is the one with the brown eyes, I thought, staring at him. He cleared his throat in embarrassment.

I said, 'I'm sorry. I don't often meet people so knowledgeable about Mary. In fact I don't often meet opera singers. I just read about them in magazines and pretend a bit of the glamour rubs off.'

'I'm not an opera singer,' he said. 'More of a concert performer. Perhaps once...' He trailed off. 'And Rathkeeran isn't glamorous.' He smiled again and jerked his head backwards at the grey, suburban sprawl. 'But I keep an eye on the opera world.' Pause. The dark blue eyes suddenly filled with concern. 'Will you tell her I'm praying for her?'

I heard myself say, 'I wonder if you could help me trace Mary's birth parents?'

'What?' Apparently astonished.

'Mary needs to know,' I said, choosing the verb carefully.

'I can appreciate that,' he said, 'but how can I help?' Sounding puzzled.

'You know Patsy Malone,' I said. In more than one sense of the word, I thought to myself.

His mouth stiffened. He said carefully, 'Mrs Molloy, would you like a cup of tea? I think we should continue this conversation in the parochial house.'

He barely waited for my nod of acquiescence before turning to lead the way round the back of the church and through a wooden gate in the perimeter wall to the redbrick rectory beyond. He opened the door and ushered me into the hallway. Pearly light through the stained glass panels in the door spattered pale green and gold Celtic whorls on the thin grey carpet. I felt curiously calm and alert. It was past twelve o'clock but there was no smell of lunch cooking. I wondered where he ate and who would make the tea. He led me down the hallway and steered me into a sitting room. He was still in his vestments. I noticed a curling grey hair on the left shoulder of his green chasuble.

'Make yourself comfortable,' he said. 'I'll just change and get the tea. Or would you prefer coffee?'

'Tea, please,' I said, before he closed the

door and left me wondering what would happen next.

The fire had been set, but not lit. The room was plainly furnished in neutral tones. Whatever money Father Songbird earned from his concerts and CDs wasn't spent on his surroundings, I thought. There were two photographs on the mantelpiece. Father Songbird with the Pope. Father Songbird with Sister Monica. I recognised them from the website. I wondered if he lived alone. The door opened and he backed into the room carrying a tray. Now he was wearing a grey, long-sleeved, casual shirt and a black pullover.

'You're looking at the photographs,' he said, as he turned to face the room. 'I expect you've got a similar one of Mary with the Pope.' He set the tray on a small table beside a beige armchair and gestured to me to sit down.

'Three of us live here,' he said. 'We've no housekeeper. We have to fend for ourselves these days. If we're lucky we get an invitation for Sunday lunch or dinner. And today we've all been lucky.' He laughed.

'I'm keeping you back,' I said.

'Ah, not at all. I'm not expected until half past one and it's only over the road.' He poured tea into a plain white china cup and saucer and handed it to me. 'Help yourself to milk and sugar. I'll not have a cup. I don't want to spoil my lunch.'

While I poured milk into my tea, he settled into the matching armchair opposite me. He leaned forward, hands clasped on his knees.

'Why did you ask me about Patsy Malone?'

'Because you know her. Knew her,' I said.

'Know her,' he said. 'Patsy is an old friend.' His tone was steady. Not giving anything away.

'She's Mary's birth mother,' I said.

He exhaled softly. 'Are you sure?'

'One of the nuns in the home where she was born told me.'

'Monica?' Incredulous.

'No. Someone else. The nun who actually handed Mary over to me. In a solicitor's office in Tullamore.'

He didn't ask how I had tracked her down.

'She remembers Patsy clearly,' I said. 'She told me you brought her to Saint Joseph's. So I assume you know who the father is.'

He got up and took a box of matches from the mantelpiece.

'It's got cold in here,' he said. 'I'll light the fire.' He knelt on one knee, struck a match and applied it to the waxy white edges of two firelighters at the base of the coals. With his back to me he said, 'Patsy is the only person who can tell you that. And she may not want to.'

The smell of paraffin caught my throat as

the firelighters flared into action.

'Mary has a right to know.'

He settled back on his heels, still looking into the fire. Specks of coal dust floated in a beam of sunshine that lay across his back and showed up a strand of hair clinging to his pullover. It was almost within reach.

'Has she contacted Patsy?'

'Not yet.'

'But she's going to.' More a statement than a question. I didn't reply.

He leaned forward, preparing to stand up. Adrenalin surged through my veins.

'Is that a coin?' I said quickly.

He turned his head to look at me, still balanced on his toes.

'There.' I pointed into the hearth.

He hunkered down again to look.

I stretched forward, half out of my chair, and snatched the hair from his pullover.

I thought he would hear the pounding of my heart.

I pinched the hair between the thumb and forefinger of my right hand. Triumphant. With my left hand I found my handbag. I rolled the hair on to a tissue. I prayed I would find it again.

'I don't see anything,' said Father Songbird. 'Where?'

'I'm sorry,' I said. 'Just a trick of the light.'

He stood up. 'Is Mary planning to contact Patsy?'

'I don't know,' I said, breathing normally again.

'I'm worried about the press,' he said, sitting down. 'The paparazzi will pounce on something like this. Particularly at the moment.'

'The church is having a bad press,' I agreed in a level voice.

'Don't I know it?' he said. 'I used to believe there was no such thing as bad publicity. Now I know there is. Still, better these things are out in the open.'

'Better for Mary, too.'

'Good God, no!' he cried. 'That'll be different. The paparazzi will go mad. There'll be a feeding frenzy.'

'At least it's not abusing small boys.'

He looked startled.

'They will make a meal of it,' he said. 'Just the kind of twist they like on a big story.'

I stared at him in horror.

'Read Saint Paul,' he said. 'First letter to the Corinthians, chapter thirteen. You know it.' He recited fluently, *'If I speak without love, I am no more than a gong booming or a cymbal clashing... If I am without love I am nothing... Love is always patient and kind; love is never jealous... Love does not rejoice at wrong-doing, but finds its joy in the truth.'*

He has said this to many people, many times, I thought. I glared at him stonily. Now his face took on a worried expression.

'The paradox of love is that it can lead us into wrongdoing, breaking God's commandments. But God is loving and merciful. Take Psalm 51. David wrote it after seeking God's forgiveness for his adultery. And God forgave him.'

'Adultery?' I said sharply. 'More like fornication.'

'No,' he said. 'It's adultery when one of the...' He swallowed. 'One of the...' Another pause as he rummaged for the right word. 'One of the ... parties,' sounding embarrassed now, 'when one of the parties is married.'

So Patsy was married when she had his baby! I was suddenly desperate to get away from him.

'I'll not keep you any longer,' I said, standing up.

'You sound upset.'

I didn't answer. I moved towards the door. He jumped up and held it open for me.

'Try not to worry.' He followed me up the hallway and reached past me to open the front door. I flinched.

'I've upset you,' he said. 'But please don't worry. These things blow over.'

I almost ran up the path to the gate into the car park, allowing no time for a handshake.

He called after me, 'God bless you. I'll pray for you. And for Mary. Tell her.'

I didn't look back.

Chapter 34

I was agitated after this first encounter with Father Devine. But underlying my agitation was a sense of triumph at the progress I had made. I had all the information I needed to put in my letter to Mary. I had a hair for DNA analysis. The clinching evidence. I pulled in at the parade of shops and bought a packet of envelopes in the newsagents.

In the car, I transferred the hair from Father Songbird into an envelope, sealed it and wrote 'Father D' on the envelope. I looked at it for a moment. I crossed out the D. I transferred the lock of Maggie Kane's hair from the inner pocket of my bag to a second envelope. I didn't need it now. But I couldn't bring myself to throw her hopes away. I put both envelopes back into my handbag. My hand encountered my mobile. I wanted someone to share my triumph and my agitation. I dialled Alma's number.

As soon as she answered, the words tumbled out of me. 'Patsy Malone is definitely Mary's birth mother and I've met Father Songbird!'

'Lena, where are you? Are you in Mayo?' she said. 'I've been trying to ring you. Have you seen...?'

Excitement made me cut in. 'I'm on my way to the airport. Alma! I've met him. I tossed a coin and decided to drive to Dublin instead. Mary's arriving this afternoon. I found Sister Dervla on the Internet. She's a university lecturer. Dr Dervla Jagoe.'

'Good God,' said Alma. 'Dervla Jagoe as in gender roles in Shakespeare?'

'Yes,' I said. 'Yes. I went to see her on the way here. She told me Mary's mother was definitely Patsy Malone. Father Songbird brought her to Saint Joseph's.'

'She's a big name in post-feminist criticism,' Alma said.

'She made everything fall into place.'

I told her how Dervla had overheard Sister Monica's conversation. 'It explains the lot,' I said. 'Monica realised Mary was her brother's child. She wanted her out of the way as quickly as possible.' I paused for effect. 'I went to Mass in Father Songbird's church. I spoke to him afterwards. And he admitted it!' I was tingling with excitement.

'He admitted it?'

'As good as.'

'What did...' Her voice faded, '...say?'

The screen winked 'Low battery.' Damn. I'd forgotten to recharge it.

'He said Patsy was an old friend. And he said not to talk to the press about it.'

'I can ... press ... love it,' Alma said.

296

'...Sunday papers?'

'What?' Her voice was breaking up.

'...Sunday...'

'Alma, you're breaking up. My battery's low.'

'Papers ... today ... hear me now?'

'What?'

'...read ... it,' she said. '...singers ... lives ... drama ... Mary.'

'There's something in the paper about Mary?'

'Hello!' she shouted.

'Hello,' I shouted back. 'Are you still there?'

'No!... Hear?... Magazine... Hello ... hairdressers.' This was getting ridiculous.

'*Hello!* magazine?' I bellowed. 'Something in *Hello!* magazine?'

The line died. The luminous screen went black. I went back into the shop and looked at the Sunday papers along the front of the counter. Nothing left but the tabloids. They were unlikely to be previewing the concert. I checked the magazine rack.

'Have you got *Hello!* magazine?' I said to the boy at the till.

'Is there none on the rack?'

'No. Is there another shop where I could get one around here?'

'There's nothing between here and the airport,' he said.

It took longer to drop off the car than I expected. I wheeled my suitcase through the car park and across the road to the arrivals hall. The tinny echo of the tannoy, announcing the arrival of a flight from Barcelona, briefly drowned the bright hum of conversation. I saw from the board that a flight from Frankfurt had landed. Was it Mary's flight? The 'baggage in hall' sign was not yet illuminated. I had time to go to the shop. I picked up *Hello!* Magazine and a selection of Sunday papers. The commotion broke out as I queued for the till.

Angry shouts. English and Italian. *Attenzione! Bastardo!* Fuck off! *Basta, basta!* Hey! Bang. Clatter. Tinkle. Every head in the queue swivelled right, then further right as a video camera came spinning along the dull brown shine of the floor and crashed into the wall outside the shop. Two men, jabbing at each other, pulling each other's ties, kicking and yelling, lurched into the shop. The queue jumped sideways. Three security guards sprinted across the hall and wrestled the men apart.

'They're all waiting for some film star,' said the woman just ahead of me in the queue.

'I thought she was a singer,' said the man behind me.

About a dozen photographers and three camera crews jostled for position outside barriers of white tape forming a path from the frosted glass doors of the customs hall into the arrivals area. Every thirty seconds or so the automatic door swung open and a small group of travellers emerged, pushing trolleys, mystified by the writhing line of feet and elbows, the impatient photographers swiftly registering their non-celebrity. Most pushed their way quickly along the line, towards the group of relatives, friends and taxi-drivers standing further away. I steered my trolley towards them.

'Here she comes!' *'Qui è!'* 'Watch out!' The photographers surged forward. Groups of chatting relatives turned to look. Three taxi drivers stepped in front of me, holding up cardboard signs, obstructing my view. I angled my face into a three-inch gap and saw a line of security guards, arms linked, shuffling sideways, along the bank of cameras. They were trying to shield two people from the shouts, the blue-white flashes, and the matt-black microphone poles. Two people walking swiftly, almost running, heads down. One dark. One blonde. One Mary.

As they reached the end of the tape, the guards formed a barrier behind them. The photographers trampled each other. I tried to call out. My voice died in my throat. I jabbed my elbows sideways, digging into the bulk of the taxi-drivers. Pushing my way through with my trolley. Gasping for breath.

'Take it easy, missus,' one protested. ''Tis only some fella's bit of fluff.'

I looked back at him in horror as I stumbled after the chase.

The scrum of photographers blocked the entrance to the terminal. I found a gap at the plate-glass window in time to see Mary's head disappearing into the back of a limousine. Her tall, dark-haired companion stepped in after her. I thought I had seen him somewhere before. But where? I leaned my forehead against the glass and closed my eyes as the limousine gathered speed and headed for the ramp marked 'exit'.

Someone was tapping my side. 'Hey, excuse me? Hello?' A child's voice. I turned. A girl of about eight looked up at me.

'You dropped your newspapers,' she said.

'Thank you,' I said, taking the papers. I tried to manufacture a smile but my face felt numb.

The story was in all the papers. I read them in the airport café. The *Observer* had a feature about opera singers whose lives reflected the roles they sang. There was a half-page photograph of Adela Contini in Tosca, captioned: '*As jealous as Floria Tosca.*'

Hello! magazine had a double-page spread of photographs. Mary and Ricardo Marsili, holding hands, blinking at flashbulbs as they emerged from a nightclub in Frankfurt. Adela Contini, alone on a winding, marble staircase, clutching her black-eyed bichon frise. Mary and Ricardo, running a gauntlet of photographers at San Francisco airport.

The tabloids and the *Sunday Telegraph* carried the painful details. *'The affair that set the opera world alight – literally!'* chortled the *Mail on Sunday*. *'Latest drama in a stormy marriage.'*

'Ricardo, star of La Gelosia, *this year's runner-up for best foreign picture at the Oscars, met Mary Molloy when his wife invited her to the Villa Ermosa,'* reported the *Sunday Telegraph*. *'She betrayed my friendship. He betrayed my trust.'* This in the *News of the World*.

They all reported that Adela set fire to the stage curtains in San Francisco and fired blanks at Mary; and that Ricardo and Mary, 'now inseparable', went together to Frankfurt. *'The couple are flying to Dublin where Mary Molloy opens a concert tour of Europe's capital cities with the Frankfurt Symphony Orchestra.'*

A waitress came to clear the table.

'Are you all right?' she said.

'What?' I looked at her through the gauze of tears.

'You look a bit, you know, upset like,' she said. 'Are you all right?'

301

'Yes,' I said dully.

'Only you've been sitting like a statue for the last half hour.'

'Sorry,' I said. 'I didn't realise.'

'Are you sure you're all right?' she said. 'Can I do anything?'

She had a kind face. 'Can you tell me where the nearest telephone is?' I said.

Jack said, 'What's wrong?'

'I've phoned you too early,' I said. 'I thought you mightn't have your phone switched on.'

'You sound awful. Where are you? What's that noise in the background?' I began to cry.

'Mary...' I managed to say through my sobs.

'Good God, Lena, what's happened?'

'I didn't know. I never guessed. I'm at the airport. All the photographers were chasing them. She didn't even see me.'

He exhaled. 'She's all right?'

'Yes.'

'But you're not all right.'

I couldn't speak.

'You poor darling. I thought you knew. Mary said she told you. She told you she was bringing him to Dublin. That's why I thought you'd be shocked.'

I blew my nose. 'She said his name was Rick. I thought he was an American. They chased them like animals! It was awful.'

'I know,' he said. 'It's all over the papers here too.'

'In New Zealand?'

'Adela Contini has sung with Kiri Te Kanawa,' he said. 'According to her, La Contini is wildly temperamental. It's in the *Gisborne Herald*.'

'It will wreck Mary's career,' I said.

'Nonsense. There's no such thing as bad publicity.'

'Yes there is,' I said.

'It will blow over,' he said. 'The press will get bored. Adela Contini is in San Francisco. They're in Dublin. There'll be nothing new to report.'

I thought of Father Songbird saying, 'Just the kind of twist they like on a big story.' He'd known. I thought of Alma, trying to warn me. She'd known.

'The whole world knew except me, Jack.'

'That's not true, Lena. I only heard about him yesterday.'

'He's married, Jack. He'll have to get divorced. They won't be able to get married in church. That's terrible.'

'Who said anything about getting married? I don't think they've known each other that long.'

'Why do you say that? How long has this been going on? Why didn't Mary tell me?'

Jack said, 'Listen, Lena. I think they were

303

just having a fling. Then Adela Contini found out and it all got out of hand. If she hadn't found out, they'd have had their affair and none of us any the wiser about it.'

'Jack! That's an awful thing to say.'

'For God's sake, Lena, Mary's twenty-seven. Do you think she's been living like a nun? He's probably had affairs before. There's a good chance this will blow over. The press will get tired of them, and they'll get tired of each other. It's just a fling. Seven year itch.'

'What about Mary?' I cried.

'Mary needed a bit of romance in her life. He's an attractive man. They're both human.'

'She's going to wreck her life and her career over this man.'

'I don't think so,' Jack said. 'I give it three months. Six months max. You wait and see.'

'You sound sure.' I dried my eyes.

'I am sure.'

I felt a great surge of love. 'Oh, Jack. I wish you were here.'

'So do I,' he said. 'Go and see them. Stay cheerful, and enjoy having your hand kissed.'

Chapter 35

I hurried to the reception desk in the Conrad.

'Mary Molloy, what room is she in, please?'

Three blonde receptionists in emerald-green blazers with gold identity badges moved towards me as one. They looked at me, then at each other. The eldest of the three flashed a professional smile.

'I'm sorry, but we don't divulge room numbers,' she said. She looked about thirty. Her badge said, 'Catherine O'Brien, Chief Receptionist.'

'I'm her mother. She's expecting me,' I said.

Catherine O'Brien took a moment to study me, before motioning me to where the wall met the long sweep of counter. She leaned across the desk towards me, locked my gaze, then slid her eyes sideways towards and back from a group of men armed with cameras, moving in a phalanx towards her colleagues.

'Press,' she whispered. 'They're all over the place. The bar's full of them.' She pulled a pink memo pad towards her, scribbled three numbers on the top square of paper, and handed it to me.

'I've put Ms Molloy and Mr Marsili in one of our suites,' she murmured. 'They won't open the door to anybody without a call first.' She indicated a cream telephone by my elbow, and reapplied her smile, before advancing on her high heels to engage the photographers.

I dialled the room number. Busy. I tried again.

'*Pronto?*' said a man's voice.

My voice was trapped in my rib cage.

'*Prensa,*' said the voice sharply, '*bastardi.*' Click.

I stood for a moment, dismayed and confused. The massed photographers were moving back across the lobby to the bar. Catherine O'Brien glanced at me.

'Engaged,' I mouthed.

She hurried towards me. 'If they find out who you are they'll be all over you,' she said. 'Where are you staying?'

'The Shelbourne,' I said. 'I'll go back and try her from there.'

I had left my mobile on charge in my room. When I tried Mary's number the answering service kicked in. I didn't leave a message. I paced up and down, tired and restless at the same time, feeling angry and excluded. The bedside telephone rang. I sprang forward and lifted the receiver to my ear.

'Mum?'

'I was at the airport,' I said tearfully. 'Are you all right, darling?'

'I'm fine, Mum. Don't worry. Just a minute.' I heard her speak interrogatively in German, before continuing. 'The concert manager is here. He and Eddy have sorted something out with the press.' She sounded excited and in command.

'Eddy?' I said faintly.

'Yes. He's booked into the Shelbourne. He should be there now.'

I heard a knock. 'There's someone at the door,' I said.

'That'll be Eddy. Love you, Mum,' she cried. I stood with the receiver in my hand, feeling stupid. I felt I was in the middle of a frantic dance to which everyone knew the steps, except me. My mouth was dry. My head hurt. I was fighting tears as I replaced the receiver and walked in a daze to the door.

I took one look at Eddy's kind, intelligent face, and began to weep. He took me gently by the arm, and steered me into the armchair by the window. I leaned back. The skin on my face felt salty and tight. Eddy hunted through the mini-bar. I heard the rattle of bottles, the clank of tumblers on the glass-topped coffee table.

'Whiskey, gin or hemlock?'

I attempted a smile.

'That's better,' Eddy said. 'I'm having a whiskey and water. No ice. Same for you?'

I nodded.

'I talked to the concert manager and the PR at the Conrad. We've fixed a press conference for seven o'clock. Time enough for the papers in the morning and the TV tonight. Then we can all have dinner in peace.' He handed me a tumbler of whiskey. 'Cheers.' He pulled over a chair from the dressing table.

'It's just the shock,' I said. 'Mary running past me like a frightened hare. The pack of photographers chasing her. I had no idea, Eddy.' I looked down into the golden liquid. 'How long has it been going on?'

'A month, five weeks?' He shrugged. 'I only found out when Adela Contini got her sacked from *Suor Angelica*.' He downed half his whiskey in one swallow. 'You look surprised,' he said.

'I thought you were great friends.'

'So did I,' he said.

Dusk descended. We sat in silence looking across at Saint Stephen's Green. The park was closing. Three figures emerged through a gate in the railings opposite the window. A young man in a tweed suit, holding a small boy by each hand. The boys, in matching rainbow-striped jerseys, pulled at their father's hands and jumped up and down. Two pairs of entwined lovers wearing college

308

scarves and blue jeans came out of the park and stood laughing and chatting as they waited to cross the road.

'What's he like, Eddy?' I asked.

'I only met him once. Charming. Clever. Moody, I'd say. Women like him.' He downed the rest of his whiskey and stood up. 'The publicity's great for her career. As her agent, of course, I hope the affair lasts till the end of the tour at least.'

Cynicism didn't suit him.

'And as you, Eddy?' I said quietly, looking up at him.

'I'd like to punch him,' he said. 'Excuse me.' He delved into his inside pocket and brought out a mobile phone. It vibrated in his hand. He looked at the green letters on the screen. 'Dietmar,' he informed me. 'The concert manager.' He fastened the phone to his ear. 'Yeah,' he said. 'Right. OK. That's a relief. Thanks, Dietmar.'

He stowed the phone in his jacket.

'The press conference went well. Dinner at eight, in the Conrad. I'll go to my room and change. Meet you downstairs in twenty minutes?'

I stood up and kissed him on the cheek.

'Thanks, Eddy,' I said. 'You're a brick.'

A sad smile crinkled his eyes. 'Steady Eddy,' he said.

Mary jumped up from the round, candlelit

table in the centre of the restaurant and threw her arms round me.

'Mum! It's wonderful to see you.'

The two men on either side of her got to their feet. One was taller than Mary, broad-shouldered and balding.

'Dietmar Eppleman, the tour manager,' Mary said, introducing me. Dietmar bowed. His surprisingly fine-boned hand shot out from a generous cream shirt cuff and shook mine.

The other man was Mary's height, with narrow brown eyes, dark blond hair, and a patrician nose. He took my proffered hand and raised it to his beautifully shaped mouth. I couldn't help laughing. He laughed too.

'All Italian men kiss hands, right?' He had a slight American accent. I guessed he was about forty.

Mary blushed. 'Mum, this is Ricardo Marsili. Rick.'

Her eyes shone. Her hair was piled loosely on top of her head and secured with a black velvet ribbon. She spoke with confidence, despite her blush. It took me a moment to find the word that fitted her. Womanly, I decided with a queer lurch of the heart. That's it. She is no longer girlish.

Rick pulled out a chair for me beside him. Eddy sat on my other side, next to Dietmar. Rick laid a proprietary hand on Mary's forearm, summoned a waiter with a graceful nod of his head, and took charge of ordering.

I am being entertained by my daughter's married lover, I said to myself. I felt unreal. As though I was both on stage, and part of the audience. I looked around the room. No one was paying particular attention to our table. The air was busy with conversation and occasional outbursts of laughter. Mary seemed perfectly at ease, but she was unconsciously tapping her cheek.

Rick talked about food and wine, and commended a wine from his hometown in Piedmont. 'Tell your husband. It's special. Only a few hundred bottles produced every harvest.'

Dietmar explained the mechanics of the tour. 'A 727 cargo plane, or two articulated trucks. Over a hundred trunks for the instruments and concert clothes.'

Eddy chatted to me about his plans for Mary. 'Stockholm is auditioning for *Carmen*,' he said. 'I think she could go for it.'

'Stockholm?' said Rick, overhearing. 'She's way beyond Stockholm. She's going to have a career in films.'

Mary looked uncomfortable. 'I'm not sure about that,' she said. 'I need to talk to Eddy.'

Rick pouted and waved his hand dismissively. Eddy looked pleased. The atmosphere changed. Dietmar said, 'Tomorrow will be a long day. Initial rehearsal at ten.'

The men tussled for the bill. Rick won. He leaned back and laid his hand again upon Mary's arm.

Mary said, 'I'm going to be busy tomorrow, Mum. Eddy has arranged interviews with the *Irish Times* and Irish television. We'll talk after the concert.'

Half of me was disappointed. The other half was relieved. I needed a breathing space. Time to think about what to say to her about Ricardo Marsili, Sister Monica, Father Songbird and Patsy Malone.

Chapter 36

Eddy had gone by the time I came down the next morning. I took a copy of the *Irish Times* from the desk in the lobby to read over breakfast. The report of the press conference was on the inside front page. Five paragraphs and a photograph across four columns. Mary was quoted: *'Obviously my association with Rick made things difficult in San Francisco. But that is all behind me now. I am delighted to have been given the opportunity to sing with one of the world's finest orchestras in a programme of songs I love.'*

'Rick (Ricardo) Marsili said, "The present

situation is difficult and painful for everybody concerned. I hope you will now permit us to get on with our lives." He announced he would be *going to Hollywood in the near future to begin work on a new film to be directed by Martin Scorsese. Ms Molloy would not be drawn on the subject of a possible role in the film.'*

There was little new in the rest of the story. *Suor Angelica* was a sell-out in San Francisco. The American Century concert was sold out in Dublin, and was expected to sell out in every other city on the tour.

The day stretched ahead of me and I had thoughts enough to fill it. The sky threatened rain. I put on my yellow raincoat and walked down Grafton Street, past Trinity College to O'Connell Bridge. On the far side of the bridge, I turned left along the quays.

Rain pitted the fast-moving, mossy brown surface of the Liffey. Questions crowded my mind. Why hadn't Mary told me about Ricardo Marsili? Why hadn't I guessed? Some people were naturally reticent, I supposed. I consoled myself with the recollection that Rosemary's daughter had suddenly produced an eligible, if conventionally boring accountant, long after Rosemary had despaired of her ever finding anybody. Jack hadn't told his parents much about his girlfriends until the day he brought me home. His mother welcoming but astonished. His grandfather pleased and relieved. 'Thought he'd never settle down. My dear, you came right out of left field. I see he waited till he got himself a beauty.'

Was Jack right that this was just an affair that had been outed? Left on its own, it would run its natural course. 'Just a fling.' Did I want to think of Mary as someone who had flings? I never had a fling. Three boyfriends, and then Jack and utter fidelity for thirty-two years. Is that why I had missed the clues?

I crossed the river on a curving, wrought-iron bridge with wooden slats that bounced gently under my feet. The rain had stopped. I was cold, damp, and in need of a hot drink. I caught a whiff of coffee, mingled with the darker smell of peat smoke, and followed my nose to a low-ceilinged pub in a narrow alleyway. I shook myself out of my wet raincoat, ordered a pot of coffee and sat at a table near the fire to address the next question in my head. Should I go to Patsy Malone's concert?

It seemed a more deliberate action than going to see Father Songbird. I was a Catholic, after all. I went to Mass on Sundays. I wasn't a folk or country music fan. But I wasn't intending to speak to her, I told myself. I only wanted to hear her. I was curious. I wanted to assuage my feeling of stupidity. If I had missed clues about

Mary and Rick, this was more than offset by my detective work tracking down Patsy Malone.

I stared at the languid tongues of flame licking the turf, warming my outstretched feet. I could unwind in the warm sensation of a job well done, I thought. There would be none of the nervous fencing I'd done with Father Songbird. I could listen for Mary's voice in the music of Patsy Malone. Should I stay an extra night to see her? Should I toss a coin?

'One punt eighty. Anything else?'

I looked up with a start as the barman pushed a round metal tray with a cafetière, cup and saucer, milk jug and sugar bowl across the counter. He had a round, smooth face and a bald, shiny head.

'I'd say your thoughts are worth more than a penny,' he said.

'I'm just asking myself a few questions,' I said, getting up to take the tray.

He took the bank note I offered and tapped on the till. He pursed his mouth reflectively. 'My mother used to say, if you have to ask, the answer is probably no,' he said. The till slid open. He extracted my change, and handed it to me. 'If that's any help,' he added, with a quick smile.

I took his words as a sign. I would go home, as planned, the next day.

I shopped, took a bus tour of Dublin, visited Trinity College. As I fingered Irish linen and lace, and studied the intricacy of the human figures and animals shimmering on the parchment page of the Book of Kells, I was aware of a slight feeling of disappointment, as though a coin had landed the wrong way.

Chapter 37

At seven thirty, I sat between Eddy and Rick in the front row of the balcony in the concert hall. Amber lights warmed the cream walls and pale wooden seats. I glanced around. Every seat was taken. Donal was edging towards the middle of a row in the stalls below me. He looked up and waved before sitting down. I opened the programme. A page had been inserted with a biography and photograph of Mary. I wanted to stand up and shout, 'Look, everybody! She's my daughter!' I glanced at the programme. Mary was opening the second half with Six Songs by George Gershwin.

The orchestra filed in to enthusiastic applause. The leader took his place. The audience stopped clapping and settled down in their seats. The hum, bumpum, oompah sounds of tuning filled the air. The leader nodded in satisfaction. Silence. Then louder clapping as the conductor entered, shook hands with the leader, bowed, and took his place on the podium. Relaxed by the familiar routine, I was hardly conscious of Eddy and Rick on either side of me as I lost myself in the music.

'Are you nervous for her?' Donal said, as we waited for Eddy to fetch our drinks during the interval. Rick had gone backstage.

'She's been a soloist before,' I said, 'but this is big. I wish Alma had been able to stay for it.' I paused, before adding, 'Did she tell you about my conversation with Father Songbird?'

Donal nodded. 'I'm surprised,' he said, in a mild tone. 'I must say I didn't think he had it in him,'

'I thought you were trying to protect your brother's old friend,' I said.

He looked away. 'No,' he said. 'It wasn't that.' Before he could add anything else, Eddy arrived, all elbows, his hands around three flutes of champagne. 'Right ho!' he said. 'Time for a toast. To Mary!'

We stood in the shimmer of the crystal chandelier that lit the stairwell, and raised our glasses in the air.

Generous applause greeted Mary's appearance on the platform. Her bare shoulders gleamed above a bodice of green velvet and a full skirt of green shot silk. She wore elbow length black gloves. A diamante clasp in her artfully tousled hair sparkled in the spotlight. Eddy sighed. Rick murmured, 'Bella.'

The conductor turned to the orchestra, raised his baton, and glanced at Mary. The strings began a wistful introduction to 'Someone to Watch over Me.' Mary's voice flowed, sweet as honey, into golden space.

'There's a somebody I'm longing to see:
I hope that he
Turns out to be
Someone who'll watch over me.'

A ripple of delight ran around the auditorium when she began the second song.

'The way you sip your tea,
The mem'ry of all that–
Oh no they can't take that away from me.'

My feet were already longing to tap. By the time Mary began the last song, I could sense the rest of the audience wanted to get up and dance.

'I got rhythm,
I got music,
I got my man–
Who could ask for anything more?'

Mary seemed to float on the music, totally in tune with the exuberance of the song.

Stamping feet and whistles joined the clapping when she finished, arms outstretched. We clapped until our hands were sore. I heard the snap of a seat folding back.

I turned around. Three rows away, directly behind me, Father Songbird was on his feet. Seats banged as row after row stood up, calling 'More!' When Mary was called back for the third time, she exchanged a nod with the conductor. The audience fell silent, resumed their seats. She began to sing 'Summertime.'

'One of these mornings you going to rise up
  singing
Then you'll spread your wings and you'll take
  the sky…
But 'til that morning, there's a nothing can
  harm you,
With Mammy and Daddy standing by.'

I wondered if Patsy Malone was in the audience. Apart from the fading Polaroid image, I had no idea what she looked like. I glanced over my shoulder at Father Devine. He was sitting between two priests in dog collars.

Mary retreated from the stage. The applause died away. I tried to compose myself to listen to Bernstein's 'Symphonic Dances.' But my ease was gone.

At the reception after the concert, Mary entered the room to more applause. She had changed into a short black velvet skirt, and loosened her hair to tumble around her shoulders. She took my hands and leaned towards me, skipping with delight on impossibly high-heeled shoes.

'I was good, Mum. I know I was good,' she whispered.

Concertgoers congregated around us, clutching programmes for Mary to sign. I kissed her, and began to weave through groups of chatting guests in search of Donal. When I came back with him, the crowd around Mary was beginning to break up.

'You were fantastic,' Donal said, when I introduced him. 'Alma's booked for your concert in Paris. I'm going to join her. I'm really looking forward to hearing you again.'

'I wouldn't be offended if Alma missed the housewarming,' I said, surprised and pleased.

'I like Paris,' said Donal. 'It's as easy for me to get there as London.'

'There goes a man in love,' Mary said, after he took his leave of us.

That was my cue. 'Mary,' I began hesitantly. But her eyes were roaming the room. A cluster of female violinists surrounded Rick. He was signing autographs. She waved to him, and said, in a distracted manner, 'We'll have a real talk, Mum, I promise. When the tour's finished, I'll come for the weekend and see the new house, and we'll talk properly.'

I went to the cloakroom to collect my coat. When I returned, Mary was talking to Father Songbird. My mouth dried. Mary called, 'Mum, come and meet Father Devine!'

'Frank to you,' I heard him say. 'Call me Frank.'

I moved towards them on heavy, mechanical feet.

'We've met,' he said.

Mary looked puzzled.

'Your mother came to Mass at Rathkeeran yesterday. We spoke afterwards.' He gave her a bright, unembarrassed smile.

Their eyes were level. Mary beamed back at him. 'Frank and I sang at the concert for the Pope,' she said to me. 'He sang Schubert too. *Ave Maria*. Magnificent.'

I fixed what I hoped was a smile to my face.

'You have a great future in opera, Mary,' he said in a serious tone. 'What's this I've been reading about Hollywood?'

'Silly speculation,' she said. 'I'm a singer. It's in my blood.'

A pause. He nodded with satisfaction.

Rick waved his fans goodbye and beckoned to Mary.

'Excuse me,' she said. 'I'll be back in a moment.'

Rick held out his arms. Mary stepped into his embrace. He spoke softly into her ear. Father Devine, regarding them, said quietly, 'Hate the sin and love the sinner.'

I turned to glare at him as I wrestled with

my coat. He was still looking at Mary as he gathered the shoulders of my coat to help me. 'Sins can be forgiven,' he murmured. 'Remember that.'

My left arm found the sleeve and slid through the silky lining. He took my right hand and said, 'She's a great girl. Try not to worry. Goodbye, now.' He waved farewell to Mary, and headed for the door. A cool gust of air invaded the room as he pushed through the door to the lobby.

Mary returned to my side. 'Wasn't Frank nice?' she said, happily. The chandelier tinkled faintly, above my head. A million particles of light seemed to swirl and stop. She likes him. I felt a great calm descend upon me. That's it, I thought. Everything will be all right now. He will speak to Patsy Malone. She will contact Mary. I can confess the whole story to Jack. Moisture returned to my mouth. 'I'd like to go home now,' I said.

Chapter 38

Alma met me at Heathrow the following afternoon. 'You seem pretty relaxed about it,' she said, when I finished telling her about meeting Ricardo Marsili and Father Devine.

'I feel OK about it all,' I said. 'I even feel OK about Sister Monica. I don't want to crow over her any more.'

The M4 was closed. We were driving along the industrial belt around Slough in a light drizzle. I closed my eyes to picture black rocks and a wild sea and listened to the rhythmic swish of the wipers against the windscreen.

Alma said quietly, 'Will you try again to find your own birth parents, Lena?'

'It's too late,' I said. 'I'm just glad I was able to do it for Mary.'

On Wednesday morning I collected the keys of the new house from the solicitor and oversaw the delivery of our furniture. Janet and Rosemary arrived with a bunch of bronze and gold chrysanthemums, a packet of tea, a litre of milk and a freshly baked loaf.

'How was Ireland?'

'Did you have a nice time?'

As we moved from room to room, checking labels and unrolling rugs, I rhapsodised about the fulmars flying high above the Cliffs of Moher, the stone-walled fields sweeping gently to the pebbled shore, and the first-class cooking of Eileen Collins. I knew they were longing to ask about Mary, but I wickedly gave them no opportunity until we had finished our tour of the house and they had made the appropriate approving noises about the view over the Thames, the sloping garden, and the sunny kitchen. As I poured tea, I said, 'Mary's Dublin concert was a great success.'

'She wasn't upset by all the newspaper stories?' said Rosemary.

'Did you meet him?' said Janet. 'Mary's...'

'Lover? He's charming,' I said airily. 'But I think this is just an affair that has been outed. Left alone it would have run its course. Now all the fuss has died down, it probably will.'

I gave no hint of Alma's conquest. My discovery of Mary's birth mother stayed a proud secret in my heart.

When they left, in a flurry of good wishes, I stood contentedly in the gleaming kitchen and telephoned Jack.

'Everything fits,' I said. 'You're the only thing missing.'

'Not for long,' he said. 'I'll be back on Sunday morning.'

'I have a lot to tell you,' I said. Feeling comfortable. Not needing to explain it all on the telephone. My heart beating peacefully. I would light a fire in the sitting room, I thought. I would snuggle against him on the sofa, and tell him the whole story. Jack would shake his head and say I told you not to do it, but I suppose it has all turned out for the best. I can't be surprised at anything the clergy do these days. Mary's not easily shocked. I'm glad she likes him. Jack would stroke my hair. I would be absolved.

Jack was talking, 'Find out what's on.'

'What? Sorry. I was daydreaming.'

'Next week. When I'm over my jet lag. Let's go out. A concert. The theatre.'

'All right,' I said. 'I'll have a look.'

'What if Patsy Malone doesn't get in contact with Mary?' Alma asked that evening.

'I'm going to put it all in a letter,' I said, cutting a slice of apple pie. 'Including the hair. For DNA testing. Though I don't suppose she'll need it.'

'Won't you be tempted to tell her?'

'I can keep a secret.'

Alma said, 'One thing I learned when I was having the affair with Gerry. You don't keep secrets. Secrets keep you.'

Alma's question unsettled me. I found it hard to sleep that night. I had prepared myself for Mary's telephone call to tell me Patsy Malone had been in touch. I had even imagined the conversation. Mary's wonder and gratitude. Her report of Patsy's joy. Now I could feel myself being dragged into a vortex of doubt. What if Patsy Malone didn't get in touch? What if Mary never said she wanted to trace her birth parents? Could I really spend the rest of my life keeping this knowledge to myself?

I burrowed deeper into the bed and pulled the duvet around me. The pillow felt hot and damp. I turned it over. Jack will know what to do, I said to myself. When I've told him, he can decide. The thought calmed me. I fell asleep.

On Friday afternoon, I was on a stepladder in the sitting room, hooking a curtain to the window rail, when a rattle, followed by a series of thuds, announced a second delivery of post.

I carried the pile of envelopes into the kitchen, made a cup of tea, and sat at the table to open them. More cards wishing us happiness in our new home, a garden catalogue, a local business directory, a bank statement and a brochure from Reading Arts. I looked through the brochure as I sipped my tea. The Hexagon; the town hall; South Street. I put down my cup and pressed my knuckles on the spine of the brochure to flatten the pages. City of Birmingham Symphony Orchestra; the Tokyo String Quartet; Patsy Malone, plus support.

Patsy Malone! Playing at South Street arts centre! I checked the date. Saturday night.

'Patsy Malone on the road again, and

attracting a huge amount of interest for her first British tour since the 1970s. Her unique blend of country and folk is rooted deep in the lyrical tradition of the west of Ireland.'

I studied the black and white photograph. Half the size of a postcard. Head and shoulders. Short, well-cut hair, a thoughtful expression, delicate ear lobes.

I sat back in my chair and considered this second chance to see Patsy Malone. I really wanted Jack's advice. But it was the middle of the night in New Zealand. He needed his sleep. He was going to fly from Dunedin to Auckland, and then non-stop to Heathrow. I wouldn't be able to reach him once he was airborne. I would have to catch him before he boarded the flight in Dunedin.

When I telephoned that night, Jack's mobile was switched off. 'What do you think?' I said to Alma. 'Should I go? Should I speak to her?'

Alma cut a wedge from the camembert and set it on her plate.

'You didn't want me to contact people when we were in Ireland,' I said. 'That day on the rocks? Remember?'

She coloured. 'I just didn't want you to get hurt,' she said. 'Things are straightforward now.'

'Come with me,' I said. 'Moral support.'

'What are you planning to do?'

'I just want to see her,' I said. 'And maybe get an address.'

'If that's all,' she said. 'I'll come.'

Chapter 39

Alma and I bagged the last two seats at a table near the stage in South Street arts centre. The space between the stage and the bar was occupied by about fifteen tables, each seating between six and eight people. There was standing room for a few more at the bar.

A single spotlight followed a small, female figure on to the stage. The figure reached centre stage and stood for a moment beside a gleaming guitar, half her size, on its stand. She lifted her head. The spotlight encircled the face of Patsy Malone. A wide, dimpled smile. 'Hello, everybody!' A pause. She wore blue jeans with high-heeled boots, a white silk shirt and a spangled denim jacket. She looked about forty-five. Her short, red hair showed no traces of grey. Impossible to see the colour of her eyes. 'And a special hello to my friends Len and Nancy who've come all the way from Swindon to be here tonight!' The young couple sitting beside Alma waved excitedly.

The circle of light flared into colour. Patsy Malone hefted the guitar from its stand, adjusted the tuning, played an introductory chord, and began to sing. I heard Mary's voice echo in the shadows above the stage. Mary's voice, with a smoky edge and a smaller range, but at its centre the same purity of tone, and the familiar, rounded sweetness of the top notes. She had, too, the attention to phrasing that singles out the perfectionist.

'She's good,' I whispered to Alma. Patsy's Swindon friends smiled and gave me the thumbs-up.

A mix of emotions churned inside me. Enjoyment. Relief. Jealousy. Mary would like her. Love her. Patsy looks honest. Sings with sincerity.

She sang about love and betrayal, death and emigration, dreams and disappointments. The stuff of opera, I thought to myself, calmer now. Young girls moved through fairs, stood in gardens, and waved at departing lovers. She sang old and new Irish folk songs, and country and western favourites. I recognised some of them. Jack was a fan of Patsy Cline and sometimes played country music when he was driving.

The audience clapped, whistled and demanded encores with shouts and stamping feet. When she returned to the stage for the third time, Patsy Malone said, 'This is one of the first songs I ever recorded, nearly thirty years ago, when I began my career with the Melody Kings Showband.'

A memory stirred in the deepest recesses of my mind. Patsy began to sing,

'I don't want your lonely mansion with a tear in every room,
All I want's the love you've promised beneath the haloed moon.
But you think I should be happy with your money and your name,
And hide myself in sorrow while you play your cheatin' game'.

I tried to wrestle the elusive memory to the ground.

'Silver thread and golden needles cannot mend this heart of mine.'

She hoisted the guitar above her head with both hands. 'Bye, everybody! *Slán abhaile!* Safe home! Thank you very much!' Lights came on in the emptying hall.

Alma said, 'Are you all right Lena? You've gone white.'

I felt tightness in my ribs. The memory I hadn't been able to pin down was jumping around in my brain.

'She's coming to speak to us,' a voice said. Patsy's high-heeled boots click-clacked across the wooden floor. This wasn't in the script. I didn't want to meet her. Something was bothering me.

Patsy's voice, a soft, quick brogue, lacked

the dark edge of her singing voice. ''Tis great to see you. How's everybody at home?'

Alma was helping me to my feet.

Patsy said, 'Is your friend not well? Can I get her a glass of water?'

'No, thank you. I'll be all right when I get outside.' I raised my head to acknowledge her offer and looked straight into her cornflower-blue eyes.

A man's voice barked in my head. 'Two blue-eyed people can't have a brown-eyed child. Chance in a million.'

I said out loud, 'Two blue-eyed people can't have a brown-eyed child.'

'What?' Startled.

I stared at her like an idiot, my brain frantically processing information. Father Devine has blue eyes. Patsy Malone has blue eyes. My mind screaming, 'Stop! Something's wrong! Say something!'

'Nice to meet you,' I said. 'I enjoyed the concert.'

'What did you say?'

'Nice to meet you. I enjoyed the concert.'

'Before that. Something about blue-eyed babies and brown-eyed mothers.'

Patsy's expression dared me to deny I'd said it. Alma's grip tightened on my arm. Patsy's two friends looked at each other, baffled by our lunatic exchange.

Patsy said to them, 'Will you go ahead and I'll see you in the hotel?'

She stood in front of me, arms folded. 'Why did you say that?' she said.

In for a penny, in for a pound, I said to myself.

In a low voice I said, 'I adopted a brown-eyed baby girl. But her mother has blue eyes.'

Patsy stiffened. Stared at me as her brightness faded. 'Wait here,' she said. She hurried after her friends and spoke briefly to them.

Alma said, 'Would you like me to wait in the car?'

I nodded, and sat down again.

Three men in shirtsleeves came into the hall and started pushing tables to one side and stacking chairs. As she walked back towards me, Patsy called out, 'Can you give us a few minutes, boys?'

'That's OK, Patsy,' one of them called back. 'We won't be locking up for another half-hour. We'll load your stuff in the van for you.'

'Thanks a million,' she said. 'Now,' turning to me, voice composed, 'what's all this about brown-eyed babies?'

She stood in the space between the table and the stage. Arms folded again, head cocked, eyes wary.

'Two blue-eyed people cannot have a brown-eyed child,' I said.

'So?'

I felt tired. 'You have blue eyes,' I said. 'My adopted daughter has brown eyes. I thought you were her birth mother. But you have blue eyes. I'm sorry. I seem to be getting everything wrong these days.'

'When is her birthday?' Patsy said quietly.

'Mary was twenty-seven on the tenth of August this year,' I said, wearily. 'That's the date on the certificate they gave me.'

Patsy dropped her arms. She stood pale and still as a statue.

'My daughter was born at ten minutes past three on the tenth of August, twenty-seven years ago.'

Again, that tightness in my ribs. I managed to say, 'Where?'

'In a home for unmarried mothers, near Tullamore.'

I tried to think clearly, but everything was jumbling up.

She said, 'Funny thing. I've imagined this moment, countless times. But I always imagined it with her.' A tear ran down her cheek. 'I need to sit down.'

She sat down at the table. Just one empty chair separated us. She stared straight ahead at the stage. 'Tell me about her,' she said.

'She's an opera singer,' I said. 'Her name is Mary Molloy.'

'That's funny,' said Patsy. A half-smile creased her cheek.

'Not really,' I said. 'It's in her genes. Bound to be a singer.'

She looked at me oddly, not smiling. 'Does

333

she know about me?'

'I'm sorry,' I said. 'I shouldn't have come. I didn't mean to say anything. I didn't know you would come over to this table. I was so surprised to see you had blue eyes it just popped out.'

Now she looked mystified.

'I thought...' I began in confusion. 'Well, he brought you to Saint Joseph's. I went to see him. He has blue eyes.'

'What are you saying? Who has blue eyes?'

'Father Frank Devine,' I said. 'The singing priest.'

We stared at each other. I felt hot waves of blood rushing to my face.

'What?'

She dropped her head into her hands, shaking it from side to side. Her shoulders quivered. She was laughing!

'I don't believe it!' She shook her head again and laughed out loud. 'You thought... Jeez... I don't believe it. My God. You thought it was Frank Devine?'

I felt I was in the middle of some mad circus.

'Frank's not interested in women. He's the kindest soul in the world. A good person. An old friend. But he's not... I can't believe you thought...'

I managed to say, 'I'm not the only one... It's just ... well, he brought you to Saint Joseph's. He kept ringing up about you ...

everybody thought...'

She was still shaking her head from side to side in astonishment.

She said, 'I've known Frank since I was a teenager. We were two misfits in the same small town. Both mad about music and playing in bands. Frank used to sneak out of his grandparents' house. We'd hitch a lift to Dundalk and play in a pub.'

I swallowed. Tried to quell a rising tide of panic.

'When I got pregnant, I'd nobody else to go to. The baby's father didn't want to know.' She shrugged her shoulders. '"Brown Eyed Handsome Man." The song could have been written for him.'

That bothersome memory jumping around my brain again. Impossible to pin down. I felt hot.

Patsy said, 'Chuck Berry. I don't sing it much. You'll appreciate why.' She paused. 'Oh, no. Not Frank. Not the priest. But just as big a cliché. The married businessman. Only I didn't know he was married at first. Funny thing was, I knew I was pregnant when I couldn't stand the sight of what he was buying and selling. Smoked salmon.'

Her voice seemed to be coming from the other end of a tunnel.

'I went to Frank for help.' She was looking at me strangely, 'Are you all right?'

From far away came the sound of a chair

scraping the floor, toppling with a crash. A distant voice said, 'Molloy. That's funny.'

Darts of light pierced my eyeballs. My heart thudded to a stop.

Chapter 40

Voices a long way off. Coming closer. Sounding worried. A man's voice, in command mode.

'Give her a bit of space, there. Open the fire exit, let some air in. Get some water from the bar. What happened? Did she bang her head?'

Patsy's voice, above me.

'She just keeled over. Buckled at the knees. I don't think she banged her head. I got a hold of her as she fell.'

A cool hand on my brow. Patsy's voice beside my ear.

'She's fierce hot.'

I realised I was lying on the floor. I pressed my left hand on to the dusty boards and raised myself on my right elbow. The chair lay awkwardly beside me, its black legs sticking up like an upturned beetle.

Patsy helped me to sit up. I looked around. A man in shirtsleeves was punching numbers into a mobile phone. Another was hurrying towards me with a glass of water. Cold air gusted through the fire exit doors.

'I'm calling an ambulance,' said the man with the mobile phone.

'No, please. I'm all right. I just fainted. It was the heat. I'm all right really.' Every nerve and muscle concentrated on not bursting into tears. My head throbbing.

'Are you sure you're all right? I can have an ambulance here in minutes,' the man said.

'No, really. I'm OK. Just a glass of water please.' I tried to hide the effort it took to speak.

Patsy crouched on the floor beside me. 'In these scenes I'm supposed to be the one who faints.' She had no idea.

She took the glass of water and handed it to me. I drank from it, sitting on the floor. I avoided her eyes.

'I'm sorry to have caused such a fuss.'

'Well, if you're sure,' said the man with the mobile phone. He righted the chair. Patsy helped me to my feet and steered me gently on to it. Through the blurry beginning of tears I saw her motion the men to leave. She put her arm around my shoulder. I began to cry. Great, heaving sobs. I cried as though my heart would break.

'It's all right,' said Patsy Malone. 'Everything will be all right.'

A spurt of anger at her glib optimism

helped me gather the remnants of my self-control. Twisting sideways in the chair, I reached down to the floor for my handbag.

'Would you like to see a photograph?' I said. I slid Mary's publicity photograph from the folder and offered it to Patsy.

She took it as though it was made of gossamer, laid it on the table, placed her hands on either side of it, and bent her head to study it. After a long pause she lifted her head and said quietly, 'She's beautiful.'

She bent over the photograph again, before adding in a sad tone, 'She doesn't look a bit like me. She's the spitting image of her father. He'll never be dead while she's alive.' She hadn't made the connection between me and Jack.

I dragged words from the hollow space inside me and forced a false smile. 'What was he like?'

The caretaker, shuffling his feet behind us, said, 'Excuse me, Patsy. I need to lock up the hall.'

Patsy stood up. 'We can talk in the van, if you like.'

I followed her out to the car park. We sat in the front of her white transit van. Patsy smoking. Her suitcases and guitar and stage equipment stored in the back. She travelled alone.

'I met him in O'Connor's in Doolin,' Patsy said. 'It was a great place for traditional music. Still is. I'd seen him come in on his own a few times. One night I sang a song. "The Nightingale". He came over to compliment me. We got talking.'

'He made a date?'

'Not exactly,' she said, turning to blow smoke through the open window at her side. 'I was always in O'Connor's on a Monday night. I was playing the dancehalls with the Melody Kings. There were no dances on a Monday night.'

'When did you start sleeping with him?' I said. Trying to sound casual. If she thought the question intrusive, she gave no sign.

'About the fourth time I saw him. I took him to a traditional music session in Inagh. It went on till about four in the morning. I had no way of getting back to my flat. He took me to his hotel.'

'How long did it go on?'

'About four months,' she said. 'He'd ring up and say he was coming over. I'd stay the Monday night with him in the hotel.'

Mr Monday, I thought.

'You'd stay in his room without paying?'

'Oh, no.' Shocked. 'That was only the first time. After that, he booked a double room.' She was straightforward. Unemotional. 'He even came to a couple of dances when we were playing.'

'You didn't know he was married?'

'Not the first time.'

'Were you in love with him?'

'I suppose I was,' she said. 'He was,' she paused while she selected the right word, 'exotic. He was exotic to me. Tall, blond, English accent. Like yours. But he loved the music and he wasn't afraid to join in. He played the piano in the sessions a few times. He sang too. "The Auld Triangle".' She gave a short laugh.

'Was he in love with you?'

She was looking straight ahead, her profile in shadow. 'For a time,' she said. 'I like to think our child was a child of love.'

Suddenly I wanted the conversation to stop, but Patsy had found the tempo of her story. Had I not been there, she would have continued talking to the night and the silent street. I felt as though I was outside the van, watching myself inside, in the passenger seat, striking a match for Patsy as she took another cigarette from the packet on the dashboard.

'I never thought he would leave her. I never wanted him to. I thought I could be a kind of secret orchard. Until I got pregnant. I don't know how it happened.'

'The usual way, I suppose.'

She seemed not to hear the bitterness in my voice. She continued in the same, calm, musical voice. 'He said you can't have a baby. It would kill my wife. She can't get pregnant. It was the first thing he said. He was phoning from England. He was frantic. Then I knew I would be on my own. So I went to see Frank. He said he would help me. The next time Jack phoned, I told him I'd lost the baby.'

The trembling began behind my cheek-bones, travelled in a wave down my shoulders, my back, my stomach. 'Did he believe you?'

'I think he wanted to believe me,' Patsy said slowly. 'When he rang that last time he was beside himself. When I said I'd lost the baby he said, "Thank God." Then he said, "That's a terrible thing to say." He was nearly crying on the phone.'

And then I really was inside the van. The leather seat sticking to the back of my knees. My hands reaching for the solidity of the dashboard. I cried out, 'Swear to me he didn't know!'

Patsy turned towards me. Harsh yellow light from a streetlamp fell on her puzzled face. 'What?'

I tried to keep my voice steady. 'Did he know you were still pregnant?'

She was staring at me, horrified.

'Did you tell him you were going to Saint Joseph's?' Insistent now.

She said it slowly. Not moving. 'Molloy.' I could feel the stillness. The van was a capsule, suspended in time. 'I thought it was a coincidence.'

'Tell me, Patsy. I have to know.'

'He got my baby,' she said. 'Our baby. His baby.' Bewildered. Her voice rising. 'I don't believe it!' she cried. She wrapped her arms round herself and rocked back and forward in the seat.

'How many people knew you went to Saint Joseph's?' I said.

'Stop. I can't think,' she cried, still rocking.

'Did Jack know?'

Her breath came in great, shuddering gasps.

'Did Jack know?' I repeated.

The rocking stopped. 'I never spoke to him again,' she said.

I imagined Jack telephoning her flat, asking about her.

'Where were you living? Did you have flatmates?'

'I shared a flat in Ennis with a girl called Carmel,' Patsy said, lifelessly. 'I've lost contact with her. She went to England.'

'Damn you, Jack,' I shouted, beating my fists on the dashboard.

Patsy resumed her rocking, shivering now. 'It's not fair. He got her. I lost her.'

'The only winner is Jack,' I said.

The tip of Alma's cigarette glowed behind the windscreen twenty yards away. I can't keep Alma waiting all night, I thought distractedly. I reached for the handle of the door, preparing to descend from the van.

'What are you going to do?' Patsy said.

'I don't know.' I looked at her pale, unhappy face. 'Will you be all right?'

'I'll phone my husband,' she said.

I was relieved there was someone she could speak to.

'Are you going to contact Mary?'

Patsy bit her lip before replying, 'It's up to her. Now I know where she is, who she is, I can follow her. Keep cuttings. It's more than I expected, or even hoped for. When she's ready, she'll get in touch.' Her voice was tired. 'I assume you're going to tell her about me.'

'I'll leave that to Jack,' I said.

Chapter 41

Alma refused to drive me to the airport unless I told Jack where I was going and why.

'Fine. I'll take a taxi.'

'Lena, you can't just vanish with no explanation. Whatever he's done.'

'I'm not vanishing. I'm going to La Colline.'

'How is Jack supposed to know that? The first thing he'll do when he finds you're not at the airport to meet him, and you're not at home, is telephone me. What am I supposed to say?'

'I don't care,' I said.

'Lena, listen to me. I understand why you want to go away. I can only try to imagine how you're feeling. But I cannot be the one to tell Jack why his wife has left home and won't speak to him.'

'You knew.'

She said gently, 'I didn't know. Donal guessed. He saw the resemblance. He picked up on the fact that Jack travelled to Ireland a lot around the time Mary was born.'

'Why didn't you say something, Alma? You and Donal speculating behind my back, saying nothing. What kind of a friend does that?'

'A worried friend,' she said. 'What was I supposed to say? Have you noticed your adopted daughter looks like your husband? What if we were wrong? And then you told me Mary's father was definitely Father Whatshisname, Thornbird.'

'Father Devine.'

'Whatever.'

'I have to get away, Alma. I can't move into the house with Jack. I need time to think.'

'Then tell him that,' she said.

I drove to the new house, went to the kitchen, unlocked the door to the garage, found the light switch. The boxes were stacked in a corner. I found the box marked A–M and took out *The Melody Kings: Ireland's Premier Showband with Ireland's Queen of Song*. I removed a large photograph from a box of albums. Mary, two years old, in a pink frock, sitting on the sofa between Jack and me. Then I took scissors, sellotape and a felt-tipped pen from the box marked Study. I laid the record album and the photograph on the kitchen table, and cut myself out of the photograph. Cold anger kept the tears at bay. I cut Patsy-sitting-on-the-wall from the album cover and sellotaped her into the empty space. I put the photograph into a foolscap envelope and wrote in capital letters with a black felt-tipped pen, I KNOW PATSY MALONE IS THE MOTHER OF YOUR CHILD. HOW COULD YOU DO THIS TO ME? ALMA KNOWS WHERE I AM.

Alma was waiting up for me when I got back. 'I've left him a note. The keys are under a flower pot.'

'What about Mary?' she said.

'I can't think, Alma!' I shouted at her. 'I can't breathe. I have to get away. I have to work this out. Please.'

She put her arms around me. 'It's all right, Lena,' she said. 'It's all right.'

'It's not all right,' I said. 'I don't know if it will ever be right again.'

Chapter 42

I could hear the telephone ringing as I got out of the taxi in La Colline. I let it ring while I paid the taxi-driver, unlocked the front door, and set my suitcase down in the hallway. When I heard Jack's voice I replaced the receiver.

For the first few days I just lay in bed, only getting up to make a cup of coffee and spread some jam on a cracker. After a while I thought I should eat some vegetables and fruit so I drove to the supermarket as soon as it was dark. It was easier to brave its bright, impersonal aisles than the *boulangerie*, the *alimentation* and the *boucherie* in the village. When I heard the church bells ringing and realised it was Sunday, I stayed in bed. I didn't want to talk to anybody. 'God forgive me,' I whispered, and turned my face to the wall.

Alma telephoned morning and night that first week. 'You don't have to call every day,' I said. 'I'm not suicidal. Murderous, maybe. But not suicidal.' I was immediately ashamed of my ingratitude. 'I'm sorry, Alma,' I said tiredly.

Mary telephoned from Stockholm. She

said in a small voice, 'Dad's told me every-thing. Are you going to talk to me again?'

'What's everything?' I said.

'I know about Patsy Malone. I know about Dad and her.'

I imagined her shock, and her elation. Jealousy soured my tears. Mary said, 'Don't cry, Mum.' She began to cry as well. 'Why didn't you tell me you were looking for her? Why did you run away? Are you going to go back? Are you going to stay in La Colline?'

The concert tour didn't end until the last week of November. I knew I wouldn't see her before then. What could I say on the telephone? That her father had made a fool of three women? Mary, Patsy and me?

The answering machine allowed me to monitor my calls. Jack left messages every day for the first two weeks. They were nearly all the same. Please come home. If I come out will you speak to me? Please? Lift the phone. Please. Then he sent letters. I didn't open them. I knew I would have to com-municate with him eventually, but I needed to get everything straight in my head first. To try to make sense of it all. To try to find some meaning in a life turned upside down. Scraps of memory, snatches of conversations surfaced. Jack, arriving at Mama's funeral. 'I'm sorry Lena. I should have come sooner.' Telephone calls from the west of Ireland. 'I'll have to stay over the weekend. I can't see the distributors until Tuesday.'

I had to talk to him. I didn't want to talk to him. Could I believe anything he told me? The worm of mistrust was in my brain, burrowing away. I wanted to know. I didn't want to know.

At the beginning of November, Alma and Donal went to Paris for Mary's concert. They flew down afterwards to see me. Alma said, 'You need fresh air.' They steered me round the village like two nurses with a trolley. It was the first time I had been out of the house in daylight. They went to the *marché provençal* in Antibes and brought back mounds of vegetables and fruit, and fish that smelled of the sea. Donal tried to make bouillabaisse. I watched him struggle for about five minutes, before taking over and joining in the laughter.

'That's better,' Alma said.

We hiked along a path above the village. We didn't talk much until we reached a plateau with a view of the Alpes Maritimes and the Baie Des Anges. I took in great lungfuls of air. My fingers traced the line of mountains engraved on a table of rock.

'You guessed,' I said to Donal. 'It was the photograph, wasn't it?'

'She's his spitting image,' he said. His spitting image. In twenty-seven years I never noticed.

'Supposing Jack knew,' I said. 'Supposing he arranged it all with Sister Monica? Supposing that's why she wouldn't tell me anything? Oh God, I will go mad.'

Alma said, 'Stop torturing yourself, Lena. I can see Jack having an affair. I can't see him organising a conspiracy.'

Donal said, 'The nun thought the baby was her brother's. She wanted it out of her sight, and preferably out of the country. That's the only thing that makes sense. Think about it.'

'I'll go and see her,' I said.

I thought he would try to dissuade me. Instead he said, 'I pity the poor woman. All these years she's carried the burden of a sin that was never committed. It estranged her from her brother. It lay between them, unmentionable. She probably agonised about what to do when she found out she was dying. Whether to tell him where his daughter was. It explains her telephone call.'

I felt ashamed. I hadn't thought of it that way. 'Thank you, Donal.' I said.

That evening, I waved Donal and Alma goodbye at Nice airport, and booked a flight to Dublin the following day.

Chapter 43

Sister Monica was playing the Chopin prelude in E minor as I walked through the hallway of Saint Joseph's and climbed the stairs towards her office. As I stepped on to the landing, she sensed my presence. Her fingers faltered for a moment, before continuing to strike the plangent chords until the end of the piece. I walked across the landing and stood at the side of the piano. She lifted the music book from its stand on to her lap and half-turned on the stool to face me. I said, as evenly as I could, 'I came back because I wanted to tell you I know Mary's mother is a singer called Patsy Malone and her father is an English businessman.'

The Joy of Chopin slid from Sister Monica's lap and hit the floor. I stooped down and picked it up. She stood up jerkily, white-faced. 'We'll go to my office,' she said.

We sat at the same coffee table by the window. A muscle twitched in her jaw.

'What makes you so sure you are right, Mrs Molloy?'

'Patsy Malone told me,' I said. 'And it's obvious from photographs. Mary is the

350

image of her father. They have the same eyes, brown as treacle. Patsy has blue eyes. Mary's father had to have brown eyes. Two blue-eyed people can't have a brown-eyed child.'

'She had blue-grey eyes when she was born.' It was out before she could stop herself.

'Aren't all babies born with blue or grey eyes?' I said.

The stiff, white face turned pink. A succession of emotions flitted through her eyes. I saw puzzlement, relief, and joy. Then she smiled. She actually smiled. 'Of course. I'd forgotten that,' she said.

I found myself smiling back, almost forgetting the weight in my heart.

'How did you track down Patsy?' she said.

'I found people who'd been in Saint Joseph's at the same time. They put me in touch.' I didn't mention Dervla.

'Quite the sleuth,' she said, dryly, but with smile intact.

'I found out a lot about inherited characteristics,' I said. 'There are dominant genes for height and brown eyes, dimples and ear lobes. Mary has brown eyes and a dimple. And she's tall.'

'You have a dimple too.'

'Yes,' I said, animated. 'One of my parents must have had a dimple. It means a lot to know even one small thing about them.'

She kept her eyes on my face. 'Where were you born?' she said.

'In a home in Croydon. Saint Anne's. Run by nuns. I don't know which order. It was knocked down when I went to look. I waited until Mama died. I was too late. Well, I told you all that before.'

'I'm sorry,' she said. Her face showed real sympathy.

On an impulse, I pulled the leather pouch from my bag. I placed the enamelled brooch and the tiny, knitted teddy bear on the glass table. 'This is all I have. They were in the hem of my blanket.'

She reached over and gently stroked the blue wool of the teddy bear.

'I don't even know if my mother gave me my name. Or if it was the nuns. I was born on the feast of St Helena.'

'But you had a happy childhood?'

'Oh, yes,' I said. 'I had a happy childhood. But there's always the feeling of a bit missing.'

A comfortable silence fell. After a moment I said, 'Why did you approach me that day, at the wedding, sister? Who told you I couldn't have children?'

A lifetime passed. Then, 'I overheard you talking to your husband,' she said. 'I asked about you.'

'Whom did you ask?'

She frowned in concentration. 'I asked the

352

bride. She asked her husband.'

I swallowed. 'Did you speak to Ned? My husband's cousin?'

'No. Although Billy might have done.' Billy was the groom. 'He came back to me and said he'd heard you both wanted children but couldn't have any. Why do you ask?'

'Just curious,' I said. 'Wondering why we'd been chosen.'

'God works in a mysterious way,' she said. She accompanied me to the car.

'You'll get wet, sister,' I said.

'A bit of rain won't do me any harm. Nor you either.' She took both my hands in hers. 'I'm glad you came back,' she said. 'I think Mary is a lucky girl. May God bless you both. And your husband too.'

She must have seen something in my face.

'Put your trust in God,' she said. 'I'll pray for you.'

I took with me the image of a tall, grey figure, under a drizzling, grey sky, hand raised in farewell, smiling.

I had two more calls to make in Ireland.

Patsy Malone lived in a two-storey, white-washed farmhouse at the end of a lane in County Meath. She ushered me into a sitting room. A turf fire glowed in the hearth. A framed photograph took up most of the wall above a piano. Three red-haired, freckled-faced boys, of descending height, sitting on a sofa, each holding a fiddle. Their expressions solemn and optimistic. Patsy and a dark-haired man, standing behind them.

'They take after Dessie, except for the hair,' she said, indicating an armchair by the fire.

I didn't sit down. 'Jack didn't know,' I said. 'I'm certain of that now. I've been to see Sister Monica.'

The muscles in Patsy's face relaxed.

'She thought Mary was her brother's baby,' I said.

Patsy sat down. After a pause she said, 'Poor Monica. So that's why she changed towards me. She shouted at me to make up my mind. She called me a selfish little tart. I thought she was going to rip the baby from my arms. I never told Frank. He adored his sister.'

She stood up. We faced each other in a small space in the centre of the room.

'I've given your address and telephone number to Mary,' I said.

Patsy shook my outstretched hand. 'Thank you for telling me,' she said. 'I was tormented by the notion that he knew.'

'It doesn't excuse him,' I said. 'It just makes him less bad.'

'I'm sorry,' she said.

'It's all right.' I couldn't be angry with

Mary's birth mother. I just didn't want Jack to be her father. I didn't want Mary to be more his than mine.

There were no irises by the stream running through the rough field to the sea. The grass was clumpy and unkempt. But the hedge around Saint Dervla's bed was neatly trimmed, the sign recently repaired, the statue freshened with blue and white paint. I stood listening to the waves sucking the pebbles on the strand and a curlew crying in the milky sky, contemplating the plaster statue of the saint.

'Mysterious ways, indeed,' I said out loud.

There was a movement behind me. I turned and saw a young couple regarding me curiously. Their cheeks had been whipped pink by the wind. They were holding hands.

'Be careful what you ask,' I said, in what I hoped was a joky manner. 'It might not turn out the way you intend.'

'But is it sort of what you wanted?' the young woman said earnestly. 'Will it be all right in the end?'

'Brigid likes happy endings,' the young man said, smiling at her bright face.

'Sure what's wrong with that? Will there be a happy ending?' she said to me.

'I don't know yet,' I said. 'I really don't know.'

Chapter 44

I felt lighter when I got back to La Colline. The weight in my heart was less leaden, and my memory was released from meticulous recall for the first time in weeks. I went for a walk in the village and sat outside the Café de la Poste, drinking *vin chaud* in the lukewarm rays of the sun. It wasn't cold, but I wore my winter coat. The French like to dress warmly in winter. I can always spot the British tourists. They never wear enough clothes.

The following morning I made myself go to the *boulangerie*. I pulled the heavy oak door behind me, and slipped into the cobbled street, barely wide enough for a small car. I glanced up at the blue ribbon of sky in the narrow space between the houses as I climbed towards the Place des Arcades. A sheet, hanging out to dry, brushed my cheek. A black cat detached itself from the shadow of a doorway and padded across the cobbles. The smell of new leather wafted from the open window of Monsieur Lecoq, the *cordonnier*, but I did not call out my usual greeting, dreading the inevitable questions: *'Et comment va Monsieur? Et la belle Mary, la diva?'*

At the *boulangerie* it was easier than I thought. Madame Viret must have seen stories about Mary and Ricardo in *Paris Match*. She didn't ask about Jack. *'Et la belle Mary?'* was followed by a uniquely Gallic wink and curl of the shoulder. *'L'amour? Eh? Jamais simple.'*

A message was recording on the answering machine when I opened the door and set down my shopping bag on the stone floor. I stood listening to Jack's protestations. 'Please, lift the phone, Lena. Answer my letters. Speak to me. Patsy was the only one. I swear it, Lena. I swear to God. It was just a fling. That was my only affair. There's been no one else.' It occurred to me he was unaware of the greater crime I thought he had committed. The telephone was inches from my hand. There was a click. The recording stopped.

The white, foolscap envelope arrived a week later. It had been addressed to Hope House, in a hand I didn't recognise, re-directed by the post office, and re-directed again in Jack's looping scrawl. Not from him, then. I took the envelope to the breakfast table, sat down, and slit the seal with a knife. Inside was a handwritten letter attached to another envelope with a paper clip.

Dear Mrs Molloy,
I write with sad news. Sister Monica died on 22 November, here in Saint Joseph's. It was the feast of Saint Cecilia, the patron saint of musicians, which is fitting. Monica loved music. Her brother, Father Frank Devine, another fine musician, was with her at the end.

Monica will be missed by all who were privileged to know her and who witnessed her dedication and generosity everywhere she worked – Saint Patrick's, Drogheda; Saint Anne's, Croydon, and last but not least, here at Saint Joseph's. It will not be the same place without her.

Being Monica, she left everything ship-shape. This letter was on her desk with a note asking me to post it.

Yours sincerely,
Pauline Carroll (Sister)

There were two sheets of foolscap in the second envelope. They looked odd. I saw they had been photocopied. Empty, divided lines at the bottom. Smeary blurs at the top where information had been covered to conceal it from the indiscriminate eye of the photocopier. On the first page, three lines stood out in black copperplate handwriting.

18 August, 1948, 4.10pm, female, 7lbs 8ozs, 241142F

Edith Cecilia Morton, Castle Farm, Swin-
low, Bucks. Spinster
Henry Good, Green Valley, Monkford,
Oxon. 2nd Lieut. RAMC

Only two lines were legible on the second
page.

241142F, January 20 1949
Dr Guy Houghton, Mrs Margaret Houghton
(née Carey)
Market Hill, Uppercross, Kent.

I put my head on the table and wept.

I was writing a letter of condolence to
Father Songbird – I still think of him by that
name – when I heard footsteps in the hall
and the murmur of voices. It was about four
o'clock in the afternoon.

'Hello! Mum! It's me. Mary. I've got Eddy
with me.'

I put down my pen, jumped up and ran
into the hallway to greet her. She hugged me
as though her life depended on it.

'I couldn't be so near and not see you.'

Eddy kissed me on both cheeks. Mary
said, 'We flew to Nice and picked up a car.
I wanted to surprise you. We can only stay a
couple of hours. We have to be in Monte
Carlo this evening.'

Eddy said, 'I'm sure you'll want to talk to

Mary. I'll go for a stroll in the village.'

'Thanks, Eddy,' Mary said. She gave his hand a squeeze.

'You can't send Eddy away,' I said. 'Eddy, stay and have something to eat. I made onion soup at lunchtime.'

'No thanks, Lena. I'd really like to stretch my legs after the plane.' Tactful Eddy.

When he'd gone I said, 'Where's Rick?'

'He's gone to spend Christmas with his mother.'

'Oh.'

She warmed her hands at the wood-burning stove before sitting down at the table. I took the chair opposite, pushing the writing things to one side.

Jack's words came into my mind again. 'Just a fling.'

'Oh, Mary, I'm sorry. Are you hurt?'

She paused before replying, her voice retaining a tone of surprise. 'Less than I thought I would be, actually. It was all so intense. I suppose the secrecy added to the excitement at first.' She raised her chin defiantly. 'Guilt can be salty,' she said. 'And when Adela was throwing her tantrums I thought, poor Rick. How terrible to live with someone like that. He needs someone more even-tempered. Like me.'

She was silent for a moment. 'He said I was the kind of woman who could make him happy. That was the first time I realised

I was making an awful mistake. It wasn't about me. It was about him. When the whole media circus started, I realised it was about *them*. He'd done this before. She'd done it before. There was a Romanian ballet dancer in 1990. Adela pushed her into a fountain.'

Mary's laugh is infectious. I began to laugh too. It occurred to me that this was the kind of conversation I had always wanted to have with her.

'And Eddy is picking up the pieces,' I said.

Mary said, 'Eddy's always there to pick up the pieces.'

'Steady Eddy.'

Mary blushed. 'Steady is OK,' she said. 'It was real with Rick while it lasted, but I couldn't bear making Adela so unhappy. To be fair to Rick, neither could he. I think they'll get together again. It was just a fling for Dad, too.'

'How do you know?' My mouth tightening as I spoke.

'He's just like me,' she said, looking at me steadily.

'How do you know he hasn't had more' – I paused for emphasis – 'flings?' Spat out.

'I asked him.'

'Why should I believe it? You've just told me it was a fling with Rick, and he's had flings before.'

'Dad's not like Rick.'

'How do you know? How do I know?'

'Ask him yourself. Talk to him. He's miserable, Mum. You're miserable.'

'Don't you want to talk about Patsy Malone?' I said.

'No.' Mary said. 'Not yet. I still haven't taken it all in. I can't believe I know who I am at last.'

'I'm sorry,' I said. 'I wanted to surprise you.'

'Don't be sorry,' she said. 'I'm glad for me that you did it. I used to wonder what she was like. Why she'd given me away. I used to have this fantasy that I would find her and we would all go away on holiday together and be a big happy family.'

'Me too,' I said.

'Oh, Mum. I know why you did it. You left it too late for yourself, didn't you?'

I took the foolscap envelope from the drawer in the kitchen table. I lifted out the letter and the photocopied pages and pushed them across the table towards her.

'This came last week,' I said.

I watched as she read, tapping her cheek. How could I not have noticed? How could I have been so blind?

'Mum, that's so sad. But wonderful too. Are you going to look for them?' Then, before I could answer, she cried, 'Let me do it. Let me try to find them for you. I know how to do it!'

I stared at her. She swallowed.

'I found out how to do a search. A few years ago. It was just something I knew I would want to do some day. You were right.' She looked down at the letter. 'I've wanted to know for a long time. There wasn't time to begin a search. My life has been so busy. If you hadn't decided to start looking, I might never have known.'

But my life would still be calm and secure, I thought.

'And you wouldn't have had this letter,' she said.

And I wouldn't know the names of my birth parents. I wouldn't know that one of them had a dimple.

I said, 'If you hadn't met Rick, you wouldn't have gone to Dublin. I wouldn't have gone to Ireland.'

'If Dad hadn't met Patsy, I wouldn't be here,' she said.

My eyes filled with tears.

'Would you wish me away?' she said gently. She reached across the table with both hands and placed them on top of mine. 'I love you, Mum. Nothing will ever change that.'

'I love you too, darling,' I said.

Angels twinkled across the window as the Christmas decorations were switched on in the street outside.

'What are you going to do at Christmas?' Mary said.

I shrugged. 'Stay here. I don't much care.'

'I could come here,' she said. 'I could bring Eddy.'

'I'd like that.'

'He'll be back to collect me soon. We need to leave.' She stood up. The door bell rang. I jumped.

'That's Eddy.'

I came with her to the door. 'I'd love you to come here for Christmas,' I said to Eddy.

As she hugged me goodbye, Mary whispered in my ear, 'Talk to Dad, Mum.'

I put on my coat and walked through the Place des Arcades. White lights outlined the Gothic arches and criss-crossed the square. Yellow light, voices, laughter, spilled from the restaurant. In the paved main street, running like a spine through the village, rows of angels glowed gently above my head. I took a cobbled street that swept round the side of the hill, and stopped at a gap in the stout stone walls. Houses tumbled down the slanting hillside. Headlamps traced the ribbon of road in the valley below. In the darkness beyond lay the sea. I like it here, I thought. Do I want to stay? Mary would hate that. But she'll get married and have a home of her own.

A cold draught of air swept over the ramparts from the east. I shivered and pulled up the collar of my coat. Home? Where was home? A vision of Mary danced across my mind, her eyes sweeping over the bare walls and windows of Hope House, her arms hugging me. Home is where the heart is. I tried to listen to my heart. But it wasn't ready to tell me where I wanted my home to be.

When I got back to the house, I switched on the radio and rotated the dial until music spilled into the room. It was the Mia Madre sextet from the *The Marriage of Figaro*. I smiled in recognition, turned off the lights in the kitchen and moved my chair to the window.

The taxi must have stopped at the entrance to the village, because Jack was climbing the broad stone steps that rose from the main road and ended at the ancient gateway about a hundred metres further down the street. He passed under the stone arch and walked, head down, towards the house. He stopped, no more than his own length from the gable wall, and looked up at the dark window, his face bleak in the blue light of electric angels. His arms dropping to his sides, his bag falling with a soft thump on the cobbles. His head slumping forward.

Dove Sono, the sad aria recollecting sweet moments of marriage, and broken promises, swelled into the room behind me.

'*Dove sono i bei momenti*
Di dolcezza e di piacer?'

I was unaware of the tears sliding down my cheeks until I tasted salt. Jack was still standing, knuckles pressed into his eyes, when I unhooked the window and pushed it open.

'*La memoria di quell bene*
Dal mio sen non trapassò?'

Jack raised his head. His clenched hands fell against his heart. His face was full of hope.

I left the music playing as I stumbled through the darkness to the door.

The publishers hope that this book has given you enjoyable reading. Large Print Books are especially designed to be as easy to see and hold as possible. If you wish a complete list of our books please ask at your local library or write directly to:

Magna Large Print Books
Magna House, Long Preston,
Skipton, North Yorkshire.
BD23 4ND